CW00391963

Disorder

By

Paddy Magrane

Fahrenheit Press

For Di

"…Fix on Oedipus your eyes,
Who resolved the dark enigma, noblest champion and
most wise.
Like a star his envied fortune mounted beaming far
and wide:
Now he sinks in seas of anguish, whelmed beneath a
raging tide…"

*Oedipus Rex, Sophocles – translated by Lewis Campbell
(1883)*

Part I

Chapter 1

North London

Always the same nightmare. Always the same cold sweat on waking.

Sam Keddie didn't have the dream every night. In fact, he might have comforted himself with the thought that it occurred less frequently. But that didn't comfort him in the slightest. That was because, these days, the nightmare seemed more real and terrifying than ever before – as if Sam hadn't been listening and now his subconscious was shouting to make itself heard.

Exhausted but too rattled to sleep any longer, Sam headed for the bathroom. A quick glance in the mirror confirmed his knackered state – dishevelled, greying hair; eyes that seemed to have crept back into his skull.

In his early 40s, Sam knew that he was, on paper, a prime candidate for a mid-life crisis. He'd lost count of the male clients his age who'd complained of feeling trapped in unhappy marriages or careers, who'd succumbed to affairs or low-slung sports cars. But Sam knew such a crisis wouldn't befall him. Aging wasn't a problem. His 'issue' was altogether more timeless.

He showered, hoping the hot water would help soothe his agitated brain, then, confident that the face he now wore wouldn't unsettle his already troubled clients, headed downstairs. In the kitchen he made a strong coffee then sat to look at his diary. It was a full day that began with a client whose name sent a small charge through Sam.

Clutching his mug, Sam moved from the kitchen to his consulting room at the front of the house. The room was decorated in a calm, pea-green colour and there was a large modern desk of oak and brushed steel by the window where Sam wrote up his notes. Nearer the door, two matching leather armchairs faced each other at slight angles. Sam liked the fact that the chairs were identical, that there was no hierarchy as there was with a Freudian couch. And the slight angle ensured that therapist and client were not head on in an intense encounter.

Other subtle cues and signals littered the room. There was a certificate of accreditation, which deliberately aimed to reassure, a small bookcase – he disliked the idea of overwhelming his clients with shelves of weighty, leather-bound tomes – with some titles on Rogers, integrative theory and Jung. They were there, not just as his own reference library, but to further convince clients that they were in the right place with the right man. A large houseplant stood on top of the shelves. Sam kept it well fed and watered, keen not to upset any deeply depressed clients with the sight of decay or death in his consulting room.

There was also a print of a painting by Jack B. Yeats – Two Travellers. It depicted two figures in a mystical landscape – a neat analogy, Sam felt, of the therapeutic encounter – the paint applied with a palette knife in a crude, violent fashion. The print tended to serve as a litmus test of a client's progress. Often, late into their therapy, they would express a negative opinion about it – that it was ugly, or that 'anyone could do it'. While Sam wholeheartedly disagreed with them, their reaction was normally a good sign, one that signalled their return to better mental health. They'd begun to notice the world beyond them – and felt that their opinions counted again.

Finally, there was a complete absence of family photos. While other therapists chose to do this to prevent clients distracting themselves with fantasies or feelings about their shrink's private life, Sam had no photos on display because there was no family. Or none that he cared to think of.

The doorbell rang. Sam could make out a shadow against the glass. A tall figure. He opened the door, ready with a comforting smile.

The man before him was Charles Scott, the Secretary of State for International Development. It was Scott's second session.

Just over a week before, Sam had taken a booking for a man called 'Charles' and so had no idea that his new client was a Cabinet Minister. When Sam first opened the door to Scott, he sensed only that they'd met before. He knew that, unless he worked out why, this would nag at him. There was also a concern that, if there was an existing relationship, this might muddy the waters of the therapeutic one.

He invited the man in and, as Scott shrugged off his coat, Sam asked: 'I'm sorry, but have we met before?'

'I don't believe so,' said his new client, his voice soft and flat. 'You might have seen me in the media though. I'm a member of the Cabinet.'

Sam had practised for some years and, as his reputation grew, he'd gradually attracted – mostly through word-of-mouth but also because of articles he'd written in a broadsheet – more and more high-fliers as clients. He'd seen journalists, broadcasters, barristers, bankers, and even the occasional celebrity. But Charles Scott was his first politician.

Hiding his slight surprise, Sam directed him to the consulting room, to an armchair by a small table furnished with a box of tissues.

As Scott settled into his seat, his head turning to look out of the window to the street, Sam realised he already knew rather a lot about his new client.

Although Scott's relatively low-key Cabinet post was one that didn't bring him into the media glare as often as the Foreign or Home Secretaries, it was a well-known face nonetheless, particularly because of his much-publicised, long-term friendship with the Prime Minister, Philip Stirling. They'd been at university together and joined Parliament at the same time. Scott was one of his most loyal supporters. In fact, if Sam remembered correctly, Scott was godfather to Stirling's son.

If this was going to work, Sam needed to clear his head of all that information – and to treat Scott as a fresh slate.

The session began with the usual practicalities – fees, confidentiality, cancellations. Then Sam asked Charles Scott the question he asked all new clients.

'Can I ask how much of this process you're familiar with?'

His new client seemed edgy, which wasn't unusual for someone on their first session, but this seemed more to do with the front window, which he was still stealing the occasional glance at.

'No one can see in,' said Sam.

The Minister seemed to relax a little, slumping back into his chair. Sam was struck by his appearance. In the flesh, Scott, who appeared tall, confident and self-contained on television, was hunched and washed out. Sunk in the seat, he was older than the voice on the phone had suggested – possibly in his early 60s. His skin was pale and lined, his eyes ringed with grey halos.

Sam sensed that a nudge was necessary. 'I mentioned the process – and how much you know about it.'

'A little,' Scott said. 'I talk, you listen, offering up bon mots from time to time.'

A trace of sarcasm was a good sign. Whatever the man was facing, he hadn't completely lost his sense of humour.

'That's more or less the idea,' Sam said. 'The "bon mots" are designed to help us both draw out the important emotional strands from what you're saying so that we can begin to find ways of overcoming whatever it is you're going through.'

Scott raised an eyebrow. '"Going through",' he said, with a derisory snort. 'Sounds like it's a passing phase. Wouldn't that be lovely?'

'It doesn't feel as if it will come to an end?'

'No,' said Scott, looking now as if he were telling the absolute truth, without a trace of irony. 'It's hell right now.'

'An unbearable feeling.'

'Utterly.'

There was a pause. Sam did not speak, aware that Scott was coming face to face with his demons. But Scott did not expand.

Sam's experience of first sessions was normally of a volcanic flow of emotional content, but this wasn't to be such a session. Scott clammed up there and then, the rest of the hour dominated by talk of his wife, Wendy, who suffered with Motor Neurone's Disease. He talked of her being trapped by her condition, as if a light had gone out, but Sam had the distinct sense that Scott had already worked through this stuff, that he was merely repeating well-rehearsed thoughts. Ten minutes before the end, Scott got up to leave, saying he had an important meeting, but would be back same time next week.

Today, Scott looked worse than the previous week. His hair appeared thinner, as if about to fall out in great clumps. His eyes were dead, his skin dry and patchy.

The Minister shot another look outside. Sam wanted to repeat his assurance that no one could see in, but sensed that this would do little to comfort Scott. He watched his client, the man's eyes now downward cast but darting rapidly from side to side. Sam remained silent.

When the Minister finally spoke, Sam felt his skin prickle.

'I've done something terrible,' Scott said. 'Something that haunts me every moment of the day and night.'

'Right.' Sam knew that Scott needed little in the way of clever interventions now. He just needed to know he was being listened to.

'Something happened,' continued the Minister. 'Something I cannot talk about. And I did nothing to stop it.'

'And you feel dreadful about that?'

'Absolutely shit.'

'A deep sense of guilt.'

'It's like a bottomless pit.'

'And you're in that pit, day and night.'

Scott's head dipped barely an inch in assent, as if the effort of confirming what Sam had said were herculean.

'I'm never going to get out,' he said, his voice almost a whisper.

Sam paused again, allowing these last words to sink in. This realisation seemed more significant than the shame Scott had spoken of.

'Right now,' Sam said, 'you think you'll never escape your feelings.'

Scott's head was down. 'I know I won't.'

'You feel alone too,' Sam offered, reading into Scott's despair a sense that he faced this on his own.

Scott closed his eyes for a moment, then opened them. 'Wendy's all but lost to me. And I can't burden Eleanor with this. She wouldn't understand.'

In Sam's experience, there were moments when a little optimism was needed. 'I've seen countless people sitting where you are now who thought they'd never get out of the state they were in, countless people who managed to move on.'

'There's only one way I can move on.'

'Which is?'

Scott met Sam's eyes, suggesting to the therapist that the solution was obvious to them both.

Sam tensed. 'It might feel that way now, that life is black and white, but I assure you there are many grey areas in between. There are different ways of seeing what's happening.'

Scott looked at him, a corner of his mouth raised almost imperceptibly as if to indicate humour in Sam's assertion.

'What's happening is crystal clear,' said Scott. 'There are no other ways of seeing it.'

Sam looked at Scott, dropping his head to one side. 'Mind if I make an observation?'

'Be my guest,' Scott said, with a shrug.

'You look exhausted. You don't need a therapist to tell you that extreme fatigue can seriously mar your ability to see things clearly.'

'I don't sleep much,' said Scott. 'And when I do I have nightmares.'

Tell me about it, thought Sam.

Scott sniffed, a lifeless attempt at laughter. 'I dream that I'm running through a maze, high walls either side of me. Frantically looking for someone called Hank.'

His face suddenly took on a deadly serious look. He breathed in deeply and sat up straight, alert and tense. His attention left the room, his eyes scanning the street outside, keen to avoid his therapist's gaze. Quite what had prompted his sudden wariness, Sam couldn't fathom. He was about to say something, make a gentle observation about what Scott had felt when he recalled the dream – a sensation so visceral he needed to detach himself from the session – when a noise interrupted his thoughts.

A car had screeched to a halt across the road, double parking at an angle that suggested the driver didn't care about other vehicles trying to pass by. It was a dark blue saloon. Sam gave it little thought, but the sight of it appeared to terrify Scott. Even more so when the driver's window slowly lowered to reveal a bald man with a thick neck. When Sam looked back at Scott, it was as if his client had seen a ghost.

'Are you OK?'

Scott didn't answer. He just kept staring at the man in the car. And then, with a surge of acceleration, the vehicle was gone.

Scott seemed to be locked on the spot where the car had been and then, very slowly, he returned to the room. His face had drained of colour. His bottom lip quivered.

'I should go now.'

Sam looked at the wall clock behind his client. 'You still have over half your session remaining, if you want to use it.'

'That's OK,' said Scott, already standing. 'This has been helpful. But I should get back to the office.'

'Would you like to book another session?'

'I'm not sure that will be possible,' he said. At this, his eyes appeared to well. He quickly pulled himself together. He then reached into his jacket for his wallet and pulled a handful of notes from it. Sam was writing a receipt for Scott when he heard the front door slam shut.

Chapter 2

Downing Street

The breakfast meeting with the Chinese foreign minister had been successful. Despite the man's chronic English, Philip Stirling, the British Prime Minister, had managed, through an interpreter, to politely repeat the UK's objection to the recent incarceration of a well-known dissident – an unavoidable yet pointless task required of him by the British media – before he moved on to easier topics – welcome Chinese investment in a steel works in Wales and a festival of Chinese culture in Manchester, which the foreign minister was due to open.

The delegation had now left Downing Street and Stirling was in the Cabinet Room having a private meeting with an adviser. Out of habit, the Prime Minister had sat at his usual seat in the middle of the table. Behind him was a white marble fireplace and above it, the only painting in the room, a portrait of Sir Robert Walpole. Britain's first Prime Minister had served for twenty years. Stirling suspected that, with the current shit storm raging about him, his tenure would be over in a fraction of that time.

The adviser standing opposite him was Frears, a former officer in the Coldstream Guards. Frears had once been a minor celebrity thanks to his eloquent, reasoned dispatches from Afghanistan, published in The Telegraph. The officer had written with surprising empathy about the Taliban, helping to soften their bogeyman status and, in turn, create a useful inroad into negotiations. When Stirling had appointed him, the PR had been excellent. 'Military intellectual to advise Stirling on terror'; 'Army's measured voice to shape Government's fight against extremists.'

Stirling was, like most decent heads of Government, a master at masking his emotions. But now, with no one but Frears to observe him, he could feel the tension releasing – and his temper rising.

The former soldier stood across the table from him, a tall figure in a pin-striped suit sporting the Brigade tie of blue and maroon diagonal stripes.

'Correct me if I'm wrong,' said Stirling, his hands gripping the arms of his chair, 'but this isn't going very well, is it?'

Frears, ram-rod straight, smoothed back his already immaculately combed hair.

'I don't agree, sir,' he said, with clipped vowels that, even in the midst of this hideous mess, amused Stirling. The officer's diction suggested order and authority, but of course Stirling knew better. The man had a messy secret, which the PM had used to his advantage when engaging Frears for the extra-curricular work they were discussing.

'In situations like these,' the officer continued, 'there are always unexpected developments. We merely adapt.'

'"Situations like these?",' snapped the PM. '"Unexpected developments?" We haven't gone to Tesco and discovered that they're out of milk.'

Frears said nothing.

'This morning's events are going to shine a very big light on Charles Scott,' continued Stirling. 'And if that wasn't bad enough, now you're telling me that he's had two sessions with a psychotherapist.'

When Frears spoke again, his tone was more conciliatory. 'I admit that the actual issue at stake is rather unusual, but the work involved – containment – is what my men do for a living. They're professionals.'

'You think they can sniff out this shrink – what's his name?'

'Keddie.'

'And find out what he knows?'

Frears nodded.

'And we're not talking water-boarding, are we?'

The Guardsman managed a sly smile. 'Just a chat.'

Stirling appeared to relax. 'Good, good. Because this thing has to stay contained. We're not just talking about my job and yours. We're talking about the country's reputation. If this Marrakesh business were to leak, the impact would be fucking cataclysmic.'

If Frears was shaken by the implications, he didn't show it. Stirling observed the Guardsman's impassive face and drew comfort from it. Emotional chaos had created this whole mess. He was hoping to God military detachment would contain it.

A little later, as Frears left 10 Downing Street, two figures appeared at a window above Number 11. One was Charlotte Stirling, the PM's wife. Her dark hair was cut in a severe bob and she wore one of her trademark peasant-style long-sleeved smocks, a look the fashion press loved to deride. The second figure was Aidan Stirling, Charlotte and Philip's twenty-five-year-old son, his face framed in a mop of curly locks. Had anyone been able to see Aidan clearly, they'd have noticed a face devoid of expression, as if a shock had reduced him to an android state. They'd have then seen his mother wrapping a protective arm around her son's shoulder.

Chapter 3

North London

It was 11am the following day, and Sam was between clients. He allowed himself about twenty minutes to make a coffee, write up notes and attempt to clear his mind of one person's inner world before he entered another's. He'd returned from the kitchen with his mug, settled behind the desk in his consulting room and was about to begin writing when there was a loud knock on the door, accompanied by the doorbell ringing.

Sam leaned back in his seat to look out of the front bay window. There was a short, bald man on the doorstep. Sam tensed. The figure outside, he was sure, was the driver of the car from yesterday – the person who'd so rattled Scott.

The man had been looking out at the street and turned towards Sam when the door opened, a poor attempt at a smile on his face. He wore an ill-fitting suit that seemed to accentuate his truncated legs and barrel chest.

'Mr Keddie?'

'Yes.'

'I work for the Government,' said the man. 'I need to talk to you about one of your clients, Charles Scott.'

Sam took a moment to register what the man was saying, then instantly became defensive.

'Firstly, I do not discuss my clients with anyone else and secondly –'

The man raised the palm of his left hand. 'It's OK,' he said. 'We know Charles Scott is one of your clients. We're not asking you to reveal whether he was bullied at school.'

'You say you work for the Government,' said Sam, who was now angry, 'but you haven't shown me any identification.'

The man looked Sam in the eye, as if assessing him. He softened a fraction. 'I'm sorry.' He reached into his jacket pocket and pulled out a leather wallet. He flicked it open for Sam to see. It appeared to be an identity badge – a royal coat of arms sat next to the man's face above some printed words and numbers – but before Sam had a chance to study it, the badge was whipped away and replaced in the wallet.

'May I come in?' said the man. 'I'd rather not discuss this matter outside.'

'No,' said Sam. 'I'm expecting another client in a few minutes.'

The man ignored him and moved past the therapist, turning into the consulting room to sit in Sam's chair. Sam stood behind the seat his clients normally took. He hoped his stance was clear, but the man was ignoring Sam, his eyes slowly scanning the room.

'I'm afraid Charles Scott is dead,' he said abruptly. 'He committed suicide last night.'

Sam closed his eyes in disbelief, half-hoping that, when he reopened them, the bald man would have evaporated. But when he looked again, he was still there, staring at Sam.

'Obviously this is devastating for Scott's family,' said the man, 'but – and excuse me if I sound a little callous at this point – there are also political implications. We need to ensure that his work within Government is not exposed in an unmanageable way.'

'You said he committed suicide,' said Sam.

The man looked distracted, as if he were now the one in a hurry. 'Yeah.'

Sam was reeling. He remembered Scott's phrase: 'There's only one way I can move on'. Alarmed at the time, Sam's response had been therapeutically off-kilter, a comment about Scott's black-and-white reading of life, a distraction rather than an acknowledgment of the man's obviously dark feelings. He cursed himself. Had he somehow precipitated this?

'Mr Keddie?'

Sam re-focused on the bald man, gripping the top of the seat to steady himself.

'We need to know what Scott said about his work.'

Sam's brain was spinning. 'I never divulge what my clients tell me in counselling.'

'You've made that clear,' said the man, struggling to appear patient. 'Now let me be clear –'

'This is really simple,' said Sam, who now wanted the man to leave as quickly as possible. 'Whatever Charles Scott told me stays in this room.'

The man leaned forward in his seat, a hand raised, the index finger pointing in Sam's direction. The doorbell went.

'You have to leave,' said Sam. 'My next client is here.'

The bald man stood and moved towards Sam, squaring up to him. He appeared about to say something, but thought better of it.

He then shoved past Sam, sending him backwards into the wall. Sam was stunned by the man's aggression and straightened, ready to say something before the man left. But it was too late. By the time the therapist made it to the door, the man was exiting, storming out past Sam's next client, an elderly man who was almost knocked to the ground.

Chapter 4

North London

During the sessions that followed the man's visit, Sam
struggled to concentrate on what his clients were saying. He
spent every break scouring the internet for signs of the story
in the news.

It broke at lunchtime on the BBC and was the lead story.
The news reader announced that the body of the Secretary
of State for International Development, Charles Scott, had
been found at his London flat. The screen then switched to a
street in Battersea. It was a sunny autumnal day – the cheery,
optimistic light quite at odds with the unravelling tragedy.
The reporter was positioned across the road from a mansion
block, the area immediately around the entrance ringed off
by police. Two officers were standing guard.

The reporter claimed that the body had been found at
around 10am by a cleaner who had keys to the flat. Little was
known of the exact circumstances of the Minister's death but
a police spokesman had stated that they were not treating it
as suspicious. At this point the news reader interjected,
asking if they thought it was natural causes. The reporter on

the street replied that this had not been mentioned, but that it was probably too early to say.

The hint had been dropped. If it wasn't suspicious and didn't turn out to be natural causes, there was only one other possibility – suicide.

The news reader thanked the reporter and then began talking about Scott's career. Sam watched footage of the Minister during a recent trip to Africa, standing in a field of maize talking to a farmer, before older images appeared – him walking the streets of his constituency, then a still of Scott as a much younger man with his arm around the shoulder of another – a beaming, tanned individual instantly recognisable as the man who was now Prime Minister. To the right of the PM was his wife and a young boy, the PM's son – Scott's godchild.

The news reader promised to return to the story when more details became available. He then turned to Marrakesh, where police had broken up a large street protest with tear gas.

Sam kept his eye on the news throughout the afternoon. At around 3pm, there was a press conference from Downing Street that was relayed live on the BBC news website.

A podium had been positioned outside Number 10. The famous door opened and Stirling, his wife, Charlotte, and son, Aidan, walked slowly out. They all looked shell-shocked.

Stirling stood at the podium, Charlotte and Aidan to one side, a couple of steps behind. The PM was in his late 50s, a man of average height whose most distinguishing feature was his wavy and slightly unruly grey hair. That and the fact that, unlike other, more immaculately turned out leaders, Stirling always looked as if he'd dressed in a hurry. The tie was often off-centre, the suit jacket slightly crumpled. These elements added up to an impression of someone who'd found himself in power by accident, when it was never his intention.

Today, his face looked tired and sad. His eyes lacked their usual animation, his skin seemed paler and looser. He pulled a pair of glasses from a jacket pocket and, from another, a piece of paper. This was unusual. He was known for speaking without notes. When he glanced up at the assembled media, he looked fragile, the tough politician beaten down by tragedy.

'Most of you will by now know that Charles Scott, the Secretary of State for International Development, was found dead this morning,' said the PM, his voice, with its slight Yorkshire lilt, quiet and soft. It was a tone Sam had heard before, the one the man adopted for sensitive statements – the death of a soldier in action, a natural disaster overseas – but this time it came with an apparent choke, as if the PM were struggling with each word.

'Charles was a very able minister who did so much to help countries who needed the expertise and resources of the UK. I know his energy and enthusiasm will be missed across the globe. Charles was also a close friend of mine. He and I had known each other since we were at university together. He had been an integral part of my family's life ever since. Naturally, I cannot expect you to refrain from reporting this story – or making enquiries of your own – but I politely implore you all to show respect to his widow, Wendy, and daughter, Eleanor. Thank you.'

There'd been no mention of suicide, and Sam briefly wondered whether the Government employee had got it all wrong. But then he checked himself. The law required a coroner to sign off the death in unusual circumstances like this, which often meant an autopsy, and even an inquest. The PM was hardly likely to pre-empt a coroner's findings, let alone talk about it at such a sensitive time.

No, Sam knew he was merely trying to comfort himself. The bald man and his grim tidings reappeared in his mind. His client had committed suicide.

Chapter 5

Clerkenwell, London

Sam cancelled the following day's clients and made an arrangement to meet Kate for lunch. Despite their split some years back, they'd managed to salvage a friendship, one which he greatly valued.

That they achieved this was quite something. Spectacular rows had preceded their rift, arguments in which their very incompatible agendas had become fatally exposed. Kate, it was evident, wanted long-term commitment and, in time, a family. Sam, as he gradually discovered over the course of the relationship, was not ready for either.

Sam had been hoping for a long boozy lunch and, if he was honest, that his ex would take the afternoon off and come back to have sex with him at the home they once shared. He could sense from the moment they sat down in the bar in Clerkenwell that Kate was not up for it. She was in a hurry, keen to get back to her studio round the corner where she was due to take some shots of a young actress for the cover of Red.

She groaned when Sam said that he hadn't heard of her.

'What's happened to the man who used to be so on the pulse?' she mocked.

Sam shrugged. Being aware of the latest cultural phenomenon was, like so many of the interests he'd once shared with Kate, a thing of the past.

'So what's up?' she asked. Her hair was cut short and croppy these days. In fact he might have struggled to recognise her compared to the long-haired woman he'd once gone out with. She'd changed a great deal – blossomed, if he was going to be truthful – since they'd split. Her career had thrived and, while she remained for the most part single, she seemed supremely content. He had no reason to resent this but it still occasionally hurt.

'One of my clients committed suicide.'

Confidentiality, as he'd told the short, bald man, was one of psychotherapy's cast-iron rules. But this wasn't about divulging what Scott had said; it was about how Scott's death made him feel.

Kate's hand reached across the table and grabbed Sam's.

'Oh sweetheart, I'm so sorry.'

She squeezed his hand. A waiter arrived with the bottle of wine Sam had ordered and poured them both a glass.

Alcohol had been a regular feature of their relationship and often precipitated the fiercest of their quarrels. Sam had a sudden, discomforting memory of how he'd broken several bones in his right hand after punching a hole in the wall during an argument over some domestic – and now long-forgotten – trifle. Later, feeling very foolish in A&E, he'd marvelled at his over-reaction, one that was vastly out of proportion with the petty matter they'd been quarrelling over.

Kate sipped her glass tentatively. Sam took a deep gulp.

'I know it's a cliché,' said Kate, 'but you know it's not your fault, don't you?'

Sam smiled weakly. 'I should think that. But right now I don't.'

'I'm no expert,' said Kate, 'but your job isn't to save people. If someone's got it into their head to kill themselves, it's never going to be easy to persuade them otherwise.'

'I should have been more careful.'

The hand slipped from his. The friendship had certain limits. And one of those was too much introspection, which Kate had grown tired of.

Self-examination had become Sam's obsession in the latter years of their relationship. Outbursts like the one that led to A&E had made him increasingly aware that beneath the façade he presented there lay a number of unresolved issues, damaged pieces of his psyche that had far more influence than he'd realised, let alone acknowledged.

'You going to eat?'

She shook her head. 'I'm a bit pushed for time. I'll probably grab a sandwich on the way back.'

He smiled. They needed to talk about something else.

'Hey,' she said, her voice suddenly brighter. 'You'll never guess where I'm off to next month.'

As Kate began talking about an assignment in the Grenadines, Sam felt himself drift, remembering a definitive row they'd had, when she'd implored him to confront his demons.

Sam had heeded her advice, finding himself a therapist, a Jungian in Highgate, whose consulting room was filled with leather-bound volumes on Jung and Freud and shelves groaning with African masks and sculptures of stunted tribal figures.

Sam's early memories provided the substance that was raked over between them, the Jungian remaining aloof and mirror-like, so that Sam never really knew the man's true reactions or feelings.

In time, while much useful insight was gained – including the understanding that Sam was not ready for marriage or fatherhood and his career in the often superficial world of advertising was probably not the ideal choice for an introspective man – he tired of the analyst's studied indifference. After four years in therapy, he called time on the Jungian.

' – and if that works out, we could be talking American Vogue.'

Sam recognised the definitive pause, the moment when a response was necessary. He was a good listener – his job demanded it – but not today.

'Sounds like you're doing brilliantly.'

Kate gave him a suspicious look. 'You're not really here, are you? You're in your bloody head again.'

'Sorry. I'm a little preoccupied.'

He watched her face flush, sensed her anger, then saw it subside.

'You can see why I found you so irritating at times,' she said.

Sam nodded. 'Totally. I'm a navel-gazing pain in the arse.'

Kate smiled, then glanced at her mobile on the table. 'Shit, gotta go.'

She stood, gave him a peck on the cheek, then paused briefly to examine him like a concerned mother.

'Look after yourself,' she said. Then she rushed to the door.

Sam was still in the bar an hour after Kate had left. He'd polished off the bottle, keen to obliterate the day.

As he left, a chill breeze hit him hard in the face and he felt twice as drunk as he had in the bar's warm interior. Unwilling to face his home – and consulting room – at that point, he decided to take the slow way back, and walk.

Sam drew the collar of his jacket up, walking north with little thought for the route he'd take.

Seeing Kate was a mixed experience emotionally. It was good to have friends who knew him as well as she did – and to feel comfortably connected to the past, as he so often urged his clients – but equally, he preferred not to revisit certain thoughts too often.

As he crossed the road from the restaurant, pausing momentarily to let a black car pass at speed, Sam wondered again whether terminating his own therapy had been wise. The presence of an irritating phobia, as well as his recurring nightmare, provided confirmation that things were far from resolved. He was middle-aged, yet still haunted by the same figure from his childhood.

It was dark by the time he returned to Stoke Newington. As he rounded the corner of his street, he was sure he saw a light on in his house. But as he neared it, the light went out.

Sam tensed. Unlatching the gate quietly, he walked very slowly up the short garden path, then unlocked the door, as if in slow motion. As soon as the door edged open, Sam heard the sound of rapid footsteps at the rear of the property and the back door slamming. Sam rushed in, anger replacing the caution he'd felt as he became convinced that he'd disturbed a burglar. The small back garden was bordered by a brick wall about four feet high. As Sam reached the back door, he saw a figure – a tall man in a dark bomber jacket and jeans – disappear over the wall with an athletic movement.

Sam ran to the wall and looked over it. The figure was already at the other side of his neighbour's garden, about to bound over it into the street beyond. Sam attempted to leap his wall, but his hand became snagged on a rose thorn, ripping the flesh.

'Fuck,' he cried out in pain.

When he looked up, the man had disappeared. Sam knew there was no point pursuing. By the time he'd made it over both walls, the burglar would be on the high street, blending in with the crowds.

Sam returned to the kitchen, turning on the tap to wash his hand, which was pouring blood. Wrapping paper towels around it to stem the flow, he then walked slowly through the house, looking for signs of disturbance. Upstairs, his bedroom was untouched, as were the guest rooms and bathroom. Downstairs, the sitting room was as he'd left it.

He then went into his consulting room and flicked on the light.

It was clear that this was the place the burglar had been interested in. One of the filing cabinets had been emptied and the contents – Sam's case notes – spread across his desk.

Sam had a sickening thought, and rushed to the piles of paper. He leafed through them rapidly, then turned to one of the other cabinets. Within seconds – and to his intense relief – he found what he was looking for, a file with a tab entitled CSM14 – named after Charles Scott, his gender and the year. He opened the cardboard sleeves and looked inside. The notes were still there.

To Sam, the conclusion was simple. Because he had refused to play ball, the Government employee had decided that more direct action was necessary – and an attempt had been made to steal Scott's notes. Why else would a burglar zone in on that one place in his house?

Sam slammed the desk with his fist in rage.

He reached for the phone, called 999 and asked for the police.

Chapter 6

Downing Street

Sometimes, while lying in bed in the morning, the house already buzzing with activity below him, Aidan Stirling would stare at the ceiling and compare his life with the home where he now lived.

Like him, the house suggested familiarity from the outside, yet inside, was more complex. It was a building where rooms led to more rooms, where concealed staircases took you from one place to another, bypassing other areas to deliver you, as if teleported, to a completely different part of the house.

He'd read about its history and it fascinated him to think of the place at the turn of the 20th Century. Then it had been close to falling down, its floors buckling and walls cracking because of the soft soil and shallow foundations below. Now concrete held the building up, subsidence a thing of the past.

The concrete's effect was comparable to the Valium he was often encouraged to take.   In the house's case, it had clearly worked. This place wasn't going anywhere. In his case, however – if he was to believe his parents and the professionals they'd taken him to – there was still movement.

But of course that was the problem. He never believed anything his parents said. Why would he take them seriously when they could never be relied on to deliver what they promised?

As a child, Aidan remembered overhearing his father – on the rare occasion his parents were conversing and not arguing – referring to him as 'an awkward little shit'. Quite how he'd drawn this conclusion when he'd hardly spent any time with his son was beyond belief. And yet that definition had stuck in Aidan's mind. That he was not a child, or a son, but an inconvenience.

He had heard a lot worse in the last few days. Uncle Charles's death had stirred things up.

Aidan had seen less and less of Uncle Charles as he got older – and his godfather became busier. But he remembered him as a thoughtful man. Someone who could always be relied on to remember birthdays, to show kindness whenever they were together.

But then he remembered the last time he'd seen him. Aidan suddenly felt every ridge and fold in the sheets and mattress below him. He turned on to his side to study the poster on the wall of Frank Lloyd Wright's most famous building, Falling Water. He focused on the image, the concrete terraces seemingly hovering in space over the waterfall, the rectilinear shapes contrasted with the soft woodland, the feeling of perfect balance.

His breathing slowed. The bed softened beneath him.

Like never before, there was a sense that architecture gave his life structure and meaning. That he'd nearly lost that career, by continually missing lectures and arguing with tutors – scraping a 2:2 on his BA – worried him. But all too often the confrontations at college were because he fundamentally disagreed with something a tutor had said.

Wasn't that what college was about – challenging as well as learning?

Now he was doing his professional experience at a firm in Islington. He got on OK there, and had even managed to make friends – or at least that's what he thought he'd made; he could never be sure what actually constituted friendship – but again he was finding it hard not to disagree with some of the opinions the partners expressed.

Now he was on semi-permanent sick leave, a situation that was deeply frustrating. But he was sure he'd return. That he'd qualify and set up his own practice. And that, in time, he'd design buildings that would leave people breathless.

Chapter 7

North London

Sam cancelled his clients again the next morning, aware that he was in no fit state to offer empathy or that other mysterious pre-requisite for good counselling, unconditional positive regard. The fact was, he was angry, and he knew it would show.

He sat at his kitchen table, drinking coffee after coffee as he raged at the events of the previous evening.

The police had arrived quickly enough, but as he attempted to explain what had happened, he soon realised how flimsy his story sounded, and their interest rapidly waned.

The trouble was, he'd been reluctant to tell them about Scott, not just because of the confidentiality he'd been so keen to impress on the Government employee, but also just in case one of the attending officers decided to make a little money by telling a newspaper that the dead Minister had been seeing a shrink.

It meant that everything he did tell them sounded slightly hollow. He explained that one of his clients had recently died and that he'd had a visit from someone concerned about what the dead man might have revealed about his work. Sam told them how he'd refused to talk about it and how, a day later, his house was broken into and the case notes targeted.

'So what you're saying,' said the interviewing officer, a man in his early 30s with tightly cropped hair and a goatee beard, 'is that you believe this man –' he paused then to consult his notes, ' – or someone in league with him, broke into your house to steal your client's notes.'

'Right.'

The policeman ran a hand across his head. 'I'm sorry to tell you this Mr Keddie, but your story is a little light on leads. We could attempt to trace this man, maybe see if we can find a match for any prints in your house. But there's little to link one event with the other – the men you describe are, as you say, physically quite different – and nothing has been stolen.'

'Because I interrupted the burglary.'

The policeman grunted in agreement.

'So basically,' said Sam, 'if you can't find the man, or any prints, there's nothing you can do.'

The policeman sighed. 'This is a break-in,' he said, his voice lifeless. 'Of which there are plenty round here. We will investigate it, but I can't promise anything.'

Sam could see the man thought he was a time waster, an impression that merely compounded the frustration and anger he felt.

These thoughts were still tormenting him when, around lunchtime, he decided to go out to clear his head.

He walked up to Church St and crossed the road to the entrance of Abney Park Cemetery.

Sam liked the cemetery. In an area that had become increasingly gentrified, this was a place of genuine natural wildness. While there were some memorials that were well maintained, for the most part the vegetation had run riot: statues of angels strangled by ivy, headstones collapsed and crumbling into the graves of the men they were meant to commemorate, mausoleums where the rain had found entry and the tombs within had become dank pools of fetid water.

While others might have found the rampant nature rather upsetting – and unsettling – Sam found it comforting. It seemed to offer confirmation of something he knew only too well.

Even though death was all around, the place made him think of life. How it was not a tidy process and anyone who tried to con themselves into thinking they could control it was a fool. As his own experience – and those of the hundreds of people he'd treated – had taught him, life could not be lived neatly. He was reminded of all those clients with apparently orderly façades – the tailored City boy who despised his job and had murderous thoughts about the other traders in his office, the middle-class mother who'd been sleeping with a teenage friend of her son. Eventually our true feelings and desires had a habit of coming to the surface. In this way, most people were no different to a crisp new headstone that, before long, is overcome by nature.

Sam had wandered deep into the cemetery. There was a sudden rustle of leaves and a snap of twig. It made him jump, which annoyed him because he knew his anxiety was only heightened because of the burglary. There was no reason to be spooked. There were a number of broad, well-maintained paths in the cemetery. Other people were bound to be around.

Just to put his mind at rest, he turned round. There, no more than ten metres behind him, was a tall figure dressed in a dark bomber jacket and jeans. Sam felt a chill run through him. The burglar – what little he'd seen of him – had been similarly built and dressed.

He berated himself. There were loads of tall men dressed like that in London. Sam looked back again. The man was moving faster.

Sam began to run, urged on by an instinctive feeling that he was now in danger. As he picked up pace, he could hear the man doing the same.

There was a clearing ahead, an area where a disused chapel stood. The surrounding lawns and gardens were often busy, a peaceful haven close to the cemetery's east gate.

Sam turned. The man had begun to close the distance between them. His face was gaunt, with pale skin and narrow, hard eyes.

Sam accelerated. Suddenly he was out in the open, the chapel standing before him. There were, just as he'd hoped, more people around. An Asian couple – him bearded, her in a hijab – seated on a bench and cooing over a pram; an elderly man walking, his arm steadied by a middle-aged daughter.

Just then, the man who'd been chasing him burst from the path. He took in the scene around him – Sam and the others – and appeared to make a quick calculation. And then Sam saw something glint, and his blood ran cold. A knife, held tightly in the man's right hand, was stuffed into a coat pocket and, as quickly, the man withdrew the way he had come.

Sam was rooted to the spot as he rapidly processed what he'd just witnessed. Had that man intended to scare him into talking? Or silence him forever?

Sam's thoughts came in quick succession. Were the police an option? Perhaps. But again, unless he was prepared to speak about Scott, he could imagine his story being met with incredulity. Besides, he thought, with rising panic, even if he did decide to talk about Scott, would the police offer any protection? As the men targeting him had demonstrated, the law was no barrier.

An image entered Sam's head, one that made his stomach contract – his pursuer now heading for the house, breaking in by the back door to surprise Sam on his return and finish the job.

Sam felt his body go rigid. How had all this happened? In a matter of days, normality had been replaced by this. He thought of clients whose lives had been turned upside down by an unexpected event – a bereavement or job loss – but none who'd suddenly found themselves in grave danger.

Even in his confused, frightened state he knew one thing. It wasn't safe to go home.

With trembling hands, Sam checked his pockets. He had his phone and wallet, enough cash in the bank to get by. And something else that he'd taken the precaution of folding into his jacket pocket before he left the house. The case notes.

Sam needed to find somewhere safe. Somewhere he could think straight and work out why the content of Charles Scott's sessions was worth killing for.

Chapter 8

South London

'What do you mean, "he's disappeared"?' Stirling's words were accompanied by a fist slamming down on the leather of the car's seats.

He and Frears were in the back of the PM's armour-plated Daimler, en route to an Islamic community centre in Camberwell where the Prime Minister was due to give a speech on multi-culturalism.

Of course that was the plan. Right now he could barely concentrate.

As he was leaving Downing Street, Stirling had politely excused another adviser, a Moslem peer who'd arranged the engagement, and asked Frears, who was in the building most weekdays, to join him in the back of the car.

A short message sent from Frears to the PM's BlackBerry – 'Need to talk' – had prompted the meeting. These get-togethers were becoming a little too frequent for Stirling's liking. This was meant to be an invisible operation, one that Frears had assured him he would not need to be overly involved in. But recently Stirling had been seeing far too much of the former soldier. The Prime Minister was acutely aware that, to others, there was only so much he and Frears could be discussing in private – particularly given the other issues on his desk. People were bound to begin wondering what the hell was going on.

'It's like I said, Prime Minister,' replied Frears, 'my man talked to Keddie but was interrupted before he could get any sense of what the shrink knew.'

'So he decided to burgle the man's house and take the case notes.'

'Keddie was harping on about confidentiality. It seemed the most sensible way to find out what Scott had talked about.'

'But your man was disturbed before he could get the notes. And then Keddie called the police. And God knows what he told them.'

'That's why we stepped things up. Tried to confront him. Scare him into talking.'

Stirling closed his eyes in disbelief. Was this really the operation he'd set in motion? A pack of wild dogs let loose on the streets of London. 'But your thug let him get away.'

'It was a public place, Prime Minister,' said Frears, the exasperation showing in his voice. 'We couldn't afford to attack him in front of witnesses.'

'And how can we now be sure he hasn't told the police or a bloody journalist about what's happened to him?'

'The events cannot be linked in a coherent way. A deniable visit from us, a burglary, a possible aggravated mugging.'

'What about what Scott told him?'

'I doubt he'll reveal that.'

Stirling gave him a withering look. 'Oh you do, do you? And what makes you so sure of that?'

'Keddie made a big deal of client confidentiality. I don't think he'd tell the police or a hack that Scott was a client of his.'

'Believe me. When there's money on offer, people will do all sorts of surprising things. As you yourself will attest.'

Frears flushed and Stirling enjoyed the Guardsman's discomfort. After leaving the army, Frears had failed to cash in on his notoriety and reverted to the world he knew best, earning his crust in the private sector, latterly in Nigeria. It was here he was involved in a disastrous attack on the camp of rebels who'd targeted an oil facility. The intelligence had been ropey and the event resulted in the deaths of hundreds of civilians. The Nigerians had covered it up, but Stirling knew the truth.

'All I'm saying,' hissed Stirling, 'is that this has become bloody complicated. I thought it would end with Scott's death, but it's become more and more of a fucking mess.'

'We're tying up the loose ends, Prime Minister,' said Frears.

'And creating a few more in the process.'

He paused, trying to make sense of it all.

'Let's now assume Keddie knows someone is after him,' he said. 'We cannot afford for him to start sniffing around. So just locate him. And when you do, find out what he knows and who, if anybody, he's talked to.'

'And what should we do with Keddie?'

Stirling tensed in his seat. How dare Frears ask a question like that? The Prime Minister looked at the former soldier and spotted the faintest hint of amusement on his face. He'd embarrassed Frears and now the soldier was having his petty revenge.

Turning away from Frears, he said: 'Just make sure he keeps his fucking mouth shut.'

Stirling pressed the intercom button on the door by his side, asking the driver to stop. This was totally against protocol but Stirling wanted Frears out of the car. The Daimler slowed to a halt on a street corner. A group of black teenagers who'd been watching the convoy fly by were now nudging each other. Good, thought Stirling. Frears will stick out like a sore thumb here.

The car behind had stopped too and now the PM's Daimler was surrounded by four policemen in suits.

'That'll be all, Frears,' said Stirling, signalling to one of the officers to open the Guardsman's door. 'I don't want to talk about this again unless it's absolutely necessary.'

Frears' door was opened and he stepped out. Stirling pressed the intercom again and told the driver to move on.

The Prime Minister turned to look at the Guardsman standing by the side of the road. The small posse of hooded teenagers were beginning to point; the man in a Gieves & Hawkes suit could not have been more out of place had he beamed down from an alien mothership.

Stirling ran both hands through the dense curls of his hair. How could he be expected to deliver a speech on multi-fucking-culturalism when he had this hanging over him?

What if Keddie had blabbed to a hack? Of course he could throw the weight of Downing Street's comms team at the tale, discredit both the shrink and the journo, dismiss it all as the delusional fantasy of a clinically depressed man. God knows, other stories had been buried in similar ways. But what if this one refused to die? What if it sucked up oxygen, became a raging fire? Stirling felt his shirt cling to the sweat on his back.

Pull yourself together, he thought. This was what being PM was about. Juggling a load of balls at the same time. Unfortunately this particular ball happened to be on fire.

He looked ahead through the plate glass, past the heads of his driver and a bodyguard to the streets in front. The road was clear. Police cars and motorbike outriders had carved a path through the London traffic. If only the problem in hand could be dealt with as simply.

Chapter 9

King's Cross, London

The front page headline chilled Sam's blood.

SCOTT 'KILLED HIMSELF'

The newspaper lay next to him on the bed. Sam had booked into a grimy bed & breakfast off the Euston Road, a place of paper-thin walls, dirty sheets and shared bathrooms. Perfect for a man who, for now, needed to disappear below the radar.

The room was paid for from the wad of cash he'd withdrawn over the counter at his local bank, an amount he hoped would tide him over and remove the need for a visit to a cashpoint. A precaution, he had told himself at the time, though he could see he was already acting like a paranoid, hunted man.

He wanted to ignore the newspaper, to throw it away, but he couldn't. He re-read the article below the headline.

According to a police 'source' who'd been present at the autopsy, Scott had 'allegedly' overdosed on Co-proxamol. The suicide assertion might have been couched in careful language but Sam suspected the paper wouldn't have dared talk of the presence of Co-proxamol had it not been true. He hoped to God Scott's family had been told in advance and not read it first in this rag.

As to why Scott might have done this, the journalist had no concrete theory but clearly enjoyed offering up his ideas. He mentioned Wendy Scott's Motor Neurone Disease which had, according to 'friends of the Scotts', put unbearable strains on family life. He also mentioned the Minister's 'disappointment' at being passed over for higher office in recent Cabinet re-shuffles, despite his close friendship with the PM.

Sam cast the paper aside in disgust. Lives, as he knew all too well, were far more subtle and complicated, yet newspapers like this felt it was their God-given right to publish utterly poisonous bullshit and pass it off as fact.

He turned to the other items on the bed, his case notes, hoping he'd find a better understanding of why Scott had ended his life – and why he was being pursued so intently.

But as he re-read the notes, he realised that there was nothing in them that provided even the most meagre of leads. The main problem was Scott's obvious caution, fuelled by paranoia, which meant he was determined to remain as opaque as possible. There was the mention of him having done 'something terrible' and of course his dream, the recalling of which produced such a physical reaction. Scott running through a high-walled maze, looking for Hank. The maze was sure to be a metaphor for his own state, a place from which he couldn't escape. But who was Hank? Without more knowledge of the Minister, it was impossible to make any sense of it.

One over-riding, toxic thought kept spinning round Sam's head. Had Scott, by the time he left, already decided to kill himself? And if so, what had prompted that decision? His interventions? No, uncomfortable though Sam felt about his brief time with Scott, he simply couldn't accept that. What about the Government employee's arrival – something that seemed to affect Scott's mood more than anything else?

Another thought cast a long shadow over the room. Had it really been suicide? Sam remembered the weapons inspector, Dr David Kelly, whose death, despite official findings, was still the subject of endless speculation on the web.

Sam shook the thought from his head. Right now, he had to build on what he knew, rather than enter a world of supposition. If he was to have any hope of removing the threat that hung over him, he urgently needed answers. But who could he turn to?

His eye drifted back to the newspaper. And it was then that he realised there was someone he could contact. Someone who, like him, would be seeking answers of their own.

Chapter 10

Sussex

The Scott family home was not hard to find. Mention of the farmhouse in Sussex had been in the media repeatedly. A quick surf in an internet café soon coughed up the relevant information.

Just over an hour later, Sam's train pulled into Haywards Heath, the town that was, according to the map he'd consulted at Victoria, nearest the Scotts' hamlet. Outside the station, he gave his destination to a minicab driver.

'You're the sixth today,' the man said. 'Journalist, are you?'

Sam climbed in the back. 'No,' he said, with a vehemence that surprised him. 'I'm visiting family.'

Fifteen minutes later, the cab was heading down a narrow lane towards the hamlet. As it came into view – a church, pub and cluster of old cottages – Sam realised that there was no need for further directions. Just ahead there were a number of large vans crowned with satellite dishes and, standing by them, a throng of reporters. Despite the PM's plea for privacy, it was clear the media still considered Eleanor and her mother fair game.

He now knew the location of the Scott house, but getting to it was still going to be a problem. He'd have to get past all the reporters and photographers, causing them excitement and drawing attention to himself in a way that was simply not sensible. Maybe, he thought, he could bypass the track and reach the house on foot across country.

He asked the driver to stop outside a small terrace, paid, and then waited for the car to pull away, before moving at a pace back up the lane on the opposite side to the gathered press.

Once past them, he crossed back over. A steep hedge bordered the edge of the lane, blocking his view of the landscape below. He needed a gap to get through if he was to stand any chance of reaching the Scotts' house.

A little further on there was a farm gate. Sam paused to plan his next move. Immediately ahead was a ploughed field, the ground large lumps of dried, cracked earth after several weeks without rain. The field dropped down to a small copse. There was no sign of the house but he could make out, just beyond the trees, a little smoke rising. It had to be a chimney.

He vaulted the gate and began moving across the field. He suddenly felt exposed, despite being unaware of anyone watching him.

It took a couple of minutes before he was at the edge of the copse. It was ringed by wooden posts linked by stretches of barbed wire. As he attempted to climb over it, his foot slid. He snagged his jeans and cursed under his breath.

Sam moved on through the wood, stumbling over the uneven ground. The trees were still in leaf and the grey light of a sunless day was soon blocked out by the canopy above. He tripped over a fallen branch covered in vegetation and staggered forward, swearing again.

Soon afterwards the light increased and he could see that he was coming to a clearing. This one wasn't marked by a barbed wire fence. The woods simply ended, opening on to a stretch of lawn that ran alongside a gravel drive leading to a large stone farmhouse and a number of outbuildings. Outside the house were two vehicles – a people carrier and a Mini Cooper.

Sam was sure that this was the Scott family home. He now had to consider his next move. Did he simply march up to the front door?

His thoughts were interrupted by the sound of a twig snapping underfoot. He was about to look behind when he heard a woman's voice.

'Move an inch and I'll blow your bloody head off.'

Chapter 11

Sussex

'If you are what you say you are – a therapist – then you'll know that, as a recently bereaved daughter, I'm out of my mind with grief; capable of acting in ways that I cannot be held responsible for.'

Looking at the woman before him – her eyes blazing with anger, hands wrapped tightly around a shotgun – Sam had no doubt she was telling the truth. 'I am a therapist,' he repeated. 'Your father's therapist.'

'Prove it,' said Eleanor Scott.

They were standing in one of the farm outbuildings, an old stable block with a floor strewn with straw, the air tainted with the smell of manure. Eleanor Scott wore an over-sized overcoat – perhaps, thought Sam, her father's, and an attempt by her to stay close to him. Above this dense, protective layer her face, despite raging eyes, seemed fragile and delicate – pale skin etched with fatigue and sadness.

'He came to see me for a session the day before he died,' said Sam, immediately regretting his choice of words.

Eleanor said nothing, which made Sam even more edgy. Right now, she had every reason to hate him. He briefly considered mentioning what Scott had said about her, but as quickly decided against it.

'All I can say is that he looked a shadow of the man I knew from the media. He talked about something that was haunting him day and night.'

The shotgun dropped a fraction.

'Your father talked about being in a deep pit – one he was never going to get out of.'

Eleanor's eyes had begun to well. Sam knew what he needed to say now to finally remove the threat of a shotgun being fired into his stomach. It was cheap but, Sam was confident, guaranteed to wrench at the heart of a bereaved daughter.

'He was frightened.'

Eleanor was crying now and the shotgun hung limply by her side.

'I'm so sorry about your father,' Sam said. 'I'm also sorry for marching on to your property like this. But I couldn't think of any other way to get in contact with you. I knew you wouldn't talk to me on the phone in case you thought I was some prying journalist.'

Eleanor looked up, her eyes wet with tears. 'So why have you come?'

'Something about your father's death doesn't add up,' said Sam. 'And I have to find out what.'

Chapter 12

Sussex

They were sitting at the kitchen table, the surface scattered with unopened mail and piles of newspapers. Clearly Eleanor had been ploughing through them, reading both the good and bad stuff about her father. It was understandable. As long as he continued to be talked about, he was alive to her.

Around them, the room looked like it hadn't been cleaned for days, with muddy boot prints across the floor and a sink stacked with unwashed plates and pans. But the place had an undeniably homely feel to it. A dog – an elderly chocolate Labrador – was curled up in front of an Aga. Photos of Scott, Eleanor and Wendy in happier days – a fading snap of a family holiday from Eleanor's teenage years, the three of them in swimming costumes on an empty beach; another of Eleanor in mortar board and gown flanked by her grinning father – were pinned to a cork board.

Sam couldn't help but contrast this domestic scene with the home of his childhood, a sterile, cold house in an isolated rural spot in Wiltshire. In the absence of his father, who'd died shortly after he was born, Sam's mother, a scientist who worked at the MoD, dictated life for her only child. The home was wholly lacking in human touches, or warmth of any kind. It was a building he had revisited countless times in his own therapy – and one which he hoped never to see again.

He could see Wendy Scott, the Minister's widow, through an open doorway. She was sitting in what looked like a specially adapted armchair and a carer was helping her to drink from a beaker with a spout.

'Keep your voice down, by the way' said Eleanor, her tone still brittle. 'Mum may look gaga but she's not – and I don't want her hearing what you say.'

Eleanor took a sip of her coffee. She was, Sam reckoned, in her early thirties, slender with a mass of unbrushed, shoulder-length brown hair. She was attractive, in an unconventional way, with a trace of freckles across the smooth skin of her cheeks and straight nose, and a dimple beneath her full mouth. Tired eyes – the irises a deep, dark brown – flickered inquisitively in his direction. Sam noticed – as he frequently did of his clients – that at the end of Eleanor's long fingers, the nails were bitten and the skin raw.

Things had moved on a great deal since their initial meeting. The shotgun – Sam guessed it might never have been loaded, but he hadn't asked – was now lying in an entrance porch and Eleanor had also made him a coffee. But he knew he could still not afford to say one wrong word. She was fragile. He could not distress her any more. So while he'd mentioned her father being haunted by something, he had not revealed the other telling phrase – Scott saying that he'd 'done something terrible'. He also knew any mention of what Scott had said about his family – 'Wendy's all but lost to me. And I can't burden Eleanor with this. She wouldn't understand.' – was out of the question. This reluctance was not out of deference to his former client – he was already betraying him – but because he knew this information could lead to poisonous, destructive assumptions on Eleanor's part. And that wouldn't help him either. The brutal truth was, he needed Eleanor to be thinking clearly.

No, the only way forward – selfish though it now felt – was to keep the notes to himself and convince her, in the gentlest, most sensitive way possible, that it was worth her getting involved in his search for the truth.

He started by telling her how, during his last session, her father had been spooked by the sight of a man in the street outside and how his mood had dramatically altered afterwards, going from fear to a calm resignation.

'Of what?' asked Eleanor.

'I'm not sure,' said Sam. 'All I know is that the next day, the same man who appeared in the street turned up at my house to tell me your father had committed suicide.'

Sam paused, groaning inwardly, hardly believing that he'd been so tactless.

'It's alright,' said Eleanor. 'We've seen the autopsy report – and the papers.'

'Right,' said Sam, struggling to regain his flow. 'Anyhow, this man then asked me to tell him what your father had said about his work.'

'I'm assuming you told him to piss off,' Eleanor said.

'After a fashion,' said Sam. 'I didn't like or trust the man one bit. And there was no way I was telling a stranger what a client had told me in confidence. But he was insistent and, had another client not arrived, I think he would have happily beaten me to a pulp to get what he wanted.'

Eleanor leaned forward in her seat. 'So then what?'

'He stormed out. But later on someone else tried to break into my place and steal your father's case notes. When that failed, the same man chased me through a local cemetery with a knife in his hand. Had there not been people around, he'd have got what he wanted.'

Eleanor combed a hand through her thick hair. 'So what you're saying is, these men suspect that you know something about my father – something they deem explosive enough to steal or even kill for.'

Sam nodded.

'But you don't.'

'Exactly.'

'So you want my help to work out what this incendiary secret is.'

'I know you have your own grief to work through, Eleanor. I also know I'm trampling all over it by marching in here today. But I just wonder whether we can help each other.'

Eleanor's head dipped. He'd upset her. He knew it. When she looked up she was crying. But what came out of her mouth was not what he expected.

Eleanor turned to look at her mother in the room behind them. Her voice then dropped. 'Most widows in my mother's state, with maybe a year to live – two at best – would have given up with this news. But not her. She's found a new appetite for life. She's eating and drinking more.' She leaned forward, as if afraid her words were still carrying into the other room. 'I know why,' she said. 'She's angry. Angry with my father possibly, but more likely with the Government for putting Dad under unbearable stress. That's how she's making sense of it all.' She paused, looking out of the window at an indeterminate point.

'But you're not sure?'

'No,' she said, her eyes returning to the room. 'I think there's something else. I mean, I know he was under stress, but I don't think that unduly affected him. He knew what he'd signed up to.'

She raised her fingers into an arch and pressed them to her lips. 'Dad was such a steady man. Not always the most expressive emotionally, but he was always consistently affectionate towards me and Mum. He'd get angry of course – who doesn't? Normally it was about bullshit in the media, unfair jibes from the Opposition or injustices in the rest of the world, particularly those beyond the reach of his brief.'

She'd begun gesticulating with her hands, but now they came to rest on the table. 'He got mad about Mum's illness too, really mad. But then, despite the pain underneath, he dealt with it in a calm, measured way. What I'm trying to say is that he'd get affected by stuff you'd expect anyone to be affected by, but otherwise it was like he had a really even keel. Until recently, that is.'

'Something changed.'

'A couple of months back, he began acting differently, out of character I guess. This might sound odd, but he seemed to be unusually happy.'

'Most of my clients would give their right arm to be described that way, but I think I know what you mean. As if he were on a high.'

'Exactly. And I'd seen enough people in his state to know what was happening.'

'Which was?'

Her voice became even quieter. 'He was in love.'

'With another woman.'

'Yeah. We all knew of politicians whose marriages had been destroyed by life in the Commons – the long hours, all that time away from home. But theirs had survived. They had a bond. They loved each other.' She sighed. 'Or at least they had. Her illness seemed to change all that.' She smiled at a memory. 'They'd always been great communicators. If you could have heard the conversations around this table. They were always talking – about politics, the arts, all sorts of stuff. I remember one debate that went on all night, about Hitchcock.' She smiled. 'Mum said he was a misogynist but Dad, who was a massive fan, defended him to the hilt.' Eleanor's face darkened. 'Her disease shut all that down. And he seemed to really miss that regular communication with her. But just when I thought it was beginning to take its toll, he changed.'

'He met someone?'

'That's my guess. It was my birthday and he took me out for dinner in London. I assumed he'd put on a good front for me, but this was different. He was almost unrecognisable. The only way I can describe it is exuberant.'

'And this lasted till when?'

'A week or so ago I saw him for the first time in ages. He'd been working incredibly hard on something at the Ministry. He came down for the weekend and seemed not just tired, but utterly spent, like the light had gone out. I tried to draw out what was up, but he was closed down.'

'You think the relationship had gone badly wrong?'

'That was my conclusion.'

Sam paused. He was aware his next comment would seem selfish and insensitive, but he had to ask it. 'But why would this Government employee be so anxious about me finding out?'

Eleanor shrugged, seemingly unperturbed. 'The fact that my dad may have been having an affair hardly seems of significance.'

'No.'

But then a thought crossed Sam's mind, one which coloured the whole business. 'I guess that depends on who the woman was.'

Chapter 13

Docklands, London

As the journalist who'd broken the Scott suicide story, Tony McNess was feeling rather pleased with himself. He'd been called in by the editor that morning and congratulated. The paper's sales had gone through the roof. They all knew that, when the headline was salacious enough, all those who'd normally turn their noses up at a paper like theirs happily bought a copy.

The same people – the ones with good educations and jobs and nice houses – were also capable of acting in ways that did not reflect the respectability they loved to portray.

Take the woman who'd called this morning when McNess had returned to his desk in the news room. She was clearly middle-class, but that hadn't stopped her asking, up front, exactly how much she'd get paid for giving him information about Charles Scott. Now that the truth was out about his death, she clearly thought it was open season on the poor bastard.

McNess mentioned the figure which, depending on the strength of her information, she could expect to be paid.

Unsurprisingly, she then agreed to spill the beans. She went on to describe how, around two months back, she'd been in a restaurant in Suffolk with her husband, when she'd seen Scott at the table next to them. She said she could not forget the way he and his female companion had been acting.

Scott's fellow diner was, the source guessed, about ten to fifteen years younger than the Minister, a woman with long, mousey brown hair – elegantly dressed and nicely made up. She and Scott were clearly besotted with each other but were trying desperately not to show anyone else. This is what had made their behaviour so memorable. Their eyes rarely broke off contact all evening while their hands continually inched across the table towards each other, only to suddenly retreat when they realised what they'd been doing.

As their meal neared its conclusion, they became less restrained. Scott's foot began caressing the woman's legs under the table, while the woman repeatedly and, in the source's opinion, inappropriately, stroked her neckline as if anticipating the Minister's hand doing the very same thing.

'So they were definitely shagging?' asked McNess.

The woman paused, as if suddenly confronted by the grubbiness of what she was involved with, then confirmed: 'I think they were definitely having – or about to have – a sexual relationship.'

'And if I get together some images of women who might have known Scott and match your description, you're happy to try and identify her?'

The woman said she was.

McNess confirmed he'd be in touch, then called off. He was, as he liked to put it, fucking cock-a-hoop. If he could confirm that Scott was having a little extra behind his dying wife's back, that would add a whole extra dimension to the story. Had he been in love? Had that relationship collapsed, leaving Scott bereft and, ultimately, suicidal?

McNess grinned. This story was going to run and run.

Chapter 14

Sussex

Keen to avoid the hyenas assembled at the end of the track, Eleanor left the farmhouse by a narrow, seldom-used drive that led to another lane.

As her Mini emerged on to the quiet road, neither she nor Sam noticed the car parked against a bank a few metres away. As they sped off, the figure inside the car grabbed his mobile.

'Guess who's just appeared with Eleanor Scott?'

The voice on the other end uttered a single word.

'In one,' confirmed the man on the mobile. 'Shall I follow?'

'Yeah. And don't bloody lose them.'

Chapter 15

Bloomsbury, London

McNess had, with the help of the paper's picture editor, assembled a large file of images for his source. He'd limited the search to the previous three months but there was still a mountain of photographs to sift through. With the brief description he'd been given, he began looking for an elegant woman in her fifties, with long, mousey-coloured hair.

Although a bit vague, that description soon helped narrow the search down. Staring at a screen as he went through endless images of Scott, he soon dismissed over a hundred images in which the woman near to the Minister was black, Asian, fat, in a hijab, elderly, ugly, short-haired, in a wheelchair or, for that matter, a combination of the above. After a couple of hours, he had whittled his search down to about thirty images. Among them, there were about five contenders. It was now a case of lining them up like the usual suspects.

He met his source in a bar. She was, he was delighted to discover, not bad looking herself. Possibly in her early forties, a redhead with green eyes. He wouldn't have minded giving her one but he could soon tell that she wasn't even a remote possibility. She was obviously determined to give the impression that she was revolted by him. It was, he knew, her way of coping with the revulsion she felt about her own grubby behaviour. How else could she come to terms with the fact that she was doing a deal with a gutter-based tabloid hack?

They sat in a booth. The bar was in the basement of a hotel, a neutral place frequented by tourists rather than Londoners – the perfect place to meet contacts.

After going through almost all of the prints the picture editor had made for them, the woman stopped and began studying a photo intently. The image lay on the table across from McNess and he cocked his head to get a better look. It showed Scott leaving a building – some faceless corporate headquarters with big glass doors – with a small group of others. Bar one, they were all men in suits. The exception was a woman wearing a fitted skirt and matching jacket, her hair tied back in a pony tail.

'That's her,' said the woman.

'You sure?'

'Positive.'

'Nice one.'

McNess pulled the images back into a pile and placed them in a manila folder. The woman across from him began to look shifty. He loved this bit. He was going to make her squirm.

'Right,' said McNess. 'You've been a diamond.' He stood, pulling on his jacket.

She was on her feet too, looking more uncomfortable. McNess turned to leave when she eventually spoke, her voice barely above a whisper.

'Aren't you going to pay me?'

'I'm sorry,' said McNess, feigning deafness.

'You owe me money,' the woman hissed.

'Of course,' laughed McNess. He reached into his pocket and pulled out a bulging brown envelope. 'Here you go, darling.'

Finally confronted with the nature of the deal she'd struck, the woman seemed to hesitate, as if her prim, middle-class core found it all repellent. But then a hand darted out and snatched the envelope – and she was gone.

As McNess stood outside waiting to catch a cab, he tingled with the prospect of pushing this story to the next stage. He'd go back to the picture editor tonight, confirm the identity of the people in the image and where it had been taken. And then he'd track the woman down and confront her.

He could already foresee some unfortunate outcomes. Scott's family becoming even more upset. Him possibly unjustly branding this woman as the reason why the Minister committed suicide. But frankly, they weren't his concerns. His job was to keep the story alive, and if that involved pouring a little petrol on the fire, then so be it.

Chapter 16

Fulham, London

The lead had taken them to a tree-lined avenue of houses off Fulham Road.

On the way from Sussex, Eleanor had called the person they were visiting to warn her of their arrival. She was pretty sure the woman in question would be in. After all, she'd just lost her job.

Diana Tennant, Charles Scott's former secretary, opened the door with tears in her eyes, immediately wrapping Eleanor in a tight hug. It was as if the sight of the woman's tears gave Eleanor permission to cry. She began sobbing, her shoulders heaving as she clung to the older woman like a life raft. A moment later, she peeled away, a look of slight embarrassment on her face, and Diana Tennant ushered them indoors and up to the top floor flat.

They were now seated in the secretary's small living room. In between polite prints of English landscapes, there were countless photos of the Scott family. As Eleanor had explained, Diana had been her father's secretary for over twenty years. Remaining unmarried, she'd devoted the best part of her adult life to Scott, and the Minister had responded by making her virtually a member of the family. Diana Tennant had been at almost every family gathering Eleanor could remember.

But Sam could see that there might be limitations to her loyalty. While she was clearly fond of Eleanor, her allegiance would always be to Scott. It was this they were about to test.

'I'm so sorry, Eleanor,' said Diana.

She was, Sam guessed, in her late sixties, with a bun of grey hair and a gently wrinkled face.

'Your father was my dearest friend.'

'Thank you, Diana.'

If the Minister's former secretary had any theories about Scott's death, she was far too sensitive to reveal them now. Eleanor, by contrast, seemed more determined to get to the nub. Having given into her grief outside, she now sat on the edge of the sofa, her back straight, face full of resolve. This was, Sam realised, a distraction from Eleanor's pain and sadness, and she was seizing it with both hands.

'I can't explain why, Diana, but Sam and I desperately need to find out why Dad committed suicide.'

Eleanor had explained Sam's presence simply by saying that he was a 'friend'. It was way more simple than telling her that he was Scott's psychotherapist. He'd already seen the effect that had on people close to Charles Scott.

Diana Tennant looked blankly at Eleanor, as if the sudden change in tone had caught her off-guard.

Eleanor pressed on. 'I think Dad was having an affair.'

Diana Tennant blushed. 'I'm sure you're wrong, Eleanor,' she said.

Eleanor, who was sitting next to Diana on the sofa, placed a hand over one of the secretary's. 'It's OK. You don't need to protect him now.'

At this, the tears suddenly began flowing freely. 'Oh God, Eleanor,' Diana said. 'I so desperately wanted to shield you and your mother from this.'

'I wouldn't ever have wanted to deny him some happiness. Please tell me what you know.'

Diana looked at Eleanor, as if weighing up the implications of what she was about to say. Then she sighed. 'While I was privy to much of his correspondence, there were still matters, understandably given his position in the Government, to which I had no access. But one thing I was sure of, was an increasing number of calls from a certain woman. When this woman telephoned at the beginning, her voice had a distinctly formal tone to it – but later it began to change. It was as if she were trying desperately to sound business-like but couldn't manage it.'

Sam wasn't sure where this was heading. It was hardly proof of anything. If Scott could shield his secretary from matters of State, an affair would hardly prove a challenge.

'But then, one day,' continued the secretary, 'I met her.'

Diana shifted on the sofa. 'I was arranging a small conference on your father's behalf at the Houses of Parliament, and I noticed her name on the attendees list. Charles asked me to be in the room at the beginning, to ensure all those attending had what they needed. That's when I saw her take a seat by the place name I had put on the table.'

'Forgive me, Diana,' said Eleanor. 'I don't doubt your female intuition, but so far you've only suggested that this woman had crossed a line from business to something more personal.'

Diana Tennant looked utterly stricken. If this had been a therapy session, Sam would never have pressed his client in the way Eleanor had Diana. Awkward, painful information – which was, Sam was sure, what Diana was about to reveal – needed to come out when the client felt safe and ready. But he recognised that they had no such luxury.

'That was all I suspected,' said Diana. 'Until the end of the day. I was heading back to the room an hour or so after the meeting had finished to clear up. But when I got there, I found it locked. I had a key and tried the door, but realised it was locked from the inside. It was then that I heard the key turn and the door opened.'

She stopped, clearly too embarrassed to continue.

'Please go on, Diana,' urged Eleanor. 'I need to know.'

'Your father had opened the door just wide enough for me to see beyond him and that was when I saw her again. She had her back to me, but I recognised her hair and outfit. And what she was doing.'

Diana paused again, every word now excruciating for her. 'She was buttoning up her blouse.'

With that, Charles Scott's former secretary broke down again. Eleanor squeezed the hand she still held.

'Diana,' she said, her voice soft but firm. 'Who was she?'

As soon as Eleanor was back in the car, she began furiously tapping and stroking the screen of her phone. They had the woman's name – and where she worked.

'Ah,' Eleanor said, a note of triumph in her voice. 'Future Systems is a renewables firm, a big one by the looks of things. HQ near Reading. They work for multi-nationals. Governments too. There's a case study of a wind farm they helped set up in Uzbekistan.'

She began tapping again. 'Where are you?' she muttered under her breath.

There was a pause: 'Gotcha. Jane Vyner, Senior Vice President, Communications. And a picture.'

Sam leaned across the car to look at the image. It was a corporate head-and-shoulders shot of a woman in a white blouse and dark jacket, face immaculately made-up, mousey coloured hair drawn back. Eleanor was staring hard, as if hoping the image would cough up some clue as to why her father had been pitched into such a rollercoaster of emotions.

She looked up, eyes moving as she thought. 'Sod it. Can you have a look in the glove compartment? There should be a pen and something to write on in there.'

Sam rooted through it, producing a biro and an old envelope, which he handed to Eleanor. She jotted down a number, breathed in deeply, exhaled, then dialled.

'It's getting late,' cautioned Sam. 'She's probably gone home.'

Eleanor shot him a brief look, then snapped back as her call was answered. 'Hello, could I speak to Jane Vyner, please?'

Sam heard the indistinct sound of another voice.

'Eleanor Scott,' said Eleanor.

There was a pause, the faint strains of on-hold musak, then another voice. One that seemed faster, though just as indistinct. Then the call ended.

Eleanor turned to Sam, her face flushed. 'She's calling back,' she said. 'She sounded terrified.'

About ten minutes later, as the avenue around them began to darken and the streetlights flickered on, her phone rang again. Eleanor put the mobile on speaker, breathed in, then answered.

'I'm sorry,' Jane Vyner said, her voice calmer. 'I wanted to talk more easily, so I had to get out of the office.'

'We need to meet,' said Eleanor.

'Of course.'

'Tomorrow.'

'I can't do tomorrow.'

'I'm sorry,' said Eleanor, her voice barely containing the anger, 'but what could be more important than this?'

There was a pause at the other end.

'You're right. How about lunch?'

Vyner gave them directions to a pub in a village south of Reading and said she'd be there tomorrow at 1pm.

Chapter 17

Green Park, London

To Aidan Stirling, the architecture of central London was suffocating. The grand gentlemen's clubs and Whitehall buildings, the regimented Georgian squares and terraces, not least his own home in Downing Street. It all screamed compliance and conformity, which was of course something he struggled with enormously.

But there was a spot on Queen's Walk in Green Park, roughly midway between the Mall and Piccadilly, where he'd found something he did like looking at. At that point there was a very noticeable break in architectural tone. Next to fussy Spencer House was a block of flats designed by one of Aidan's architectural heroes, Denys Lasdun. He was better known for the National Theatre, a Brutalist building defined by chunks of bare concrete, hard angles and walkways. Aidan admired the theatre's otherness, the sense that the architect had been trying exceptionally hard to produce something simple and pure, a true combination of form and function.

In a sense, the block of flats before him was not a fraction as innovative, but in the midst of all the formality of this part of town, it allowed Aidan to escape.

Of course simply getting to this place in the park was an escape, slipping not just his minders, but also the grip of the Olanzapine he'd been prescribed.

For the past two days, he'd been trusted – naively, as it turned out – to take the little pills. He'd abused that trust, flushing the capsules down the toilet where they were now no doubt slowing the frantic, libidinous rats in the sewer to a sleepy shuffle. He could still feel the toxins in his system. On full whack, the pills acted like a malevolent treacle, slowing every reaction, movement and desire. He was reduced to a zombie, a daytime television-watching simpleton whose only need was a constant stream of sugary snacks.

It was early evening, the fading sunlight sending long shadows across the grass and lighting up the windows of 26 St James's Place so that they appeared on fire.

Aidan sat on a bench to enjoy what he knew would be a limited moment. The park would soon be closing. He'd shortly be discovered.

A girl passed by in a black mackintosh, slim legs in fishnet tights. She wore a pair of heels that were clearly uncomfortable, a slight hobble defining her gait. Perhaps they were new, or she was unused to wearing shoes like that. She was young, about 18 or 19, with short blond hair. Maybe she'd just started working.

The girl moved past him towards Piccadilly, looking briefly in his direction. Checking him out? His nose picked up her one-dimensional scent. He couldn't help comparing it to the more multi-layered perfumes his mother wore.

Having felt calmed by the sight of 26 St James's Place, he now began to feel discomfort, as if his clothes were riddled with lice. He studied the girl's stumbling legs as they moved up the path. Would she turn round for another look?

He never found out. A hand gripped his shoulder. He then heard a familiar voice in his ear.

'Shouldn't you be at home?' said a man, the tone sarcastic, but also impatient.

Aidan closed his eyes, hoping the presence behind him was some spiteful spirit coughed up by what remained of his medication. But when he reopened them and turned his head, he was there. One of his shadows.

'You'd best come back with me,' said the man.

Chapter 18

It was just after 10pm when one of the members of Team Kilo reached the front door that Keddie and Scott had exited earlier that evening.

Frears had seven men in his unit – professionals he already trusted or whose reputations he'd admired while in the private sector – each chosen for their absolute discretion and established skills in distinct areas. There was Team Alpha, which consisted of four surveillance experts, former members of the police and army intelligence. Then there was Team Kilo, made up of three ex-soldiers chosen for their ability to follow orders that required both inventiveness and a certain moral elasticity to carry out.

The bald, stocky figure in a suit carefully studied the names of the different residents, written on small framed cards next to the buzzers of their flats. Recognising one from a list Frears had furnished him with, he pressed the bell. A moment later, an uncertain voice spoke over the intercom and asked who was there.

The man told Diana Tennant he was a Government employee, there on urgent business concerning the late Charles Scott.

'How do I know you're not from the press?' she asked.

'You don't,' he said. 'But if you refuse to let me in, I can't give you Philip Stirling's personal message.'

As expected, the door opened.

He found her in a dressing gown, long, grey hair tumbling down both shoulders, standing at the doorway of the flat. He asked if he could come in. She seemed to hesitate, then relented.

Diana Tennant shut the door behind him and then stood by her mantelpiece. He was not invited to sit.

The man apologized for visiting at such a late hour, but said that he was here on a matter of national security. He briefly flashed his identification badge. Diana Tennant, used to being close but not privy to such things, jumped to attention at this point. With her fully compliant, the man then asked what Eleanor Scott and Keddie had wanted. For a moment, the older woman seemed torn between her loyalty to the Scott family and to the State. The man smiled, a reassuring gesture that said: 'You can trust me.'

Minutes later, he was back on the street.

Upstairs, Diana Tennant was getting ready for bed again. Her mind briefly grappled with what had happened, how she'd betrayed the family of her former boss. But then she remembered the phrase, 'a matter of national security' and the man's parting words: 'Philip Stirling wants you to know he values loyalty to the Government very highly'.

As she pulled the sheets up around her, Diana Tennant felt her cheeks glow.

Chapter 19

Sussex

Sam woke with a jolt, the room around him unfamiliar. He rubbed his eyes and then realised where he was.

The room was cold, the small window dripping with condensation. He had a sense that this was a forgotten corner of the house, a place to which he'd been banished by Eleanor to avoid him coming into contact with Wendy Scott, or indeed herself.

He got out of bed and went to the window, wiping a section clear of moisture. It was an overcast day, the woodland he'd emerged from the day before indistinct in the misty morning light. He felt a sudden twinge in the stomach, a memory of the fear he'd experienced in the cemetery. He breathed in deeply, trying to relax.

Downstairs, Eleanor was pacing the kitchen.

'There's coffee over there,' she said, pointing to a half-filled cafetière. Sam sensed a cooling of relations. This was understandable. Initially deeply mistrustful, then more open, she seemed to have swung back in the original direction. He predicted that today, bar the task in hand, there'd be little in the way of conversation.

Last night, on the way home, Eleanor had talked about her workplace, an overseas development charity. They then briefly discussed her role there, as head of fundraising. Sam had remarked that the job was a natural choice, given her father's Ministerial post, and this had gone down really badly, with Eleanor clamming up immediately.

He understood her reticence. She'd just lost her father. And rather than processing this in a private way, she was being forced to share time with his mind-probing therapist, about whom she was bound to have conflicting feelings. Did Sam, for example, tip her father over the edge?

Fortunately, thought Sam, as he sipped lukewarm coffee at the table while Eleanor, finally seated, consulted a map, today was not about chatting, but about pursuing their next line of enquiry.

An hour and a half later, their near silent journey – punctuated by short exchanges of information about the route they were taking – was nearing its destination. They drove down a street past thatched houses, a cluster of Victorian cottages, a school, hall and shop.

'Where's this bloody boozer?' muttered Eleanor impatiently.

They rounded a corner and there was a sign just ahead for the pub. They turned into the car park. Jane Vyner had said she'd be standing by a silver BMW. They got out and surveyed the car park. There were about fifteen cars but, as they soon realised, no silver BMWs and certainly no-one waiting to meet them.

'Do you think she got cold feet?' asked Sam.

'I don't know,' said Eleanor. 'But I'm not letting her off this easily. I'll give her ten minutes, then if she hasn't turned up, God help her.'

Chapter 20

Reading, Berkshire

Jane Vyner distinctly remembered the moment Charles
Scott's death was announced. The team had been called into
the boardroom and told by the Chief Executive. Everyone
had gasped, hands were placed over open mouths. The Chief
Executive gave them a minute to absorb the news, then
ploughed on. Tragic though the Minister's death was, the
project would not be derailed.

A little later, locked in a cubicle in the ladies toilet, Jane
had given into a flood of emotion. She sobbed, the tears
accompanied by great heaves of her shoulders. Her nose ran
uncontrollably. Waves of nausea swept through her stomach.

Afterwards, she examined herself in the mirror. Her face
was red and puffy, her cheeks stained with mascara-
blackened tears. Rooting in her handbag and retrieving her
make-up, she set to work to repair the damage.

It was amazing what a little foundation, lipstick and
mascara could achieve. Her eyes were still red but then
whose weren't? They'd all been working incredibly hard to
ensure the biggest deal in the company's history went

through. Late nights had become the norm, with meetings either here at head office, or up in London with various mid- and high-level members of the Government.

At that moment, looking at the mask she'd applied, she realised something. It was all about the face she presented. She had to remain calm and measured. What had happened had to stay secret – unbearably painful though it was. This had the potential not only to destroy her, but the firm as well. A piece of information that could bring a mighty FTSE company to its knees at the very moment when it should have been riding high.

She'd only recently patted herself on the back for maintaining such a composed demeanour, for so skilfully compartmentalising the sadness she felt.

And then she'd got the call.

She'd expected a journalist, or maybe her boss. But Scott's daughter?

She'd hardly been able to sleep last night, as her mind went over and over the potential outcomes of today's lunch. Now, as she walked towards the lifts that would take her to the reception of Future Systems' huge corporate headquarters, she returned to the same treadmill of thoughts. Denying it – claiming that the two of them had simply been friends – was not an option. The chances were that Eleanor Scott already knew. Why else would she be calling?

She tried to calm herself. This wasn't necessarily a disaster. Eleanor Scott had not sounded hostile. She probably just wanted to talk to someone who'd been close to the man she missed.

Jane reached a bank of lifts and pressed the button. There were a handful of colleagues she knew but she acted as if she were deep in thought – head down, brow furrowed – in the hope she wouldn't be disturbed.

What if Eleanor Scott blamed her for her father's suicide? What lengths would she go to to make her pay? It was something Jane had considered herself numerous times since she'd heard the awful news. She'd repeatedly been over the final moments of their relationship, looking for signs that she had caused the kind of damage that might have tipped Charles over the edge. Sometimes – when she was alone, late, in the office – she wondered whether she should have given him another chance. But when she felt strong, she knew that she couldn't possibly have acted in any other way. She had not been responsible for pushing a man like Charles – a thick-skinned Cabinet Minister who'd dealt with any number of crises, both personal and work-related – to take his own life. Something else had.

To explain this to Eleanor, she knew that it was important to establish why she'd ended the relationship. It would be painful for both of them, but give Eleanor an idea of her father's mental state at the time.

Charles, the man she'd fallen so spectacularly for, had suddenly changed. Jane could pinpoint exactly when that change had occurred, but had no idea what had caused it. In true politician's style, Charles had kept that particular card very close to his chest. All she knew was that something poisonous had insinuated itself into Charles's mind, and his easy, intimate way with her disappeared overnight. Without some guarantee that things would return to how they'd been – and Charles had given none – she knew she could not stay with him.

The lift doors opened on to a vast reception area. Four storeys above her was the glass roof. To her right was a white wall hung with a huge abstract painting.

As she moved towards the doors that opened on to the car park, her progress was halted by one of the girls on the front desk, who called out to her.

'Miss Vyner, there's a gentleman here to see you.'

Jane had been so deep in thought that she hadn't noticed the man leaning against the long bank of polished walnut that fronted the reception. He was 40ish, with balding hair shaved close to his scalp and a pot belly hanging over the waistband of his jeans.

'Tony McNess,' he said, thrusting out a hand. He then said two more words that froze her blood – the name of a British tabloid newspaper.

'Can I have a word?'

She had to think fast. 'You should talk to our press office.'

'It's not about your firm,' he said. His voice then dropped to a hiss. 'It's about you – and Charles Scott.'

Jane shot a glance at the receptionists. They appeared not to have heard. She smiled weakly. 'I'm not quite sure what you're referring to. Whatever it is, I cannot talk now. I urge you to make an appointment.'

She knew she sounded like a lousy liar, but this was all happening too fast. First Eleanor Scott, now this. She couldn't think straight. She began moving towards the entrance. McNess quickly caught up.

'We both know you were sleeping with Scott, Miss Vyner,' he said. 'Now we can either get your side of the story, or go ahead and print what we know.'

Jane stopped in her tracks just before the entrance. 'I would urge you to be very careful what you print,' she bluffed. 'Future Systems is a very big company, with a formidable legal resource. You do not want to get on the wrong side of us.'

McNess smiled. 'Like I said, Miss Vyner. This is nothing to do with Future Systems. This is about you.'

Afraid that whatever she said would get her deeper into the shit she was already wading through, Jane walked through the doors, desperate to get away from this viper. She was soon running, sprinting to her car so she could shut him – and the rest of this nightmare – out of her life, even if for just one moment.

McNess was running after her, obviously not ready to give up yet. As she approached her car, she unlocked the doors with her fob, and was then in, starting the engine. McNess was suddenly in front of the vehicle, arms outstretched in a vain attempt to halt her. Fuck him, she thought, as she put the car in gear and slammed on the accelerator. The journalist leapt out of the way just in time, as Jane, with a skid of tyres, headed for the exit.

At the barrier, which seemed to rise agonisingly slowly, she looked in the rear-view mirror and saw a dark car approaching in her wake. She had to get away.

Finally she was out. Turning left and putting her foot down, she glanced backwards again. The dark car had somehow managed to gain on her, and was now just metres behind. She slammed her foot down without realising that the lights ahead had changed.

Her car shot forward as traffic from both sides began to move into her path. As she crossed the first lane, she missed, by a whisker, the back end of a white van. A split-second later, as she moved into the second lane of vehicles, her good fortune ran out, and a large shape, which was all she saw in her peripheral vision, smashed into the passenger side of her car. Before Jane lost consciousness, she had the distinct sensation that her BMW was flying through the air in slow motion. As the ground came towards the window at her side and she began to lift up, she realised that, in the rush to escape McNess, she'd forgotten to put her seatbelt on.

Chapter 21

Reading, Berkshire

'If this goes to bloody voicemail, I'm heading straight for her office,' said Eleanor, as she waited for Jane Vyner to answer her phone.

'Hello,' she said, her impatience barely contained. There was a pause. 'I need to speak to Jane.' When she spoke again after another moment, her voice was softer, quieter. 'Right. Thank you'

Eleanor's face, when she turned to Sam, had paled. 'A policeman answered her phone. He said that there's been a traffic accident. Two casualties have been taken to hospital in Reading.'

Eleanor stared into the middle distance, then snapped back into reality. Her face seemed to flood with rage, with the look Sam had seen when he'd first met her and she was clutching a shotgun.

'She cannot do this to me!' Eleanor cried. 'She cannot deny me my right to know why Dad died.'

Sam had watched enough hospital dramas to know that Jane Vyner would probably be unconscious and, once in hospital, in surgery almost immediately.

'We need to get to that hospital,' said Eleanor.

'That might not be a great idea,' cautioned Sam. 'It makes us very visible.'

Eleanor looked sceptically at Sam. Of course, he thought, why would she be scared? To her, talk of knife-wielding pursuers was still just that, talk. It wasn't real to her. He hoped to God it stayed that way.

'This is my one chance to speak to her,' said Eleanor. 'I'm not missing it.'

She jumped in the car. The engine started. Sam inwardly railed against this, but knew that any discussion would not be welcome. Besides, he'd dragged Eleanor into this. He had to protect her.

Chapter 22

Reading, Berkshire

Behind the glass-fronted reception of the hospital's A&E department, the nurse on duty, an Asian man whose bloodshot eyes suggested sleeplessness on a grand scale, asked how he could help them.

'A friend has just been admitted – Jane Vyner,' said Eleanor. Sam could see her anger was barely contained. The prospect of being robbed of the chance to speak to Vyner had been further compounded by a frustrating hunt for a parking space and then A&E. 'She's been involved in a car accident.'

The nurse looked blankly at Eleanor. 'You're not a relative?'

'No, but –'

'Then I can't talk about a patient with you.'

'But I need –'

'I'm sorry,' said the man, his voice calm but unyielding, as he returned to the screen in front of him.

Sam drew Eleanor away. 'Listen,' he said. 'Chances are she's in ICU. Why don't we try and find her? And prepare our lines a bit better?'

Eleanor nodded. Nearby was a long list of wards, departments and theatres. Finally, they located the one they were looking for – Kennet Ward – and, thanks to a map of the site, a route to it.

They were soon jogging down a corridor towards a bank of lifts, dodging hospital staff and slow-moving patients shuffling along in dressing gowns.

On the hospital's third floor, the reception at Kennet Ward was manned by three nurses – one with her head deep in paperwork, two others sharing a joke as they adjusted a saline drip. The corridor beyond was alive with activity – families sitting outside rooms, doctors clustered in small groups with nursing staff – and it was only as Eleanor approached reception that Sam saw, much further down the corridor, two policemen.

'Stop,' whispered Sam, grabbing her arm.

Eleanor looked at him. He nodded in the policemen's direction. 'I bet they're here for Jane Vyner,' he said, his voice still low. 'It's a road traffic accident. They will need to interview her. I'm not sure we want to be drawing attention to ourselves by lying.'

Eleanor's arm, which had tensed against his hand, relaxed a fraction.

The people in the corridor parted as a trolley was wheeled through their midst. A small group in green scrubs accompanied it. As it neared, Sam could see that the figure on the trolley – what was visible of her – was a woman.

The patient was in a surgical gown, spotted with blood on her legs and arms. There was a large dressing to the right side of her head. Her eyes were closed.

As they passed, one of the figures in green handed a piece of paper to another in the group.

'What do you see?'

'Crescent-shaped deformity so...'

'Come on, come on. No time to hesitate in these situations.'

'Subdural haemorrhage?'

'Good. But not good for our patient. That said, for a car crash of this severity, she's bloody lucky it's not worse.'

The group moved on.

'It's her, isn't it?' said Eleanor.

'Yup.'

'Christ,' said Eleanor, with a shudder. 'She's in a right bloody mess.'

'And unconscious for some hours yet.'

Sam, who still held Eleanor's arm, felt her tense again.

'I have to talk to her.'

Chapter 23

Reading, Berkshire

It was 8pm when Eleanor and Sam returned to the hospital. Five hours had passed since they'd seen Jane Vyner on her way to surgery. They'd hidden in a dark corner of a pub for the afternoon, nursing one soft drink after another. Sam had insisted on a table with a view of the front and back doors.

Returning to the hospital seemed to Sam like tempting fate. There was also the matter of the lie that needed to be told to gain access to Jane Vyner, who just might be out of surgery and awake, if still heavily sedated. If her family were present – or the police – it was out of the question.

The lift doors opened on to Kennet Ward and a view of the town spread out in front of them, a mass of lights in a darkening cityscape. To their right was the reception desk and beyond, the corridor, now dimmed. Compared to earlier, it was eerily quiet. The reception was unmanned. Further down the corridor, there was no sign of the police, nor indeed anyone else.

They moved down the corridor, through a set of swing doors into a ward. There were around twenty beds, about a quarter of which were occupied. Patients, many of whom were on drips and connected to heart monitors, appeared heavily sedated, barely reacting to the presence of two strangers wandering through their midst, scrutinising them.

The doors ahead of them suddenly swung open and a tall male nurse in a lilac uniform rushed past before either of them had a chance to ask where Jane Vyner was. As the man passed, Sam caught a glimpse of his face – narrow eyes that flared briefly as they took in Sam and Eleanor.

Sam felt an inexplicable chill run through him, as if he'd seen a ghost. He took Eleanor by the elbow, moving her swiftly through the next set of doors.

They were now on a corridor of private rooms. Sam and Eleanor scanned the windows to see if they could spot Jane Vyner. As they began to wonder whether they were in the wrong ward, they heard a commotion at the far end of the passage.

The door to a private room was open and Sam and Eleanor saw two nurses and a doctor moving about the bed. The doctor was standing over the patient conducting chest compressions while one of the nurses was pumping a bag connected to a mask over a woman's mouth and nose. Despite the commotion, Sam could hear the sound of an automated, American-accented voice: 'Analysing rhythm,' it said. There was a pause, then: 'No shock required; resume CPR.'

'It's her, isn't it?' said Eleanor.

The doctor and nurse continued their ritual for a few more minutes. Then the metallic voice uttered the same three phrases. The doctor stopped for a moment, feeling the woman's neck. He shook his head, then looked at his watch.

'Time of death, 8.10pm,' he said.

'I just don't understand it,' said one of the nurses. 'I passed by a quarter of an hour ago and Miss Vyner seemed comfortable.'

Sam's blood ran cold. Suddenly he remembered where he'd seen that face before. The narrow-eyed nurse was the man who'd chased him through the cemetery.

The hospital, a place packed with skilled staff and sophisticated equipment dedicated to preserving and prolonging life, now felt as defenceless as the woman lying on the bed before them. Sam glanced over his shoulder. The walls of the empty corridor seemed to close in on him, their escape route suddenly loaded with danger.

Chapter 24

Reading, Berkshire

The narrow-eyed man reappeared in Sam's mind more menacing than ever before. This had to be his work.

A thought occurred to Sam, one that made his mouth go dry and the breath catch in his throat. They'd led the man right to Jane Vyner.

Eleanor was standing in a state of shock, staring at the now slower activity around Jane Vyner's bed. The doctor was filling in a form while a nurse pulled the sheets back over Vyner, as if making her comfortable. Another nurse gently closed her eyes.

Sam was desperate to get Eleanor out of here and by as public and busy a route as possible. If the narrow-eyed man was prepared to snuff out a woman in the midst of a hospital ward, Sam suspected he wouldn't hesitate to take them out in whatever way was convenient.

'Come on,' said Sam, placing a hand in the small of Eleanor's back. 'We need to get out of here.'

Eleanor, numbed by what she'd seen, snapped into the moment.

'Why?'

'I'll explain when we're out of the hospital.'

Eleanor stiffened but still allowed Sam to lead her back the way they'd come. The ward felt darker and more threatening now, as if someone might spring from the shadows at any moment.

As they approached the lift and stairwell, Sam began weighing up their two escape options. The lift, though direct, was a confined space and a primal instinct – one forged in his early childhood – was screaming 'no'. The stairs seemed a better option – more open, and with a number of potential escape routes.

Sam closed his eyes and re-opened them. Focus, he thought. As far as he could see, the murderer was no longer on this floor. In reality, what were the chances of him being on a floor below, waiting for a lift to descend from the third floor in the hope that it contained Sam and Eleanor – and they were alone? Sam pressed the button.

'What the hell is going on?' said Eleanor.

Sam watched the red light above the button he'd just pressed. It was still on '0'. Finally it inched to '1', then stopped. He turned to look into Eleanor's eyes for signs of runaway anxiety. She was clearly hyper alert, but didn't appear to be in a state of extreme alarm. He risked the truth.

'The male nurse we passed,' he said, 'the man in lilac.'

Eleanor nodded, frown lines appearing across her forehead.

'I've seen him before. He was the one who pulled a knife on me in the cemetery.'

There was a 'ping' heralding the arrival of the lift. The doors opened to reveal a trolley on which a sedated elderly man was lying, his chest connected via a series of pads and wires to an ECG monitor. Behind him were three men in green still wearing surgical bandannas.

The sight of these professionals seemed to calm Eleanor. Sam watched her take a deep breath as the trolley moved past. They then moved into the lift.

They were silent as the lift descended, Sam experiencing every second of the journey as an eternity.

On the ground floor, they passed through the crowded corridors to the hospital's main entrance. Outside, a wiry man wearing pyjamas and a dressing gown was sucking on a cigarette as if it were oxygen and he'd just escaped a blazing building.

They crossed a road to the multi-storey car park.

The lift was out of order so they began to climb the stairs. They had two flights to ascend before they reached the level where the car was parked. The stairs, tagged in graffiti and smelling of disinfectant and urine, were well-lit, yet Sam was now sure that an attacker was behind every corner.

On the second floor they walked slowly towards the car. There were now just a handful of vehicles in the car park. If the murderer knew that Eleanor drove a Mini – which, given his knowledge of their movements, was highly likely – then he was probably waiting for them.

Eleanor reached into her coat pocket for the car fob. She pressed it and the Mini's lights blinked to attention. If the narrow-eyed man hadn't seen or heard them coming yet, he would have now. The car was on its own at the end of a row which meant that Sam could see right around – and underneath – it as he approached. There didn't appear to be anyone hiding nearby. But that didn't mean someone wasn't watching from another place.

They reached the car, Sam's mind now alive with other possibilities: the car exploding the moment the engine started; the lights of another car facing them head on as soon as they turned to leave.

Eleanor handed him the keys, clearly too shaken to drive.

Sam started the engine then eased the car slowly out of the space and towards the ramp down to the first level.

There were no explosions, no other headlights. They passed through the barrier and out into the street.

Whatever relief Sam felt soon evaporated. Traffic was moving painfully slowly, their swift escape from Reading thwarted.

Sam looked ahead and behind, to his left and right. The driver to his side, a man in his fifties; the woman on the pavement in a dark tracksuit and baseball cap. Suddenly he saw threats everywhere.

Chapter 25

Downing Street

'He did what?'

The generously proportioned private apartment above the Chancellor of the Exchequer's official residence, 11 Downing Street, had, since Blair's day, been the home of the Prime Minister. The Chancellor, meanwhile, had been forced to move next door, to the pokey one-bedroom flat above Number 10.

Stirling hadn't reversed the tradition, insisting on the larger apartment. As far as he was concerned, the business of Government went on long after you'd shut the front door of your home. If that home happened to be a broom cupboard, surely that affected the quality of the decisions made?

Right now however, seated at the kitchen table, a rapidly shrinking bottle of single malt on the table before him, the idea of superior decisions being made about the future course of the country seemed fanciful. There was nothing lofty about the conversation taking place – one that was largely conducted in strained whispers. In fact Stirling felt as if he had descended into the ninth circle of hell and was sitting, waist deep in ice, with the big man himself.

It was the PM who'd called the meeting. That morning another of Frears' poisonous little messages had appeared on his BlackBerry. It had taken till late in the evening to find a moment to talk. Charlotte and Aidan were in the sitting room, slumped in front of a film. The kitchen door was closed.

Frears had told him how Eleanor Scott was now with Keddie, what his team had learned from Diana Tennant and what had happened since, including Jane Vyner's death.

'This is an operation that requires on-the-spot decision-making. I made a call. Or would you rather I had cleared it with you first?'

'But we're not even sure she knew anything.' Stirling's voice was barely a whisper.

'She was Scott's lover,' said Frears.

According to the information gleaned from Diana Tennant, it was a short-lived affair, a matter of months. This, thought Stirling, might explain why it was news to him.

'We could not afford to have her mouthing off to Eleanor Scott and Keddie.' The Guardsman enunciated his syllables with nauseating precision.

'But your man smothered her, for Christ's sake!' The words caught in Stirling's throat.

The Prime Minister could hear the sound of a car chase from the television in the sitting room across the hallway, brakes screeching, accelerating engines, then gunfire.

He longed, right then, to disappear, to evaporate into thin air. His reality had become, in the blink of an eye, the most terrifying place imaginable. He poured himself another inch of whisky, downing it in one. The peaty liquid burned a passage down his throat to his stomach. A temporary warmth. His body felt icy.

'There were nursing staff and other patients around. He had to act fast.'

Stirling said nothing.

'He took precautions,' continued Frears.

Stirling was still silent, his eyes locked on to a set of breakfast cereal boxes arranged on the granite top opposite him.

'Where did you get this man from,' muttered Stirling, 'Broadmoor?'

'Given the task in hand, you should be grateful it's him doing your work,' hissed Frears back. 'You came to me because you had no one else to turn to. I assembled the best team I could, given the difficult circumstances. This man was thinking on his feet – we both were – which is exactly what a rapidly changing situation demands.'

'Couldn't he have –'

'Have what?' snapped Frears.

'– acted with a little restraint?'

Frears said nothing. The answer was obvious.

Stirling ran the fingers of both hands through his curly hair. He then gripped the locks and pulled till his scalp hurt in the hope that he would wake some dormant brain cells to provide a miraculous route out of this almighty mess. They didn't.

Frears was right of course, but he couldn't help but see a long trail of shit leading all the way to his door. First Scott commits suicide, then his former lover totals her car.

Think, he thought. Think. An alternate narrative began forming in his head. He felt his blood pressure lowering. Scott had overdosed. There was evidence. Vyner, driving recklessly out of her mind with grief, had been involved in a massive traffic accident. Her injuries had been so severe, she'd died in hospital. There was, if Frears was to be believed, no evidence of foul play.

But what about Keddie and Eleanor Scott? Perhaps a fresh approach was necessary. Perhaps the dogs needed to be put back on the leash. Perhaps they could negotiate, avoid a pile-up of corpses. He reached for the whisky bottle, then pulled his hand back. He couldn't think straight and the malt wasn't going to help. Whenever decision-making was required of him in Government, there was always an Oxbridge cleverdick around to sound ideas against. But now all he had was a murderous soldier.

'It's like I said the other day, Prime Minister,' said Frears, as if hearing Stirling's thoughts. 'Right now, we're in the containment business.'

'If we're really in the "containment" business,' snapped Stirling, 'then how come my son managed to slip out?'

'We were very stretched,' countered Frears. 'Besides, he was unmedicated, which wasn't our fault.'

Fair point, thought the PM. That was Charlotte's department, and she'd screwed up. Another thought, one that made Stirling feel even colder, suddenly entered his mind. What if Frears himself needed 'containing'? If, even with the considerable payments he received from a trust buried deep in Charlotte's family's accounts, he decided to blackmail him?

Stirling shook the thought from his head. Too much. This had to be taken one day at a time. One hour at a time.

'Where are they now?' he asked, his voice still quiet.

'We're not sure. We lost them outside Reading.'

Stirling groaned. 'You "lost them".'

Frears titled his head a fraction. Stirling sensed that sarcasm was on its way. 'We don't have the resources of MI5 at our disposal to track calls or monitor CCTV. Unless you'd like to ask them to give us a helping hand.' Frears smirked. 'But we do have people at all the base points – the family home in Sussex, Eleanor Scott's place in London, Keddie's house, Charles Scott's flat. They will show up.'

Stirling let his head fall backwards, the weight of it suddenly unbearable. He had to assume the Guardsman was right. That Keddie and Eleanor Scott would reappear. And they weren't right now heading for a tête-à-tête with some hack from the Guardian.

He sighed, then brought his head forward, looking Frears squarely in the eye. Directness. That would help, he thought. The Guardsman clearly felt that he was not taking enough responsibility for this.

'When you do catch up with them, I'm wondering whether a new approach might be helpful? Maybe attempt to negotiate. Avoid any more bodies.'

Frears frowned. 'My man at the hospital is certain they recognised him. They know we're active. That, without doubt, we have a secret that we will kill to keep hidden. The time for conversation – for discovering what they may or may not know – is over.'

'And you think you can make it look like an accident?' He felt his stomach drop, his bowels loosen. He'd known Eleanor Scott since she was a baby. Smart child. Always asking bloody questions.

'All we require is the right opportunity.'

Stirling swallowed hard, barely able to believe he was speaking the words. 'Then let's hope such an opportunity presents itself.'

As the Guardsman exited the flat, it occurred to Stirling that, despite being Prime Minister of the United Kingdom, he was barely in control of this little operation.

Chapter 26

Reading, Berkshire

Sam and Eleanor sat in the Mini by the side of a country lane somewhere outside the town. Sam hadn't thought hard about where they were going. He simply drove, as fast as he could, out of Reading and into the surrounding countryside, his eye constantly darting to the rearview mirror. When he was confident they weren't being followed, he pulled up. It was a quiet lane, the only sound Sam could hear their rapid breathing.

'We should call the police,' said Eleanor. 'Tell them about that man.'

'Tell them what?'

'What we know.'

Sam recalled his previous frustrating experience with the police. 'What do we know? Right now, it's that your father was haunted by something and probably having an affair.'

'But you spotted that man.'

'I know I did, but what does that prove? If no one saw him in Jane Vyner's room committing the act – and you can be certain he made sure he wasn't seen – then all the police have is my word that I was threatened in London by a man who looked very like someone walking through that ward.'

'But while we do nothing, he's going around killing people.'

'The police will not protect us – or anyone else, for that matter. These people work for the Government. They're above the bloody law.'

Eleanor was quiet. Sam hadn't meant to direct his anger at her.

'I'm sorry for dragging you into this,' Sam said.

Eleanor shook her head, dismissing his apology. 'This is about my father,' she said. 'I need to know what he was involved in. What the hell happened to him. Whether he even committed suicide.'

She suddenly let out a howl of pain and slammed the steering wheel with her hands. Sam waited for her to calm, then placed a hand on her shoulder.

'Is there any way we can retrace your father's footsteps? Find the event that might explain his sudden change in mood. A diary, maybe?'

'In his office at Westminster,' said Eleanor, her voice now hushed. 'Diana Tennant would know.'

'Not sure we should talk to her again.'

Eleanor shot him a look. 'Do you think she told these people where we were going?'

'It's possible.'

'You don't think they hurt her?' Eleanor's voice had gathered pitch again.

Sam reached for one of Eleanor's hands, which were still clasping the steering wheel. He encircled it, felt how cold it was, the icy fear in her.

'Let's not get carried away.'

There was a pause, then Eleanor spoke again. 'Dad's flat,' she said. 'I've got keys. There'll be credit card statements. Receipts maybe. It's worth a try.'

In truth, Sam wanted to find a place to hide, to go underground and never re-surface. He sensed that they were running out of time. That the team that had followed them so far would, sooner or later, catch up with them. And then what chance did they have of surviving?

He glanced at Eleanor. She was looking ahead into the darkness of the night, a steely calm returning to her face. She seemed to have a tough reserve she could draw on, however upset she got. He took heart from it.

Right now, they had no choice but to carry on. Their survival depended on them discovering Scott's secret.

Chapter 27

London

Just before 9.30pm, they parked the Mini in a side street near Richmond Underground station. Sam watched as Eleanor read the parking information on a sign nearby. He could see she was going through the motions of normality, possibly about to text her number plate and credit card details. But then she shrugged, locked the car, and joined him.

'Hardly worth worrying about, is it?' she said.

The Tube was half-filled, a group of well-heeled teenagers standing by the doors, joshing and loudly taking the piss out of each other; sitting opposite, a young couple poring over a holiday brochure.

They took the District Line to Sloane Square, then weaved their way through affluent backstreets towards Albert Bridge. As they moved along grand Georgian terraces, Sam sensed a world of cosseted wealth around him, of security systems and alarmed cars, of lives fortified against crime and danger. He wondered whether anyone, if they crossed the invisible line he and Eleanor had, could ever be truly safe.

On the other side of the bridge, Eleanor led him down the west of Battersea Park and then, minutes later, along its south side. He recognised the mansion blocks from that first news report on Charles Scott's death.

'We're here,' said Eleanor, who hadn't spoken since leaving the Tube station. Sam could see this was an enormous step for her. In addition to being hounded by murderers, she was now having to confront the space in which her father had died.

Eleanor unlocked the front door and strode into the lobby area. There was a lift ahead but Eleanor took the stairs to the side of it, leaping the steps two at a time.

The flat was on the third floor and it was here, as Eleanor fumbled with her keys, that he had an inkling of the terror she was now experiencing. The landing and stairwell were near silent, a distant sound of a television and, even more muted, laughter. Strange, thought Sam, how a building could soak up so much tragedy and then, within days, present as if nothing had ever happened.

Inside, Sam was struck by the cold. Eleanor lifted a pile of mail from the hallway.

'Odd how the concierge feels it necessary to put pizza take-away flyers through the letterbox of a dead man,' she said, her voice full of irritation.

She moved into the sitting room, a generous space that looked, through large windows, on to the street and the darkness of the park beyond. She flicked a switch to her left and a series of table lamps flickered on, bathing the room in a soft light.

The place shared the lived-in feel of the Scott family home. Worn, much-loved furniture; books everywhere; a mantelpiece choked with photographs of Eleanor and Wendy.

But then there was the temperature. And the ghost in the room. Was this, wondered Sam, where Scott had been found? Or did he lie down in his bed and slowly fall asleep?

Clearly Eleanor was not hanging around to weigh such questions up. She had headed over to an old wooden desk, its top inset with ink-spattered leather, and was slowly going through its drawers.

'God knows how my father managed a Government department,' she muttered. 'This is bloody chaos.'

Sam could hear her frustration as she rummaged through office junk – the sound of pens, paper-clips and other small objects being pushed around impatiently.

Eleanor had opened the bottom drawer on the desk's right hand when she paused.

'Oh,' she said.

Sam had moved to the window where he was casting an anxious eye on the street below. He turned to her. 'What is it?'

'It's empty. And I mean completely empty. Strange, given that the other drawers are crammed.'

Sam noticed a movement just within the park, a figure emerging for a moment from the shadows cast by trees and streetlights. He squinted. Had his eyes deceived him? But then, as quickly, the figure retreated.

He felt that all-too-familiar grip of fear, the pounding in his chest. The horrible sense of life-threatening danger again.

'It may be nothing,' said Sam, 'but I'm not sure we should hang around for long.'

He turned to look at Eleanor. She was still rooting through the drawers. She raised a hand in assent to him, then continued.

Sam was unsure of the time that had elapsed since the figure had appeared, but he sensed that it was only minutes later when he heard the engine. In contrast to the usual sound of London traffic, this was a vehicle driven with serious intent. Sam looked in the direction of the noise, saw a dark saloon heading towards the mansion block from the east. It then halted abruptly outside. At that point, he saw the figure re-emerge at the edge of the park, climb and then vault the railings to join four others who'd got out of the car.

'Fuck,' muttered Sam. It was as if he'd seen it but couldn't register it. A spilt-second passed. 'We need to get out of here,' he barked. 'Now!'

He turned to Eleanor. She had laid out a pile of papers and receipts on the desk's surface and was going through them, one by one.

'We don't have time!' he said, rushing to her. 'Just grab them all.'

Eleanor snapped to attention. She swept the desk with an arm, pulling the paperwork into a wad. She then began searching frantically for something to put the papers in, settling for an old padded envelope from another drawer.

Sam grabbed her arm and ran to the door. He opened it halfway, standing on the threshold to listen. In between Eleanor's rapid breaths, he could hear a loud rattling sound from downstairs. The noise of a lock being tampered with, he was sure of it. They had, he reckoned, a minute before the door was opened and the men came charging up the stairs.

He shut the door. 'Is there a fire escape?'

'The kitchen. The back door leads on to an outside staircase.'

Sam followed Eleanor as she ran down a short corridor into the kitchen. She then began fumbling with her keys, trying to find the one that would unlock the back door.

'There's no time,' said Sam.

He grabbed the nearest object, a metal bread bin, and used it to batter the glass above the lock. The glass was reinforced. It wouldn't break.

'Fuck!'

He looked round the room feverishly, searching for a heavier object, some other way out of their rapidly shrinking prison.

He felt a hand tightly grip his arm.

'With me, now,' said Eleanor.

She led him back to the front door, which she opened a fraction. They both heard the noise. The door below had been opened. There were people on the stairs. Sam could hear the sounds of clothing rustling, hushed instructions, getting fractionally louder.

Eleanor was out first. Sam was gripped with a terror that somehow she meant to confront them, let loose her anger on a group of men she held responsible for her father's death. But she was moving left, away from the stairs down, and towards the next flight up. She then darted upwards. Sam leapt the steps in Eleanor's wake to where she'd halted, outside the flat directly above Charles Scott's.

Eleanor looked Sam straight in the eye. 'Let's hope to God this works,' she whispered, the words punctuated by heavy breaths. She then rapped gently on the door.

Sam reckoned the men were now on the second floor. He and Eleanor had a matter of seconds before they reached the third and Scott's front door which, he now realised, they'd left ajar. And then barely a minute before they discovered the flat was empty and came looking for them elsewhere.

There was no answer. Eleanor knocked harder now, but with the side of her fist not her knuckles, in an attempt to muffle the noise. Sam listened below for any sign that the men had heard. They'd reached the third floor. Eleanor's hand was raised to knock again and Sam rapidly put a finger to his lips. Eleanor stopped, her hand frozen.

On the floor below, words were being spoken in muted tones. There was a creak of hinges. They were in the flat.

Sam nodded. Eleanor hammered on the door one last time, again with the side of her fist. The door opened almost immediately, an older man's face appearing in a chink of opening restrained by a chain.

'Eleanor,' a voice boomed.

'Sssshh,' hissed Eleanor. 'Just let us in.'

The man looked affronted and pushed the door shut. Sam wondered whether Eleanor had upset the man but then he heard the chain being pulled and the door re-opened.

'What the hell's going on?' said the man before them, a lean figure in a check shirt and corduroys.

'In a minute,' whispered Eleanor, pushing past him and pulling Sam in behind her. She shut the door quietly.

'Donald,' Eleanor said. 'I cannot explain right now, but I'm in trouble. Something to do with Dad. There are men in his flat right now. Men who mean to do me harm.'

'Then we must call the police,' said the man.

'No,' said Eleanor. The man reached for a phone on a table behind him. Eleanor's arm shot out, grabbing the old man's hand. 'No, Donald.'

It was then they all heard the unmistakable sound of glass breaking. Where Sam had failed, these men had succeeded. They were out on the fire escape. There was a clatter of footsteps on metal. But then another noise, words being grunted. An order being given.

'Please,' said Sam, 'turn your lights out.'

'Who is this man, Eleanor?' muttered Donald. 'Your father and I may have been old friends but this is quite intolerable.'

Eleanor still held the old man's hand. 'Please Donald,' she pleaded, 'I can't explain now. But the police won't help me.'

How long had this old man known Charles Scott, his wife and daughter, wondered Sam? What kind of friendship had existed between them? Sam saw the old man's face melt, the hand reaching for the phone drop, another hand extend towards a light switch.

They stood motionless in the dark. Could Sam hear a man rising on the stairs outside, or was it just the sound of his pulse thudding in his ears? He couldn't be sure. But then the narrow slit of light at the bottom of the door was interrupted by two shadows. Someone was standing inches from them.

The figure stayed there for what seemed like minutes, before moving away. In the gloom next to him, Sam could see Donald opening his mouth to speak before one of Eleanor's hands darted out to clamp it shut.

Sam moved into the sitting room. Here, mercifully, the lights weren't on to draw attention from the street below. Sam opened a curtain an inch, saw the car. The men – four, then five – re-grouped. There was a brief meeting, a leader directing his team with arm movements. Three of the men dispersed in opposite directions on foot, while the other two got back in the car, which moved off at a more sedate pace.

'They've gone,' said Sam. His throat was dry and he had to say the words again before Eleanor and the old man heard.

Chapter 28

London

The three of them sat round a circular dining table in the room overlooking the street. The lights were still out.

In between the old man's questions, Eleanor managed to explain to Sam that Donald had been her father's neighbour for over twenty years. He was a retired civil servant, and he and Scott had bonded over their shared understanding of the often frustrating ways of Government.

'So who are these bloody people, Eleanor?' asked Donald. 'They don't seem to give a damn about law and order. Russians?'

'No, Donald. Possibly our own.'

There was a pause. 'Well,' he said, a trace of indignation in his voice, 'I didn't vote for this lot anyway.'

He leaned forward. 'You must call the police.'

'You've known me since I was a teenager, Donald,' pleaded Eleanor. 'Can you trust me to do the right thing? And can I ask you not to do anything? At least for now.'

Donald paused, lost in thought. 'I'm not an idiot, Eleanor. I know we don't always play fair in this country. It's just I don't feel comfortable ignoring the rules.'

'Just for a short time. Please.'

Donald grunted his assent.

'I hate to interrupt,' said Sam, 'but I think we need to move. If they can't find us in the streets, they may well come back here.'

'We need to find somewhere safe; somewhere we can look through this stuff,' said Eleanor, patting the envelope she'd taken from her father's flat.

'Take my car,' said Donald. 'It's parked in Warriner Gardens, the street running parallel to Prince of Wales Drive. It's an old green Peugeot. Here, I'll write the registration on the envelope. I hardly use it these days. Just drop it back some time and post the keys through the letterbox.'

Eleanor hugged the old man tight as they parted at the edge of the fire escape.

'Now sod off, the pair of you,' Donald said, with mock grumpiness, 'before I change my mind.'

They drove the old Peugeot in an easterly direction for about ten minutes, changing course constantly, until they stopped in a small square in Kennington.

A streetlight illuminated the car's interior. Eleanor opened the envelope and divided up the wad of bills and receipts between them.

'Christ,' muttered Eleanor. 'What a bloody mess.'

'When we first spoke at the farmhouse,' Sam said, 'you mentioned your dad changing.'

'I saw him about a week ago. That was when I noticed the difference.'

'So we're looking for something just before then. Something around the 11th or 12th.'

They slowly sifted through the paperwork. In Sam's pile there were countless receipts for supermarkets, taxi journeys, lunches at restaurants in central London, a bill from a wine merchant in Clapham, another from a plumber, but nothing, as yet, that seemed significant – or for those dates.

About thirty minutes later, Eleanor shifted in her seat.

'This might be something,' she said. She handed Sam a receipt, printed on heavy paper. It was for a hotel in the Lake District – The Burn Banks, the words printed in an Art Deco font. There was a bar bill, plus the cost of a room for a single night – the 13th September – totalling £360.

'Pricey,' said Eleanor.

'Your father stayed in the Keswick Suite, which would suggest that the room wasn't a humble single, or even a twin.'

'So we can probably assume he was with Jane Vyner,' said Eleanor, a matter-of-fact tone of voice suggesting that, for now, any feelings about her father's affair were being carefully held at bay.

'The location of the hotel is interesting too,' Sam said. 'The Lake District. Kind of miles from everywhere.'

'Perfect for a Minister keen to avoid prying eyes,' Eleanor suggested.

Sam nodded. 'And the date feels right, if what you're saying about your dad's lurch in mood is correct. Something around this time changed him.'

Sam glanced at Eleanor, but he could see she'd already made up her mind.

Chapter 29

The Lake District

It was after 4am and Sam reckoned they were now a couple of miles from their destination. Eleanor was sleeping in the seat beside him, her head slumped against the window.

For the past hour Sam had been having serious doubts about the sanity of this journey. What did they expect to find at the hotel? A body buried in the grounds?

He looked across at Eleanor. In sharp contrast to how she'd appeared hours before, her face looked calm. He knew it was a temporary state. Having had his world turned upside down, Sam had done the same to Eleanor, just as she was reeling from her father's suicide. They were now both in a parallel universe, a place where old certainties and securities had evaporated.

A car passed them on the road, filling the Peugeot's interior with dazzling light. Shadows shot briefly across Eleanor's brightly illuminated face. Her head flopped forward then instinctively pulled back.

How odd, thought Sam, to be thrown together in such an intense experience and yet still barely know each other. He wasn't sure he knew himself any more. He could feel the presence of the notes in his pocket, the glimpses of a father he'd deliberately held back from Eleanor. He was hardening, becoming more calculating.

After about five minutes down a quiet road that straddled a lake, a slither of moon reflected on its inky black surface, Sam saw a sign for the hotel. He turned off down a narrow lane bordered on both sides by thick conifer woods, branches overhanging the track so that it felt like they were descending a dark tunnel, not arriving at a luxury hideaway. Eleanor woke, tensing at the sight of the dense wooded shadows on either side.

But then the hotel appeared, white walls illuminated by carefully positioned ground lights. Eleanor relaxed a fraction. As the font on the bill had suggested, the Burn Banks was an Art Deco building, a two-storey curved construction.

The entrance sat under a cantilevered porch, the lights inside sending a glow into the dark night.

They tried the front door. It was locked.

'Guess we should have thought this through,' muttered Sam.

But then they saw a man cross the hotel's lobby and head in their direction. He wore grey trousers, a crumpled white shirt open at the neck. He unlocked the door.

'Hi,' he said, rubbing his eyes. 'Come in.'

He re-locked the door behind them, then moved behind a reception desk.

The interior was dimly lit but Sam could see that the Art Deco theme continued inside, with a staircase of polished chrome that curved in a loop upwards. On the walls were black and white photographs: two women in evening wear, their shoulders draped in fur; a man dressed in plus fours, a bow tie and large flat cap, a cigarette dangling from the side of his mouth.

'What room, please?'

Sam and Eleanor exchanged glances.

'We're not guests,' said Sam.

'Oh.'

'We need to talk to the manager,' Eleanor said.

The man gave them a slightly puzzled look. 'It's 4.30 in the morning. The manager went home hours ago. She'll be back at around 8. Can it wait till then?'

Sam nodded. In truth he was exhausted and pretty sure that he wouldn't have made any sense if he had been able to speak to her.

'I don't know about you, but I need to sleep.'

Eleanor nodded.

Sam turned back to the man. 'Have you got any rooms?'

The man frowned. 'We don't normally take guests in the middle of the night.'

'Please,' said Eleanor.

The man looked from Sam to Eleanor, assessing them. His eyes dropped to a ledger on the desk. He turned a page. 'There's the Keswick Suite and,' he said, running a finger downwards, 'the Windermere, which is a double.'

'The Windermere will do fine,' said Eleanor. Clearly, thought Sam, the prospect of staying in the same room as her father and his lover was not appealing.

'I can't register you now,' said the man. 'Our system is shut down. I'll need to take a credit card for security.

'Can I pay in cash?' Sam asked.

The man paused.

'I can do it now, if it's easy.'

The man blinked rapidly, as if courtesy was fighting with a desire to fling these two strangers out. 'Sure.'

The Windermere, despite being the cheaper of the two options they'd been offered, was still a large room, decked out in restrained greys, with streamlined Modernist furniture arranged by the window which, the man had assured them, had a partial lake view.

'And you think we weren't followed?' said Eleanor, once they'd been left alone.

'I haven't seen another car for hours,' said Sam. 'We've told no-one where we are. The car we've been driving doesn't belong to either of us. I paid cash. And that man downstairs was so sleepy he didn't even take our names.'

This seemed enough for Eleanor, who flopped down on the bed.

When Sam re-emerged from the bathroom, Eleanor was already asleep. Sam folded the bedspread over her. He pulled some cushions from a sofa and laid them on the floor. Soon he was in a deep sleep.

Chapter 30

The Lake District

Sam was dreaming.

He was in a familiar place, the images and events to come as predictable as a repeatedly viewed movie. He would have loved to run. But he knew he was powerless to escape.

He was standing by a large steel door, the kind that might open into a storage unit, or cold room. He turned the handle, and stepped inside.

He was now in a laboratory, a place that might have been conceived by Hollywood for a film about a deranged scientist. On either side of the room were long workstations cluttered with activity. Numerous lit burners sat under tripods, a rainbow selection of liquids bubbling away in test tubes or beakers, flames and puffs of gas erupting from them. As Sam walked down the middle of the room he began to feel anxious, as if any minute now, there'd be an explosion from this chaotic display.

The room was filling with smoke, the air becoming thick with the cloying smell of bad eggs.

Sam heard a cry. His name, from an all-too-familiar voice. His mother's. She was in distress. The cry was coming from the end of the room but, because of the smoke, he couldn't see her. Suddenly she emerged out of the sulphurous fog. She was wearing a lab coat and was sitting on a stool. She didn't appear to be tied up or injured, but merely paralysed, as if only he could free her from this prison. He moved through the smoke towards her.

'I'm coming, Mum,' he said.

Just then there was another noise, a terrifying clatter he knew all too well. It was the sound of hooves pounding the floor's hard surface. Suddenly out of the gloom emerged a huge black horse, sweat on its coat, nostrils flaring, white foam around its mouth and eyes bulging with fear. It was heading directly for Sam. He stepped back, petrified by the sight of this out-of-control wild animal. The horse was closer now and began rearing up on its hind, flailing at Sam with its front legs. Any minute now it would bring those hooves down on him and he'd be knocked to the ground and trampled to death.

But even above the din the frenzied animal was making, Sam could still hear the cry of his mother.

'Sam,' she feebly called out. 'Don't leave me.'

Sam decided to move forward towards his mother, who was beckoning with open arms. But soon he was again directly before the animal. It reared up once more, towering above him, a crazed beast about to strike him down. Sam screamed out.

He was awake and sitting bolt upright. His body was covered in sweat, his system still firing on adrenaline. Eleanor was sitting up in bed looking down at him.

'You OK?'

'I had a nightmare,' he said.

'A nasty one by the look of things. You're drenched in sweat.'

'It's a recurring dream,' said Sam, keen to keep the revelations to a minimum. He'd never told anyone the content of this nightmare, and he had no intention of doing it now.

'So nothing to do with the image of that man pressing a pillow against Jane Vyner's face, which has kept me from falling asleep?'

'I didn't wake you?'

'No, I was already awake. I've been watching you for the last few minutes. You were thrashing around. I wanted to wake you but I seem to remember you shouldn't disturb someone having a nightmare.'

'That's sleepwalking,' said Sam. 'For future reference, feel free.'

Eleanor turned on her side, resting her head against a hand propped up on an elbow. 'Want to talk about it?'

'That's meant to be my line,' said Sam, managing a smile. 'It's OK, thanks. It's just my mind emptying. Meaningless stuff.'

'That's not what Freud and Jung thought.'

Sam was taken aback by her comment. It was clear she could see through him – and that she wasn't buying his dismissal of dreams as meaningless. But he couldn't reveal the content of his nightmare to her, not until he'd resolved it himself.

'I should take a shower,' he said.

When he returned from the bathroom, Eleanor had turned on her side to face the other direction. He sensed she was still awake. He settled back on the cushions on the floor but knew that, as always after the nightmare, sleep would not return.

Chapter 31

The Lake District

Sam and Eleanor approached reception just before 9am. Sam's fatigue felt like a heavy coat. His body was begging to stop, to collapse on to the nearest seat and sleep. Eleanor, by contrast, was chomping at the bit. She asked for the manageress and the man behind the desk made a call. A moment later a woman with curly red hair emerged from a nearby doorway.

'Ah!' she said, 'our late-night visitors.' She extended her hand. 'I'm Fay, the manageress. How can I help?'

'It's about my father,' said Eleanor. 'I believe he was a guest here recently.'

'OK,' said the manageress, toning down her enthusiasm. 'Can I take his name?'

'Charles Scott.'

The woman looked up at Eleanor and then her eyes darted to Sam.

Eleanor rooted in her bag and retrieved her driver's license, which she showed to the manageress.

'I'm sorry,' said the woman, 'but this doesn't prove you're his daughter.'

'Oh for Christ's sake,' muttered Eleanor. She fished in her bag again and pulled out her wallet. She opened it and flashed the inside to the manageress. Sam caught a brief glimpse of a photo of Eleanor and her father.

The woman smiled sympathetically.

'I'm so sorry for your loss, Miss Scott. You can understand the last thing I want to do is discuss your father with someone from the press.'

'Of course,' said Eleanor tersely.

'So,' said the manageress, some reserve still evident in her voice. 'What would you like to talk about?'

'Can we go somewhere more private?' asked Eleanor.

The manageress led them out of reception into a snug, panelled bar. She directed them to a table well away from the only other person in the room, a waiter polishing glasses at a curved, chrome-top bar.

'Can I get you anything – some coffee perhaps?' she asked.

Sam and Eleanor shook their heads. Sam had the distinct sense that the woman was delaying Eleanor's questions.

'When my father stayed here recently,' said Eleanor, 'he came with a woman he was having a relationship with.'

The manageress looked uncertain. 'To be fair, I'm not certain that's the case.'

'They shared the Keswick Suite,' said Eleanor, flatly.

'I'd have to check.'

'Please,' said Eleanor, not bothering to hide her irritation, 'don't feel the need to protect me. I know my father was having an affair. I also believe that something happened here that might shed some light on his death.'

The woman looked at Eleanor and sighed. She then nodded gently. 'Your father was a guest here earlier in the month – and he brought a woman called Jane Vyner as his guest.'

'Do you always manage to remember your guests' names so easily?' asked Sam.

The manageress looked down at the table, then up at Sam and Eleanor, smiling uncomfortably. 'Certain guests.'

Sam and Eleanor exchanged glances.

The manageress paused, the discomfort written all over her face. 'Your father and Jane Vyner had rather a public row – in this very room, in fact – that was overheard by pretty much everyone in the bar at the time.'

'Go on,' said Eleanor.

'It was around seven in the evening and guests were drifting in for a drink before dinner. It's normally such a relaxed time at the hotel, but that night the atmosphere changed in an instant.' The manageress's eyes moved between Sam and Eleanor, as if begging them to ask her to stop.

'I was in the room at the time, ensuring the staff were looking after guests, drinks were refilled, that kind of thing. Your father,' and here the eyes again dropped to the table for a moment, 'was sitting in one of the booths with Jane Vyner. I have to say, they didn't look that happy when they walked in, as if they'd just had a row. Anyhow, whatever was on their minds soon resurfaced.'

The manageress looked at Eleanor, her eyes almost pleading. 'Are you sure you want to hear this?'

Eleanor's face was set rigid. 'Tell me everything.'

'It's an exchange I can remember almost word for word,' continued the manageress after a pause. Sam sensed her gathering momentum, keen to get this over with.

'I was close to the table when I heard your father raise his voice for the first time, saying "just drop it, will you?" Jane Vyner snapped back with "Drop what exactly? You haven't told me anything." Your father began speaking louder, his tone, if I'm going to be honest, was dripping with sarcasm. He told Jane Vyner to stop being "so bloody clever". They had the full attention of everyone in the room now and whatever conversation anyone else had been enjoying had halted. In fact, when your father and Jane Vyner weren't talking, you could have heard a pin drop. I'd had enough at this point and headed over to their booth to ask them to either pipe down or leave the room. But as I was about to intervene, Jane Vyner's voice became more of a shout. She was ranting about how it was impossible to drop the issue, and that nothing had been the same since he'd got back. Your father then slammed the table with a fist and shouted "Enough". As you can imagine, that was it. I asked them to leave.'

There was a sudden scrape of chair legs and Sam turned to see Eleanor walk out of the room. He'd been listening to the manageress so intently, he hadn't noticed Eleanor's state. This was clearly much harder than she'd anticipated.

The manageress sighed heavily. 'I'm so sorry,' she said.

'It's not your fault,' said Sam. 'She asked to hear it.'

'I'm sure this isn't how she wants to remember her father.'

Sam turned back to the table. 'To be honest, I doubt she knows him at all any more.'

Sam found Eleanor sitting on the terrace at the back of the hotel. It was a bleak day, the clouds gun-metal grey and low over the lake below them. The far side was obscured, so the view appeared nothing more than an oppressive bank of fog. He sat down beside her.

'You OK?'

'That was too much for me,' said Eleanor, her voice cold, 'the idea of my father ranting in a hotel bar.' She combed both hands through her thick hair. 'But at the same time, I want to know everything. I need to understand him.'

Sam could see now that he had to give Eleanor the case notes – the pieces of paper he'd willfully held back. To protect her from making assumptions about her father's actions, and his feelings towards her. But also because it hadn't suited him at the time.

But before he could reach for the sheets of paper in his pocket, she spoke.

'He took 28 Co-proxamol, you know,' she said. 'They found the boxes by his chair, and some barely digested pills he'd vomited. He'd had the tablets for years. He'd been prescribed them for a bad back. They must have been in his bathroom cabinet all that time. Just waiting.'

Sam said nothing, letting her speak unimpeded.

'He left a suicide note too. The police gave it to us. It just said "So sorry to let you both down". Pathetic, don't you agree? How could he leave us this way, with a huge bloody mystery, guessing why in God's name he decided it made sense to abandon his wife and daughter.'

She started to cry, her head resting on her knees. Sam placed a hand on her back.

'I should show you these,' he said.

Eleanor looked up. 'What?'

'Your father's case notes.'

The tears had stopped flowing and Sam could see the rapid calculations going on in Eleanor's head. 'You kept these from me,' she said. 'Why?'

'Because,' Sam replied, searching for words that wouldn't inflame the situation. 'I kept them from you because I didn't want to upset you any more than you were already.'

The words were true, but Sam was acutely aware that he was still not being entirely honest.

'But these amount to some of my father's last words.' She snatched the papers from Sam. Hastily wiping her tears with the back of a hand, she began to read.

'I'm sorry,' said Sam.

Eleanor did not look up. She was no longer with Sam, but intently studying the pieces of paper in her hands.

Sam slipped away.

A little later, he was sitting in the hotel foyer, a cup of coffee going cold before him, when Eleanor approached.

'I'm going home,' she said, barely looking him in the eye. 'I need to be with my mother. If the Government wants to kill me they can come and get me. I'll give you a lift to the station. I think it's best we part ways.'

Sam stood. 'Eleanor –'

Her eyes locked on to his, cutting his words dead. Sam knew what was haunting her. It was the short, poisonous phrase Scott had used when he briefly talked about Eleanor, the kind of phrase that would torture any child who'd just lost a parent. She wouldn't understand. Eleanor would now be convinced that she'd let her father down, just when he needed her most.

Eleanor broke her stare and walked away.

A little later, Sam was waiting outside the hotel entrance. The air was dense with small particles of mist that swirled around him, coating his face and clothes with a light film of water.

Sam heard footsteps behind him and turned to see the manageress.

'Safe journey,' she said, an apologetic smile on her face.

Sam nodded. As the woman turned into the hotel, Sam realised that, despite Eleanor's clear intention to stop digging, he wasn't finished.

'One other thing,' he said.

The woman turned.

'When you asked them to leave, was that the end of their argument?'

The manageress shook her head. 'There was a little more unfortunately, none of it pretty. Jane Vyner said he'd been unrecognisable since Marrakesh. Scott then bellowed "Enough" again. Jane Vyner stormed out, shortly followed by Scott. A little later she came down alone with her suitcase and asked the receptionist to order a cab. I didn't see Scott until the following morning, when he paid up and left.'

Just then Eleanor emerged from the hotel – her face like thunder – clutching her bag.

They climbed into the car in silence. As she reversed the Peugeot hard, sending gravel spinning away from the car's wheels, Sam knew that any further discussion about her father – or indeed anything else – was not welcome.

Chapter 32

The Lake District

At the top of the hotel's narrow drive, Eleanor looked briefly both ways and then accelerated into the road. The car was moving fast – too fast – into a bank of mist. The vehicle's lights were little help, the beams swallowed up by the murky haze.

'You should slow down,' said Sam.

Eleanor shot him a withering look, continuing down the road at the same speed.

The car turned a corner and the windscreen was filled with a bright, blinding light. Sam pushed back into the seat, as if his weight might slow the car. Eleanor slammed on the brakes but the car didn't stop. She yanked on the handbrake, but again the car didn't react.

Sam's arm instinctively shot out to protect Eleanor from being flung forward into the steering wheel and windscreen. The futility of the gesture was soon made sickeningly clear.

In the seconds that followed, Eleanor lost control of the vehicle as it spun right, crashing through a low-lying stone wall. There was a tearing, crunching sound, as the chassis of the Peugeot ground over the stones at high speed. Sam's other arm was at his side, clinging to the car seat, even as he felt the vehicle take flight.

The next thing he knew, the car's motion came to a sudden halt as it landed in water. Their heads were flung brutally forward into the cushion of an airbag. The sense that they'd escaped being slammed into the dashboard or windscreen was little comfort. The car was now listing violently from side to side.

Ahead, the mist briefly cleared and Sam saw the waves rippling around them, an indifferent expanse of lake ready to draw the car and its passengers into a cold, wet embrace.

Eleanor pulled frantically at her door, muttering 'Christ, oh Christ' between rapid breaths.

Sam could feel his own breathing becoming faster, his lungs desperately gasping for oxygen as his body began to panic. The claustrophobia was closing in. He experienced a sudden flash of memory from his childhood – of the dark featureless walls of a cupboard below the stairs – before he shook the thought from his head. Focus, he had to focus.

He lunged across Eleanor, pressing the window switch on her door.

'You can't open the doors,' he said. 'The pressure of the water's too great. The window's our only way out.'

But the switch did not respond. The window remained closed. Sam pressed again, punching it with his finger. He tried his. That too refused to budge. The electrics had gone. The water's first victim.

'Fuck.'

He was just about to release his seatbelt and wind down the rear windows when they both heard the dull metallic groan, as if the car was protesting. The Peugeot's front was dropping rapidly below the water's surface. Icy liquid had made entry and was pooling around their ankles.

Sam watched, with a feeling of intense dread, as the bonnet angled downwards, the Peugeot's windscreen dropping fast below the waterline. The liquid inside had now risen to waist level, a dark mass of freezing water that threatened hypothermia as well as drowning.

It was as if they were being buried alive. The dim light of the day was quickly being extinguished and Sam could already feel the air in the car being eaten up.

He knew that if the lake's bottom was deep – and he prayed to God that at this close distance to shore it wasn't – they were both dead.

Within seconds, they were below the surface, a murky, diffused light all around. A dull thud, a sound muffled by a thick wall of water, interrupted Sam's dark thoughts. The car had stopped. The water was around their chests, and rising fast. It was now a question of waiting.

Eleanor had given into panic and was pulling frantically at her door again.

'You will not be able to open that door until the car is full of water,' he barked.

Eleanor blinked rapidly, struggling to take in what he was saying.

As he spoke the next words, Sam could feel his stomach tighten. 'The car needs to fill with water to equalize the pressure. Do you understand?'

This time Eleanor nodded. He felt a hand grab one of his, Eleanor's fingertips digging into his skin.

As the water reached Sam's chin, he shouted out to Eleanor: 'In a couple of seconds you need to release your seatbelt and then take a very deep breath.'

Eleanor, her face white, nodded.

A moment later Sam gave Eleanor the signal and they released their seatbelts with hands that were already numbing with cold. Their bodies were gently pushed upwards till their heads nudged the car's roof. There were about three inches of air to spare, their heads at sharp angles to allow their mouths to take a last gasp. He blinked at Eleanor. The message was clear. They simultaneously drew in the deepest breaths they could, before the water consumed the last drops of oxygen in the car.

The car's interior was now full of water and they wasted no time. Eleanor reached for the handle of her door. It eased slowly open and she swam out and upwards. Sam's door was stiffer and, as he finally emerged from the car, there was another groaning sound and the vehicle began to drop again, this time faster than before. Sam shot forward but the door frame caught his left leg. He felt the metal scrape against his skin and was then swimming upwards, his lungs close to bursting.

His head broke through the surface, his mouth drawing in great draughts of air as he looked round for Eleanor. He saw her just feet away, a pale face framed by dark wet hair that clung to her skull.

Her teeth were chattering, the hypothermia gradually taking hold. Suddenly the effort of escaping the lake felt monumental. His wet clothes seemed to have doubled his body weight. Simply attempting to swim was exhausting.

But then he saw a light sweep across the surface of the water, and a shot of adrenaline raced through his system.

'We need to get out of sight!' he said to Eleanor. 'Dive down and swim to the bank.'

Eleanor didn't need persuading. The last thing Sam saw before he dived under was her head disappearing.

A moment later, they were huddled together under a small knoll at the water's edge. They watched the bright beam – without doubt the same one that had driven them off the road – move slowly and methodically across the water's surface, the light dense with minute spots of mist.

A few agonising minutes later, the beam cut out and Sam heard footsteps and then the sound of a car door slamming. An engine started and a car accelerated away, the sound slowly becoming more distant.

To his side, Eleanor's body was shaking violently. He could feel his jaw tightening and teeth beginning to rattle. His body had started to shiver. He suspected they had minutes to go before they were both in danger of slipping into unconsciousness.

Climbing the bank to the road was out of the question. It wasn't just the steep gradient. They'd seen how little traffic passed by. No, the only possibility was to walk back along the shore to the hotel.

'We need to go back,' said Sam. He heaved himself up, the wet clothes like an anchor, and helped Eleanor to her feet. Pulling her close to him he began to walk. The wound his leg had suffered exiting the car now made itself known, a pain that shot up his left thigh with every step.

They hobbled slowly round the headland, clinging to each other to stay warm, their progress slowed by wet clothes, exhaustion and, in Sam's case, the excruciating pain of his left leg.

Finally they rounded a corner and the white sweep of the Burn Banks Hotel emerged from the mist. A figure was standing in the near distance. Sam called out but he could barely hear the words himself. They dragged themselves up a shallow slope that felt more like a mountain and then Sam attempted another cry for help. This time the figure – a man digging a flowerbed – turned in their direction. He discarded his spade and ran towards them, just as Sam and Eleanor collapsed to the ground.

Chapter 33

Downing Street

It was over. A short text from Frears – 'problem solved' – confirmed that Keddie and Eleanor Scott were no longer part of the picture.

Stirling was in his office on the first floor of 10 Downing Street, a generous room with windows that looked out on the rose garden below. The scene of many a press conference and reception, the garden looked empty and bleak today, most of the roses pruned back for the coming autumn, the lawn, so perfectly emerald in summer, now looking the colour of mushy peas under the gloomy September skies. Outside the office door, the machinery of high office hummed away, manned by a large team of civil servants and advisers.

The never-ending nature of Government meant that Stirling was rarely alone in the room designed for his sole use. There was always someone wanting a piece of him. In fact the only time he was on his own was when he was on the phone and confidentiality was required.

Bizarrely though, the door had just closed on his Permanent Secretary and, if he ignored the pile of documents he was meant to be working through, he was finally able to think without interruption.

For the past days Stirling had been feeling certain that, at any moment, the door would burst open and he'd be dragged from the room by the police on charges of murder.

He was, he knew, giving into paranoia. There was nothing to connect him to the killings that Frears' men had carried out. As far as the hospital was concerned, Jane Vyner had died from her injuries and, while he awaited the exact details from the Guardsman, he was sure Eleanor Scott and Sam Keddie's deaths would be explained easily enough. 'Accident' was the word Frears had used.

Of course, that wouldn't stop the journalists digging. Sooner or later someone would discover that Vyner had been Scott's lover. And that the man who died by Eleanor Scott's side was his psychotherapist. And what if Keddie and Eleanor Scott had already set that process in motion? Spoken to a hack?

He breathed in, held the air in his lungs, then exhaled noisily. Yes, there would be discoveries. Connections made. But these deaths were not proof of conspiracy. Look at the bloody Kennedys, for God's sake. Assassinations, plane and car crashes, drug overdoses. The Scotts had nothing on them.

No, he had to concentrate on the original issue – the job he'd first hired Frears for. From now on, they would double the surveillance – and keep an eye on the medication. If doses were skipped again, the implications were bloody disastrous.

He paused for a moment to consider the leap he'd made giving Frears that more direct instruction, the deaths that he'd all but ordered. He shuddered briefly. But then he thought of the soldiers who'd died in action fighting conflicts at his behest. He simply had to place Eleanor and Keddie in the same category. Some deaths were necessary. He straightened his back. This was not a time for harsh self-reflection.

Besides, there were other worries. Such continuous scrutiny might simply not be sustainable in the long term. Would he have to exit early from the job? The very thought was too painful for him to consider. But surely it was better to leave on his own terms, than be driven by another drama like the one he'd just escaped?

He shook the possibility from his mind.

And then there was the Moroccan business. If things escalated in Marrakesh, and the authorities chose to react brutally out there – and that scuppered the deal they'd all been working on – then, frankly, it was a small price to pay. They'd all had a narrow escape – and been bloody lucky.

The phone rang.

'Gillian Mayer is here, Prime Minister,' said one of his secretaries. 'Wondering if she can have a quick word?'

The last thing he felt like was another meeting, but he knew that acting normal was imperative. 'Show her in.'

In any Cabinet there were always a handful of ministers who coveted the PM's role. Stirling accepted that as part of the job. What he liked about Mayer, the Foreign Secretary, was that, when the moment came for her to make her move, she could be trusted to plunge her dagger into his chest, and not between the shoulder blades.

The door opened and in walked Mayer, a small, steely woman who, while not loved by either the media or public, was admired as smart and capable.

'Gillian,' said Stirling, rising from his seat to come round the desk and plant a kiss on the Foreign Secretary's cheek. God, he was good at this.

'You're in a good mood,' said the Foreign Secretary. 'Hope I'm not about to change that.'

'I'm sure that won't be the case. Sit down, sit down.'

The Foreign Secretary sat in a chair in front of the desk and Stirling returned to his seat.

'Before I start,' said Mayer, 'may I just congratulate you on that speech on multi-culturalism, Prime Minister. Very refreshing.'

'Thank you, Gillian,' he said, placing his hands behind his head. 'Now, what's on your mind?'

'In a word, Morocco.'

Stirling felt his bowels shift and the colour drain from his face. He hoped to God it wouldn't show.

'Go on.'

'These riots –'

'I wouldn't call them riots exactly,' interrupted Stirling, already on the defensive. The hands slowly returned to the desk.

'In this part of the world,' Mayer corrected, 'as you of course know, any dissent is significant. Right now, we need their friendship more than ever. Obviously our recent activity could help safeguard that. But that could all be pissed away if we don't react to these riots – and the State's response to them – in the most sensitive manner.'

'Gillian, Gillian,' Stirling soothed, as much to calm her, as his own, frayed nerves.

'What's going on out there doesn't amount to much, certainly compared to what we've seen elsewhere.'

'You honestly think this won't escalate?' Mayer said, barely able to contain her irritation.

'If and when it does we will be ready.'

'With what, exactly? If these skirmishes do turn into full scale riots – and the Moroccans react with force, as we expect them to – we are caught between a rock and a hard place. We can't condone what they do. Equally, we cannot afford to condemn. If we do that, we risk losing everything.'

Stirling smiled a cat-like grin. 'Perhaps you can order your thoughts in a memo, Gillian. Get them to me this evening. I'll take a look and then we can meet again to shape it into something we're both happy to use in the event things go pear-shaped.'

Touché, you bitch, he thought.

He watched as the Foreign Secretary opened her mouth, then shut it.

'Of course,' she said. 'Thank you, Prime Minister.'

Just before midnight Stirling was upstairs in his apartment, heading down the hallway to the kitchen following a visit to the loo. A meeting with his Chief of Staff – lubricated by a couple of thimbles of single malt – had been ensuing. They were hammering out their strategy for dealing with the volcano of bad press that had erupted following the death of a comedian. The man, who the press called 'an 80s comic legend', had, it was alleged, lain on a trolley at his local NHS hospital for three hours unattended. That time, it was claimed, had proved fatal to the man's already weakened heart.

The fact that the comic had never been particularly funny – something Stirling and his Chief of Staff had chuckled over – was neither here nor there. His death had rallied Middle England around the oldest chestnut in the book – that the NHS wasn't working and it was the Government's fault.

As the Prime Minister moved past the sitting room and its open door, he glanced in to see Aidan sitting on the sofa. A movie was on – Stirling recognised a battered-looking Bruce Willis but couldn't name the film; he'd never watched much tv – and Aidan was staring at the screen, slack jawed and dull eyed.

Stirling knew that the medication had that effect, of deadening everything. And for that he was grateful. The boy's emotional make-up was a bloody mess. Like a lot of people the PM knew – he could think of several sociopathic world leaders – Aidan could have saved himself and everyone else a great deal of trouble by developing empathy. Had that been the case, they'd never have faced the disaster that so nearly derailed his leadership.

Aidan's eyes shifted sluggishly in his father's direction. It was, the Prime Minister thought at first, a blank look. But then Stirling caught something else in the gaze. The eyes seemed to narrow, to laser in on him with a look of utter contempt.

He could feel his blood suddenly boiling and marched into the room, heading straight for the sofa with his arm outstretched. Suddenly a hand grabbed his wrist and Stirling turned to see Charlotte. Although she'd come out of nowhere, he somehow wasn't surprised to find her lurking silently there. She was never far from her child. Now, with the added role of medication-giver, that proximity had a new legitimacy.

'Don't you dare,' she said.

Stirling shook off her grip. 'How can you defend him?' he said. 'After all he's put us through?'

'"He's put us through"?' she snapped back. 'What about you?'

Stirling groaned. 'Let's not go over that tired old ground again, for fuck's sake. The dreary therapy speak. I'm not responsible for him. And neither are you, for that matter. He's an adult, for God's sake. A fucked-up, train crash of an adult.'

The hand that had, moments before, held his own violent strike in check, lashed out, smacking him across the face.

Stirling would have liked nothing better than to punch his wife in the face at that point. Thinking of his Chief of Staff overhearing their fight or Charlotte sporting a black eye or broken nose, he managed to hold his clenched fist still by his side.

'Do what you do best, Philip,' she hissed. 'Leave us alone.'

Part II

Chapter 34

Sam woke with a jolt, unsure of where he was. He was lying on a bed, dressed in a surgical gown, a blanket draped over him. The curtain around the bed was drawn. He'd dozed off, and that worried him. He had to find Eleanor.

He tried to sit up, then felt an intense pain in his forehead, as if he'd just walked into a steel girder. He winced, his head dropping back on the pillow.

He remembered arriving here, brought by ambulance. Their wet clothes had been removed – Sam's jeans cut from his legs – and they'd been wrapped in blankets and given some warming intravenous fluids. A handful of cuts and bruises had been cleaned and bandaged, as well as the leg wound Sam had sustained exiting the Peugeot. They'd been lucky, they were told. Nothing worse than mild hypothermia. Sam was given painkillers and then Eleanor was led off to another bed. The doctor said the police would be by later, interested in knowing just how their car had ended up in the lake.

The imminent arrival of the police was not worrying Sam. It was their assailants. Once they discovered the car crash

130

had failed to kill them, they'd be back. And he knew a hospital presented no obstacle.

Sam lifted his head again, more slowly. The pain was still there, but not as bad as before. He lowered his feet to the ground, feeling an agonising twinge shoot up his left leg.

He opened the cupboard by his bed. Inside were his wallet and keys, but no clothes. He drew the curtain back. Occupying the bed next door was an older man, fast asleep. Sam was no thief, but a surgical gown, open at the rear, was not the ideal outfit for escaping a hospital. He gently opened the cupboard next to the man's bed. There was a washbag on the top shelf and below, a plaid shirt, dark trousers and a pair of trainers. He pulled them out slowly, then returned to his bed, drawing the curtain again.

He'd just buttoned up the shirt when he heard footsteps. He froze. The curtain began to peel back. And then he saw Eleanor, her brow furrowed with concern. She was dressed.

'The nurse told me you were here. How are you? Can you walk?' she asked.

'I'm fine. I can shuffle.'

'I'm scared.'

'Me too,' said Sam.

'What if they come back?'

'Let's make sure they don't find us.'

Eleanor nodded, Sam's direct talk clearly comforting. She slipped an arm around his waist and they began to move through the ward. Aside from the sleeping man, the other beds were empty.

'How come your clothes are dry?' asked Sam.

'A nurse took pity on my sob story of a romantic weekend ruined. She had them dried. By the way,' Eleanor said. 'I owe you an apology, Sam. I nearly killed you today.'

He gently removed Eleanor's arm. He could walk independently, albeit with difficulty, and if they were going to leave the hospital without interference, he couldn't afford to look like a patient in need of care.

He felt the sweat break out on his face, as the pain in his leg pulsed. 'You were right to be angry. I should have shown you those notes.'

They'd reached the end of the ward. Across the corridor was the nurses' station. A large family – a mother and father, and four squabbling children – was blocking the nurses' view of them. Sam and Eleanor slipped by.

'You and I both know it wasn't that simple,' said Eleanor. 'They were my father's words to you, not me. You knew they could have upset me more – which they did. You weren't concealing them from me. You were protecting me.'

Sam swallowed hard. It was easier looking ahead – at the corridor in front, at hospital staff and patients moving by – than at Eleanor. 'I was also trying to help myself. I was worried that if you got upset or started jumping to conclusions, I'd never find out why those people were on my back.'

'Everything I hear about my father is upsetting, Sam – particularly reading that he'd done something terrible, something he believed he couldn't burden me with.'

She reached out and squeezed his hand. 'But I don't blame you. I can see why you asked for my help – and why you needed me to be focused. Besides,' she said, turning to him with a slight grin, 'having nearly killed you today, I think we're quits.'

'I suspect tampered brakes and bright lights had more to do with it, but thank you.'

Sam felt a wave of relief, as if he'd been absolved by Eleanor. But a small niggling knot in his stomach reminded him of the calculation he'd made concealing the notes, and where such behaviour might stem from. Suddenly something else was concerning him, the sight of the doctor who'd treated them turning into the corridor ahead.

Sam pulled on Eleanor's arm, dragging her left down another passage. Up ahead was a set of swing doors. Sam turned and saw the doctor walk past. His shoulders dropped.

They moved through the doors and were now on a main corridor, a series of signs hung from the ceiling. Sam spotted one for the main entrance, pointing right. They headed in that direction, past the X-Ray Department and then Paediatrics.

Eleanor was fumbling in her coat pocket. She drew out a damp white ball.

'At least the notes are no use to anyone else now,' she said.

'I'm sorry you've lost them though.'

A repetitive beeping sound made Sam jump. He turned to see an elderly lady in a pink dressing gown being driven in a silent electric buggy towards them. They moved out of the way, prompting a sluggish thumbs-up from the porter at the wheel.

Eleanor then spoke. 'The sight of that man at the window really scared my father, didn't it?'

'Given what we've experienced since,' said Sam, 'it's understandable.'

They had reached the hospital entrance. There was a help desk to their left and glass doors in front of them opening on to a drop-off area.

Sam's eyes scanned the foyer for signs of the narrow-eyed man, or the bulky bald figure who'd visited him at the house. The coast appeared clear. They moved towards the doors, which opened automatically, and were blasted with cold air. Sam felt the stabs of pain in his head and leg dull. The pills were kicking in.

They walked on, finally stopping when they were well clear of the main building, by the hospital laundry. Steam billowed from an extractor above their heads. Blue containers on wheels, piled high with white sheets, were being dragged up a ramp by a man in grey overalls, who seemed indifferent to the two figures standing against a nearby wall.

'What do you think that man had on my father?' asked Eleanor, her breath turning to vapour in the cold air.

'I've no idea,' said Sam. 'All I know is that, once he'd seen him, he didn't want to talk any more.'

Eleanor's head dropped, as if she were hiding her distress.

Sam remembered how she'd been as they left the hotel earlier in the day, her frosty manner, the barely contained rage. She was experiencing the full gamut of emotions right now.

As he thought of their departure that morning, another memory began to emerge from the fog induced by his painkillers – his final conversation with Fay, the manageress.

'It didn't seem the right moment to mention it in the car, but just before we left, the manageress at the hotel said something else about your father's exchange with Jane Vyner. Something significant.'

'Oh God,' sighed Eleanor, 'not more ranting I hope.'

'No,' said Sam. 'According to her, Jane Vyner named the place that had so changed your father.'

'And?'

'Marrakesh.'

Eleanor paused in thought. 'I remember Dad mentioning he'd been there.'

'Do you remember the last time he went?'

She shook her head. 'Mum and I struggled to keep tabs on him from one day to the next. It was the nature of his work. He was always travelling. And while some of his trips were public knowledge, openly available on the DFID website, other visits he made were kept more secret, I guess to protect sensitive work.'

'We should try and find the date, but I bet anything we've found the place where it all happened – whatever "it" is.'

Eleanor seemed to be thinking through a series of options, her eyes rapidly moving from side to side. She then looked up, the determination Sam was familiar with back on her face.

'We need to finish this.'

There was a small spasm of pain in Sam's head, a reminder of the near-death experience they'd recently escaped. Of the lengths their pursuers were willing to go to.

'I hate to be the voice of reason,' he said, 'but our odds of success are narrowing by the day. They won't make another mistake.'

'If that's the case,' said Eleanor, 'then we need to be even more careful.' Her eyes bore into Sam's. 'I'm not giving up,' she said. 'These bastards need punishing.'

Chapter 35

Penrith, Lake District

The distant hum of heavy traffic suggested their next step, reminding Sam that the motorway was nearby. He'd peeled off it just the night before. A lift to London seemed a better idea than the train. If the local police decided to come looking for them, the railway station and any train heading south were obvious places to start.

Sam was keen to avoid wandering around the town centre, and asked the man working in the laundry if he'd call them a minicab. He looked them up and down suspiciously, then offered to drive them himself. For a fiver.

They were dropped in the car park of a service station by the motorway. An hour later, just as Eleanor was losing faith that they'd ever escape Penrith, Sam negotiated a lift with a group of climbers who, for a small donation towards diesel, were only too happy to give the couple whose car – and contents – had been stolen in the Lakes a lift back to London.

Sam and Eleanor sat opposite each other in the rear of the mini bus, wedged in between rucksacks packed to bursting point. Towards the front, the other passengers dozed.

'We've got a problem,' said Sam, his voice hushed. He didn't want the driver overhearing.

Eleanor was tying her hair back, pulling the dense locks away from her fine features. She looked at him and he was momentarily caught on the back foot – by her flushed cheeks, the dark intensity of her eyes.

'Besides the fact we're being hunted by a group of homicidal maniacs?'

She flashed him a smile and Sam had to smile back, the thoughts in his head now amplified.

'Besides that,' said Sam. 'If we're to leave the country – and that's a big "if" – we need to get our passports.'

'And in all likelihood, our homes are being watched.'

'Exactly.'

Eleanor cupped her face in her hands, then drew them slowly away, massaging the skin back to life. She tipped her head from side to side, wincing with discomfort as she exercised a stiff neck.

She looked at Sam again. He wondered whether his face was reddening. 'I've got an idea,' she said.

They reached Stoke Newington late in the afternoon. They first visited a sports shop on the high street. Sam bought a hoodie, which he put on. Outside the shop, they parted ways, Eleanor heading for a café and Sam for his house, the protests from his leg and head dulled by the painkillers he'd taken as they'd reached the outskirts of London.

Despite feeling confident his features were obscured, the adrenaline was still racing through his system. Since their near-death experience in the Lakes, it was as if they both felt bolder – reckless even – but now that he was potentially approaching one of their pursuers, he felt vulnerable and exposed.

The streets around his house were, as usual, jammed with parked cars. Sam kept his head down, inspecting each vehicle in turn. He was looking for one facing the property, one from which a decent view of his front door could be enjoyed.

He'd passed his front door and was about to turn down a side street when he spotted the car on the opposite side of the road. Sam felt his heart leap in his chest. Behind the wheel was the stocky man who'd paid him that threatening visit days ago. The man was on the phone, looking away from Sam. He seemed to be barking into the mobile, a finger prodding the air angrily. Sam passed the car, then walked as casually as his pounding heart would allow back towards the café where Eleanor was waiting.

A little later, Sam retraced his steps, stopping before he reached his street and positioning himself behind a tree where he had a partial view of the car and its driver.

It took longer than he'd expected, and for a moment he wondered whether Eleanor's call had worked, but suddenly there was a roar of engines and two squad cars emerged from a westerly direction and stopped adjacent to his pursuer's vehicle.

There was an exchange, which quickly became heated as the man's temper flared, and then he got out of his vehicle and into the back of one of the squad cars.

Sam watched the cars move off, marvelling at how Eleanor's tale – the concerned mother who'd noticed a man taking pictures of children – had worked.

With the cars gone, Sam wasted no time, moving down the side street and round the corner to his front door.

From the outside, the house looked untouched. Inside, it was a different story. The consulting room was in the worst state, with case notes pulled from filing cabinets and scattered everywhere. Other damage was more gratuitous. His Yeats print had been ripped from the wall, as had his certificate of accreditation. Both lay in a pile of splintered wood and broken glass. In the living room, chairs were upended and cushions slashed, the floor scattered with thousands of small feathers. Books had been pulled from the book cases and left in a pile, as if someone was planning to come back and use them to start a bonfire.

Sam went straight upstairs to his bedroom, concerned that his pursuers had turned it over as efficiently as downstairs and, in doing so, discovered the place where he hid his passport.

The chest of drawers to the right of his bed had been searched, the contents pulled out and dumped on the floor. But not all the drawers had been fully removed. Sam eased out the bottom one, revealing a cavity below, and a metal box. He unlocked it. Inside, sitting on a pile of old bank statements and other papers, was his passport.

Minutes later, carrying a bag stuffed with some clothes, Sam was back on the high street with Eleanor.

By late evening, they were in Haywards Heath, outside a modern house in a cul-de-sac. A car was parked in the drive and, though the curtains were drawn, the lights were clearly on inside. Eleanor pressed the doorbell.

A moment later a short, round woman with tight blond curls answered the door. Wendy Scott's carer, Jill, greeted Eleanor with a hug and then a barrage of questions about where she'd been, and how much her mother needed her, what with the funeral coming up at the weekend and so much to arrange –.

'I'm fine,' said Eleanor, cutting her off. 'And I'll be home soon to sort things out. But I need your help first.'

Eleanor's reassurances, delivered in an even tone, seemed to calm the woman.

'Where are my manners?' said Jill. 'Come in, come in.'

Seated in the living room shortly after, steaming mugs of tea before them, Eleanor explained the purpose of her visit. She had an overseas trip to make – 'an urgent one that's just come up' – and she needed her passport.

'The thing is, Jill, I'd fetch it myself but I don't want to upset Mum by rushing in and out.'

Sam watched as Jill smiled and nodded, accepting Eleanor's lie. God, he thought, she's good at this.

'I'm sure you're right,' said Jill. 'Listen, I don't want to upset you any more, but she's all over the place at the moment. Crying one minute, slapping the arms of her chair the next.'

Sam saw Eleanor's eyes glass with tears.

''Course I'll get your passport, love,' said the carer. 'And I won't mention your trip either.'

Jill shot them both a look. 'Listen, you two look exhausted. Do you need to stay? I've got a spare room.'

Neither Sam nor Eleanor had got that far in their planning. Sam was exhausted and looking at Eleanor, at the bags under her eyes, could see she was too. If they headed back to London, it would only be to find another anonymous and quite possibly nasty bed & breakfast where they could pay in cash.

'We should probably –' began Eleanor.

'We'd love to,' interjected Sam.

An hour or so later, Sam watched Eleanor as she emerged from the bathroom. The lights were out and she appeared as a silhouette, illuminated by the glow from the street outside. Long bare legs, breasts outlined in the cotton of an oversized t-shirt.

There were two beds in the room but, without hesitation, she climbed in next to him.

She moved closer to Sam, reaching out for his face in the darkness, tracing her fingers gently down his cheek.

'I don't feel scared tonight,' she said.

'Me neither,' Sam said. 'I think it's the painkillers. I might take a few tomorrow.'

She leaned into him, kissing his cheek just to the side of his mouth. She was soon fast asleep.

Sam lay awake, his mind working overtime. The truth was, he did feel scared. Hearing her slow breathing next to him, it was impossible not to dwell on his feelings for her, the attraction that had been growing, he now realised, from the moment they'd met. The fear he felt was based on one thing – a certainty that, sooner or later, Eleanor would be torn from him.

Chapter 36

Earl's Court, London

The walls of the travel agency were lined with shallow shelves, each one filled with holiday brochures – cruises in the Caribbean and the Med, trips to Disneyland in Florida, long-haul holidays in the Far East, romantic city breaks in Europe. The world they represented – one of care-free relaxation – now appeared to Sam like a parallel universe.

He and Eleanor sat with their backs to the window that faced the street. Sam kept turning to look outside. Despite a new theory about their pursuers that had been gathering weight since their experience in Stoke Newington, he felt defenceless and exposed, and knew those feelings would only increase as the day wore on.

They had bought tickets for a flight leaving early that afternoon to Marrakesh. The sales assistant had disappeared to print them off. Eleanor turned to Sam.

'This feels like madness,' she said, her voice low, all traces of last night's composure gone. 'Our details have just been entered on to a system. We're visible again. Christ, they found us in the Lakes when we'd been really careful. What chance do we have now?'

Sam placed a hand over one of Eleanor's. 'I'm coming to the conclusion that our pursuers aren't as sophisticated as we thought.'

He explained his thinking. If the people after them really had tentacles everywhere, then why had that man outside Sam's house been apprehended? It suggested the police weren't in on it.

'Think about it,' he continued. 'If you wanted to keep a secret, how many people would you involve? I think this is a tight operation, run well below the radar.'

Eleanor smiled, frowning at the same time. It was clear she only partially bought what Sam was saying. And of course this new theory was only moderately comforting to him. Eleanor was right, their pursuers had found them in the Lakes, and that was after they'd taken great pains to keep their movements hidden. Were these people simply one step ahead, all too aware of where he and Eleanor would look next? In which case, was it not wiser to just run? But then how long would they last before they were caught? No, there was only one course of action – the one they were taking.

The sales assistant returned with their tickets and wished them a safe journey. Sam smiled back weakly.

There were still a few hours to kill before check-in, so they crossed the road to an internet café to tackle the other task they'd set themselves.

Nursing watery cappuccinos and occupying stools at the rear of the café with a good view of the street, they logged on to the DFID website. The home page featured a large image of grinning African schoolchildren and the headline: 'Access to education for all finally a possibility?' Above and below were a series of other tabs including one, Sam noticed, directing visitors to a page that paid tribute to Charles Scott. If Eleanor had noticed, she didn't let on. She clicked instead on 'Diary' and a new page appeared, one that detailed the Minister's most recent movements – or at least those the Government chose to publicly reveal.

Some entries were rich in detail – the new Secretary of State's address at a conference in Edinburgh on violence against women, which was accompanied by the conference timetable and his actual speech – while others were more skeletal.

'Here,' she said, her finger resting on the screen.

Sam leaned in to read the entry.

Charles Scott, Secretary of State for International Development, attended a series of sustainability seminars in Marrakesh this month. The meetings, held at La Mamounia Hotel, aimed to capitalise on the region's existing potential while drawing on British skills and expertise.

'Is that it?' he asked.

'It's what they call transparency,' said Eleanor.

'So we visit La Mamounia,' Sam suggested.

'And the Sofitel,' said Eleanor, who had now moved on from the DFID site to a Google page listing Marrakesh hotels.

'I was racking my brains this morning, trying to remember whether Dad had mentioned the hotel where he stayed. It was the Sofitel, I'm positive.'

'Right,' said Sam, 'so we have two leads. All we need to do now is leave the country.'

Sam hated Heathrow at the best of times. Confronted now with the crowds, the low ceiling of steel beams and bright lighting, the multitude of signs and advertising messages, he could feel his chest constrict.

He thought back to their near-death experience in the Lakes. Something that had been designed to appear an accident or, more to the point, not murder. He looked at the people before him. Any one of them could be a killer, ready to brush by, to administer a dose of some lethal chemical simply by touch, or the tiniest pin-prick. A dose inducing a death that appeared to be natural.

He shook the thoughts from his head. This was no time for paranoia.

Sam looked up at the departures board. Their flight was still on time, scheduled to leave in two hours. They took the escalator upstairs to Departures. Here, it was marginally calmer although Sam took no comfort in the lack of crowds. Exposed or surrounded, neither felt safe.

They moved towards two policemen wearing flak jackets and carrying semi-automatic weapons, who stood either side of a thoroughfare that led to the desk they needed to reach.

Eleanor's sweating hand clutched his tightly. Sam cast a glance at one of the men as they passed. The man's eyes looked through him, scanning the building for dangers that, it appeared, did not include him and Eleanor.

They joined the line at check-in. In contrast to the other queues nearby, this one was short. Ahead of them were three North African men, dressed in suits and in the midst of an earnest discussion. In front of them, a family – the parents standing in silence, their teenage sons both engrossed in tablets. The stillness unnerved Sam.

Moments later they reached the desk. The woman who took their passports and tickets displayed evident disinterest, only breaking into a sentence to confirm that Sam and Eleanor had no luggage to check in.

The next challenge was security. Here the queues were longer, with every departure descending on this one part of the terminal. Sam stood protectively behind Eleanor, her back pressed into him. As the queue crept forward he was suddenly pushed from behind and turned to see an overweight man, his face glistening with sweat.

'Sorry bud,' the man said in a Midwestern accent. 'Wasn't looking where I was going.'

They inched on, Sam now rigid with tension as he examined every person near them for signs of intent. He could feel his shirt clinging to his back and knew he needed to calm down if he was to pass through the next stage without drawing attention to himself.

As they reached the head of the queue a security officer indicated to Eleanor that there was an opening to their right. When Sam tried to follow, the man raised the palm of his hand.

'One at a time, sir.'

Eleanor looked back, eyes wide with distress.

Sam was now directed to his left. He placed his bag, keys and the phone that had been switched off for days into a tray and then moved through the scanner. To his right, he could see that Eleanor was one step ahead of him. She was now in discussion with a security officer, an older woman with tightly drawn-back grey hair. The woman wasn't smiling.

Sam, who'd paused, was now urged to move on. He collected his stuff from the tray and went to Eleanor.

As he approached, he heard the tail-end of the conversation she was having, and felt his stomach relax.

'It's more than 100 millilitres,' the security officer was saying, as she held a bottle of water in her hand. 'We're going to have to dispose of it.'

'That's fine,' said Eleanor. 'My mistake.'

'Christ,' whispered Eleanor, as they moved away. 'When that woman called me over, I thought that was it.'

'We need to calm down. The way we're acting, we're going to get arrested for looking like a pair of sweating terrorists.'

Eleanor exhaled loudly. It was then, over her shoulder, that Sam saw a pair of security officers – the older woman who'd been talking to Eleanor and a younger man – walking at a pace in their direction.

Eleanor noticed the expression on Sam's face, and turned.

'What do we do?'

'We wait,' said Sam. 'There's nowhere to run or hide here. Besides, if we do, we'll certainly be arrested.'

The two officers were now a few metres away. Sam felt like a small animal caught in the headlights of a fast-moving car, immobilised, yet keenly aware of impending danger.

'Excuse me,' said the female officer to Eleanor. Her face was flushed. 'You forgot these.'

She held out a plastic bag containing the items that Eleanor had put in the tray. Keys, a mobile, her passport, some coins.

Eleanor gushed her thanks, a broad smile suggesting joy at being reunited with her belongings. But Sam knew it was an expression of something quite different – enormous relief that another moment of gut-wrenching fear had turned out to be a false alarm.

'I almost prefer genuine danger,' she said, as they walked through duty-free. 'This is unbearable.'

As they sat by their gate a little later, Sam sensed that Eleanor had now given up, no longer able to maintain the heightened vigilance they'd both shared since the start of the day. Her head rested on his shoulder, a hand on his forearm. Sam couldn't let up. His eyes darted around the room, seeking out signs that any of the other passengers meant them harm.

The flight, as the queue at check-in had suggested, was near empty. Sam counted around fifty passengers and not a single European among them. There were the three men and the family with teenage sons; an elegant couple in their fifties; a group of school children in their early teens, marshalled by a visibly irritated male teacher who kept barking at them to be quiet. As Sam studied each face in turn, he caught the eye of a small boy who was travelling with his parents. The child smiled at Sam and he found himself smiling back. His shoulders dropped.

Perhaps his new theory was right. After all, would they have got this far if the people after them had access to the airport's CCTV footage, or the Border Agency's database?

But even with this crumb of comfort, Sam couldn't help questioning the sober mood of the room. Other than the immediate coverage of Scott's death, Sam hadn't given the news a thought since this business had started. He remembered a mention of riots in Marrakesh the day Scott's suicide had broken. Was this what was troubling his fellow passengers? What united them in their dark mood?

They were calling the flight. The families with children moved off first. The little boy, the one person in the room who seemed blissfully unaware of the tension, turned and waved at Sam. His face was full of excitement, the prospect of flying clearly an adventure. Sam nodded and waved back, even as he felt a deep sense of foreboding.

Chapter 37

Whitehall, London

The Cabinet Office Briefing Room A is a stuffy, windowless room in the bowels of a bland Whitehall building. It's a place where selected Ministers, armed forces chiefs and emergency services heads are called in the event of a national crisis, whether caused by terrorism, extreme weather, a potential pandemic or other major emergencies.

COBRA meetings were, as Philip Stirling knew all too well, often a complete waste of time, dragging professionals away from co-ordinating appropriate responses to gather with a group of politicians who were more concerned with their personal ratings than anything else. Many of the MPs, even those who'd previously visited the room, still couldn't find the place and would hurry in late, gushing with apologies, brows glistening with sweat, having jogged up and down the gloomy corridors outside for ten minutes.

That said, the media loved COBRA. If it was meeting, it meant the Government was taking something seriously. Today, it was in response to the diabolical weather that Northern Ireland had been having. Following torrential downpours, several towns had experienced severe flooding and the news had been full of Biblical imagery of bridges washed away and cows and sheep floating down high streets. Stirling had convened a meeting to which he'd invited the Home, Transport and Environment Secretaries and – because he knew the man would be asked if this event was due to global warming – the Energy and Climate Change Secretary. Also in attendance were the Head of the Marine and Coast Guard Agency and the Chief Constable of the Police Service of Northern Ireland (via a video link). Frears, ostensibly because of his knowledge of the military logistics involved in such a crisis, had also been summoned.

In truth, Stirling did not give a crap how much Frears knew about erecting temporary bridges. He was here because the shit had hit the fan. The Guardsman had informed him, in a snatched and wholly inconclusive conversation in a hallway at Number 10, that Keddie and Eleanor Scott had survived their car crash in the Lakes.

The Prime Minister sat impatiently while the professionals briefed the room and then the Ministers flexed their muscles, selfishly seeing the whole business from their own standpoint. Eventually he pressed for conclusions and, finally, drew the meeting to a close.

'Could I have a word, Frears?' he said, as the now red-faced attendees began filing out of the stifling room, all visibly grateful for the air in the corridor outside, which contained a degree more oxygen than the space they were leaving.

Once the door was closed, he wasted no time. 'It's clear your men didn't hang around long enough to ensure the job was done properly.'

'It wasn't safe to stay at the scene.'

'What the hell were the two of them doing there?' asked the PM, ignoring the proffered excuse.

'We think they were sniffing around a hotel where Scott stayed with Jane Vyner.'

Stirling was silent, mulling over the implications of this latest titbit.

'So,' he asked, 'how do you intend to find them now?'

Frears looked momentarily disorientated, a look that worried the PM greatly. The man had many annoying traits, not least his clipped intonation and 'militarising' of everything, but he always displayed a confident decisiveness. The thought of Frears not knowing what to do was truly worrying.

'I'm making some calls,' he said.

'You do that.'

The door closed behind Frears. Stirling began gathering up the papers in front of him, attempting to convince himself that he was still doing the job he'd been elected to do, rather than walking a tightrope over hellfire, which was how he now felt. He stopped for a moment, running his hands through his unruly locks.

Outside in the corridor, his Cabinet Secretary and a couple of advisers were waiting. Right now, he couldn't face them. He wanted to crawl under the table and weep. Surely, with Keddie and Eleanor Scott still alive, he was royally fucked. They now knew unequivocally that an attempt had been made on their lives. They were bound to go to the press.

Stirling breathed in deeply. Proof. There was no proof that anyone had tried to kill them. And as for their presence in the Lakes, this suggested they were still some way off the truth.

He moved towards the door. Before he left this ghastly building, he'd pause to visit the gents at the end of the corridor. He was finding it harder and harder to control his bowels. Gone forever was the smooth-operating politician who had risen, almost imperceptibly, to the top. He was now a physical wreck.

Of course, Prime Ministers were allowed to look tired. But little did the people of Britain know, that the baggy eyed man at the helm was now fighting, not just for his political survival, but to avoid complete and utter annihilation.

Chapter 38

Marrakesh, Morocco

While they'd both experienced a sense of exhilaration as their plane surged down the runway and climbed into the grey September clouds and away from the UK, their arrival in Morocco quickly dispelled the optimism.

The airport certainly felt European and familiar – a terminal of white steel latticework that could have been built by Richard Rogers, flights to places like Madrid, Paris, Brussels and Amsterdam – but what was happening on the ground seemed altogether less comforting.

Appearing like a wall in front of them, a large group of dark-suited men and their wives, all dressed head-to-foot in black robes, were trying to check in. Whatever was holding them up was causing enormous stress. A couple of the women were screaming in high-pitched voices while three of the men were involved in heated exchanges with airport staff.

Sam and Eleanor passed through the group and then side-stepped a gang of teenaged Arabic girls standing by their bags. They were clad, by contrast, in tight jeans and midriff tops, but their young, thickly made-up faces seemed etched with the same tension.

Beyond them was a group of Saudi businessmen in long white robes, red check scarves over their heads held in place with thick black cords. Although clearly together, they stood apart, each talking rapidly and with agitation into mobile phones.

Watching over this scene were around forty policemen, armed and accompanied by restive sniffer dogs, agitating at the ankles of passing passengers.

Outside, Sam and Eleanor caught a cab and were soon hurtling down a near-deserted highway towards the city. The driver had one hand on the wheel while the other held a cigarette at an open window. The back of the car was filled with warm, dusty and tobacco-tainted air. The radio was on – a jaunty African pop song coming out of tinny speakers in the back of the car. Worry beads hanging from the rear-view mirror swung with the car's motion. The driver did not speak a word for the whole journey.

The Sofitel, where they'd decided to stay, merely confirmed Sam's sense of alienation. They were the only Europeans in the reception area, an atrium dominated by a marble fountain and Islamic motifs on the walls and ceiling. North African businessmen in suits huddled around the fountain speaking in hushed tones. A group of black men in jeans and football shirts were checking out, sullen expressions on their faces. The one suggestion that there was a world beyond North Africa was the tune the hotel pianist was playing, which Sam recognised as a very slow version of Raindrops keep falling on my head.

Finally, once a stressed-looking receptionist had booked them in and given them their keys, they were travelling in a lift to the eighth floor, alone in their thoughts.

Their room was airless and stuffy. Sam slid open the French doors that led on to the balcony. The sound of a siren gathering strength and a distant muezzin call filled the room. Below were the hotel's pool and gardens, beyond that a cluster of other large hotels. Sam's eyes looked further into the distance. It was as if the city unfurled before him, a vast sea of rooftops cluttered with washing lines, water tanks and satellite dishes stretching into the distance.

Chapter 39

Marrakesh, Morocco

It was Eleanor, sitting on the bed poring over a map she'd picked up in reception, who dragged Sam back into the moment.

'La Mamounia is just round the corner.'

Sam took one last look at the cityscape before him, then turned to Eleanor. 'In which case now is as good a moment as any to start asking questions. If our arrival here has been noticed by our friends in the UK, then time's pressing.'

Eleanor disappeared into the bathroom then re-emerged minutes later, drying her face. She dropped the towel on the bed then paused, closing her eyes briefly, as if summoning strength for the next stage.

As they walked through the foyer past reception, the woman who'd checked them in called out, urging caution.

'Because of the riots,' she added, when she saw Sam and Eleanor's puzzled faces.

It was late afternoon in Marrakesh, the sun still beating down hard on the city. Sam felt himself beginning to sweat, his body unaccustomed to the sudden leap of mercury.

The streets had an eerie calm to them. Just as on the road into the city, there were only a handful of cars on the move. Sam and Eleanor passed several cafés where the scene was the same – men seated at tables, their shisha pipes and coffee cups abandoned as they stared at television screens.

Watching over the streets from above, on huge banners, was the face of the King. Sam dimly recalled coverage of riots in Morocco in 2011 before events in Libya, Egypt and Syria became the dominant stories of the Arab Spring. He had a sense that protests had been met with more restraint than in other countries – and there'd been enough promise of reform that things had calmed. But the omnipresent face of the monarch was a reminder that one family still dominated life here. Sam also remembered how both the US and UK were said to have farmed out the interrogation of terrorist suspects to the Moroccans, who were, it was alleged, less squeamish about using torture to extract information. The image Sam had in his mind was of an iron fist in a velvet glove, an impression compounded by the palpable tension on the streets.

Inside La Mamounia, the entrance reached through a large gate in the walls of the medina, the staff were doing their level best to dispel the unease outside in the city. Sam and Eleanor walked into a grand, air-conditioned lobby of Islamic horseshoe arches, marble flooring and vast blood-red sofas. In the background, soft musak – laced with some hint of North Africa – filtered out of concealed speakers. The clientele was mainly Arab, men in well-cut suits seemingly immune to the tense world beyond the hotel's walls.

Neither Sam nor Eleanor had discussed how they were going to approach this. Suddenly Eleanor took the lead, marching up to reception where a man in a black jacket greeted her with a warm, five-star smile.

'Hello Madam,' he said. 'How can I help you?'

'My father came here recently. Charles Scott.'

The receptionist's eyes lit up. It was as if Eleanor had just mentioned the name of a favourite uncle. 'Of course,' he said, beaming. 'How is your father?'

'I'm afraid he died,' she said. 'He committed suicide.'

Christ, thought Sam. She isn't pulling any punches.

No amount of corporate hospitality training could prevent the man's face from falling. 'Oh,' he said. 'I am very sorry.'

Eleanor placed both hands on the dark, highly polished wood of the reception desk. 'I wonder if you can help me.'

The man's head tipped to one side sympathetically. 'Of course.'

'Morocco was one of the last places he visited. Do you remember anything strange about his time here?'

The man shifted on his feet. 'Your father was not a guest here, just a delegate at a seminar. The people at these meetings – they go into a room at 9 o'clock. We take them lunch at midday. They come out at the end of the day. We really didn't see much of him.'

'What about the meetings he was attending?'

The man smiled uncomfortably, saying nothing.

Eleanor's hands tensed. 'I'm sorry, but the way you remembered him suggested that you knew him better.'

'He was a good man, and I am very sorry for your loss. But as I have said, he was not a guest here. So no, I do not remember him well.'

Eleanor walked away, slumping in one of the sofas, her head in her hands.

Sam left her alone for a moment, moving away from reception down a broad corridor. By a door on his left there was an artfully rusted plaque etched with the words 'Le Français'. Sam looked inside. It was a restaurant, with starched white table-clothes and swathes of heavy fabric framing the windows. Just two tables were occupied. Sam moved on. The next door opened on to a more informal restaurant, with subdued lighting and dark walls, again barely inhabited. Further on down the corridor were more doors – one to a hamman, which was closed, another to a ballroom, which was ajar. Sam eased it open and found himself in a vast area, its ceilings hung with huge chandeliers. A woman in a white tabard was guiding a floor polisher, the machine slowly inching across the acreage of marble.

Sam then tried a door opposite. This room was slightly smaller but still, he guessed, capable of holding around 200. As many seats were stacked in one corner. He could easily imagine the chairs arranged in a square and Charles Scott sitting on one side with his British team. But discussing what – and to what effect? Had what happened in these anonymous-looking rooms really been so significant that a Minister would commit suicide and the Government would kill innocent people? Sam stared at the bland décor, the huge framed photographs of what he guessed was the souk in the 1920s, with French policemen in white uniforms moving among locals dressed in djellabas.

'Hey,' said Eleanor behind him, startling Sam. 'What have you found?'

Sam sighed. 'Empty rooms.'

'I think we need something to drink. I'm kind of spun out.'

Sam took another look at the photos on the wall. 'Let's go to the souk,' he said. 'Be tourists for a change.'

They took a cab from outside the hotel up to the Djemma el Fna. Sam had an image in his mind of a place packed with dancers, acrobats, snake charmers and countless food stalls. What greeted them was anything but.

Bar a couple of calèches – the horse-drawn carriages that took tourists on tours of the city – the square was deserted. Around its edges the bars and cafés were all closed, their shutters drawn. A handful of shops had remained open, but trade was clearly not good. Boxes of cucumbers, tomatoes, mint and peppers were stacked high outside a grocer. The shopkeeper stood pensively in the doorway, drawing hard on a cigarette. The frontage of a hardware store – jammed with pots, pans and a huge selection of Tupperware in every colour – seemed more like armour than goods to sell.

They paid the driver, who was then gone, accelerating away as if the place were cursed.

Sam and Eleanor moved across the square in a slight trance. They passed one calèche, the horse's weeping eyes thick with flies. In the carriage, his owner sat sullenly, staring into the middle distance.

A figure they hadn't noticed from the cab window now approached. He wore faded jeans and a dirty green t-shirt, and carried a small monkey on a chain.

'Take picture with monkey,' he said.

Sam lifted the palm of his hand in response but, in the absence of any other tourist, the monkey man seemed disinclined to give up, moving right into their path. He repeated his terse sales pitch. Sam and Eleanor sidestepped the man and tried to continue on but he was quickly at their side. The monkey made a hissing sound and bared its teeth in a snarl.

Eventually Sam turned to the man and barked 'No!'

The man stared Sam hard in the face, a look of venom in his eyes, and started spouting an angry barrage of Arabic, his free hand gesticulating violently. Then, admitting defeat, he walked away, muttering to himself.

Shaken, Sam led Eleanor on across the square, eventually reaching its north eastern corner. There they stopped and turned, Sam relieved that the monkey man hadn't followed them. Now, apart from the calèche drivers, who were being given an ear-bashing by the monkey man, the only other figure in the square was a man in a black leather jacket who appeared engrossed in the window of a closed patisserie.

'Shall we move on, see if we can find anything open in the souks?' Sam suggested.

Eleanor nodded listlessly.

They progressed up a broad cobbled avenue and moments later, the light and heat were partially extinguished as a slatted metal roof cut out all but narrow shafts of sunlight, beams in which thousands of tiny dust specks danced.

Just a handful of places were open, shops cluttered with colourful kaftans, scarves and richly embroidered shirts. But there was little sign of the pestering sales techniques the souk was famous for. The shopkeepers sat subdued in front of their stalls, the sight of two foreigners failing to ignite even a glimmer of a pitch.

As they moved on through the souk, Sam glanced back and noticed the man in the black leather jacket, about 30 metres behind. On seeing Sam, the man suddenly looked away to study a shop display. Sam tensed. He exhaled, dismissing his paranoia and the idea that anyone could be following them out here.

After a couple of minutes the darkness intensified as they moved into a narrower alleyway in which the sunlight barely registered. The few open shops here sold leather goods – wallets, backpacks, handbags and purses that were hung in floor-to-ceiling displays, filling the air with a dense and cloying smell of hide and polish.

'I need to find a bar or café,' Eleanor said. 'Somewhere to sit down.'

Sam happened to look behind and saw the man again. He was still the same distance away and was staring right at them. When he caught Sam's eyes he looked away again. A sickeningly familiar feeling returned to the pit of Sam's stomach. This was no longer a coincidence. They were being followed, again.

Sam grabbed Eleanor's hand. 'Don't panic,' he said. 'But when I say run, run.'

Chapter 40

Marrakesh, Morocco

Gripping Eleanor's hand, Sam shot left down an alleyway between two shops until they came to a low arch to their side. He looked back. His instinct had been right. The man was now running too. Sam pulled Eleanor under the arch and into darkness.

They moved rapidly down the narrow alleyway towards a source of light at the end, the cobbles of the souk now replaced by dusty, impacted earth.

At the end of the alleyway, Sam didn't stop to think, darting right and then left past gaudy displays of decorated slippers, hoping to God they'd lose the man simply by getting lost themselves.

They ran between crumbling red buildings that leaned towards each other across the street. Strung between the houses, washing lines heavy with clothes compounded the sensation that they were in a tunnel. Sam felt his throat tighten, as if a noose were being pulled taut.

They dashed towards another darkened alleyway only to halt in their tracks as a moped emerged out of the shadows, the young male rider skidding in front of them and firing off expletives as he sought to right his bike. They dodged past him into the gloom but then, as they reached light, they came face to face with a plastic barrier emblazoned with a message in both Arabic and French. The latter's meaning was unmistakeable: 'Police – Défense d'entrer.

'Shit,' said Sam.

He turned. They seemed to have lost their tail – for now. The wound Sam had sustained in the lake had begun to pulse with pain, as if his body were reminding him where all this activity inevitably led. But there was no time to contemplate other courses of action.

Sam guided Eleanor back up the dark alley and took the first left. The route was wider and Sam breathed again, sensing that this would take them to a more open, populated area. The alley wound to the left slightly and Sam saw, with enormous relief, a semblance of activity ahead. A barber's shop – the internationally recognisable red-and-white pole hanging outside – and a small workshop. As they passed, the dark interior was momentarily illuminated by sparks. A man holding a welding torch turned to watch them.

But just ahead was the thing Sam had most dreaded. Another police sign stopping them in their tracks.

He turned in exasperation – and froze. There, just metres away, was the man in the black leather jacket. He was slowly approaching them, his face stripped of emotion. Eleanor had turned now and flinched.

They had a choice. Leap the barrier and hope to run into a sympathetic policeman, or try and find refuge in one of the shops they'd passed.

Sam didn't stop to think long. He grabbed Eleanor's arm and made for the barber's shop. As they burst in, the barber, who'd been sitting reading a newspaper, leapt up. But no sooner had he registered their presence and they were running through a beaded curtain to the back door. Up ahead, past shelves packed tightly with cardboard boxes, was a closed door. Sam turned to see that the man in the leather jacket had entered the shop behind them. The barber was barking something at him in Arabic. The man said nothing in response.

They reached the door. Sam tried the handle. It was locked. He began to push his shoulder against it. But it was jammed tight. He took a small run and charged at the door. With a splinter of wood, it gave way and they ran into daylight – and a cramped and high-walled backyard.

Chapter 41

Marrakesh, Morocco

Cornered in the backyard of the barber's shop, Sam felt two overwhelming sensations in quick succession.

The first was the all-too-familiar feeling of claustrophobia. He'd just about held it together in the warren-like alleys of the souk. Now, as the walls closed in on him, Sam felt as if he were being choked. But then he saw the man approach and knew that protecting Eleanor was the priority. He felt his body flood with adrenaline. But as he tensed, preparing for confrontation, Sam noticed his pursuer's now contradictory signals. His palms were raised and when he spoke, it was with an unthreatening voice.

'Please,' he said. 'I mean no harm. I am here to protect Miss Scott.'

At this, Sam's aggression cooled a fraction.

'How do you know her name?' he uttered, between rapid breaths.

'I will explain,' said the man, 'but first let us go somewhere a little calmer.'

Sam turned to Eleanor. She nodded.

The man spoke to the irate barber, handing him a wad of notes, then gestured for Sam and Eleanor to follow him back through the maze of alleyways.

They walked, Sam still uneasy about their companion but convinced that, had he meant them harm, he would already have caused it.

At a certain stage, as if they had crossed an invisible line in the medina, Sam became aware of posters stuck on walls and doorways, all depicting the same image – a pretty young woman – and some words in a language he didn't recognise, daubed in red.

A moment later they walked through an ornate carved doorway, down a corridor of heavily patterned tilework, then turned into a courtyard open to the sky. Around them were sand-coloured walls and orange trees in large terracotta pots. Empty tables were ranged around a small marble fountain in which water gently burbled. Somewhere in the courtyard a bird was singing. Save a handful of waiters standing idle, they were alone with the man.

He signalled to a waiter then sat in silence, as if there were no point in attempting to explain anything until his order arrived.

Minutes later, the waiter returned carrying a tray loaded with a stainless steel teapot and three engraved glass beakers filled with mint leaves. He placed the tray down on a neighbouring table then, with a slight flourish, poured the tea from on high. The beakers were then placed in front of them, sending a calming cloud of minty steam into the air. Sam took a sip. The tea was laced with sugar.

The man introduced himself as Kamal. He had short dark hair and a neatly trimmed beard. He was, he said, the deputy manager of the Sofitel and, as such, he'd known Charles Scott from what he described as the Minister's 'frequent trips to Marrakesh'.

'The day I heard that your father had died,' said Kamal, his English, though spoken in a heavy French accent, flawless, 'I was so sorry.' His head dipped in a small bow.

'Thank you,' said Eleanor, clearly touched.

'When I saw your name on the hotel's computer, I wondered whether it might be my friend's daughter. Then I saw you, and I was sure. You have the same eyes – and the same kind face.'

Eleanor's eyes welled.

'I was going to introduce myself,' continued Kamal, 'but our paths had not yet crossed. But then, when I came to the hotel this morning, I heard that you were heading out and, given the atmosphere in the city, I wanted to ensure you and your friend came to no harm. So I followed you at a discreet distance.' He smiled. 'Clearly I have something to learn about surveillance. I think you saw me several times and all I ended up achieving was scaring you. For this, I apologise.'

Eleanor thanked Kamal for his kind words – and for his chivalrous attempt at protecting her.

'Kamal,' she then said, her voice a little hesitant. Sam could see that this sudden opportunity to talk to someone who, like him, had been with her father in his last few days, had taken Eleanor aback. But, resolute as ever, she was not going to miss it. 'Could you tell me everything you remember about my father's last stay in Marrakesh?'

Kamal nodded, clearly happy, after his botched attempt at protection, to help Eleanor any way he could. He then described how, one afternoon, the Minister had returned to the hotel and he and Kamal had got talking over tea. Scott had said that his visits seemed to be dominated by meetings and while these were very fruitful – he did not go into any detail about their content – he still knew little of the city. It was his last day – there was to be a dinner that evening with senior members of both the British and Moroccan delegations – and tomorrow they were all heading back to the UK.

Kamal offered to take the afternoon off and show him a little of Marrakesh. Scott seemed delighted. The next few hours were his last opportunity to see the city and he accepted gladly.

'Your father was an enormously knowledgeable man,' Kamal said. 'His understanding of Morocco's history and culture was exemplary.'

They visited the Kotoubia Mosque, Scott apparently bowled over by the building's simplicity and the feeling of peace.

'Your father,' Kamal continued, 'said that people in the West often chose to ignore the connections between religions and focus only on the differences. He talked about how Jesus Christ and John the Baptist are prophets in our faith and, more surprisingly, how the design of the mosque's minaret had influenced many church towers in Spain and Eastern Europe. I didn't know this myself.'

They then wandered the souks, visiting the different markets. A little later, Scott asked if he might visit a good antique shop so that he could buy some presents.

Kamal led him to a street south of the Djemma el Fna and to a shop run by a man called Marcel Hadad, a famous antique dealer in the city. But as they neared it, Kamal realised it was already hosting some illustrious visitors. Two men, clearly some kind of Moroccan security, stood outside scanning the streets. As Kamal and Scott neared the door, the men tried to bar their entrance. But then Scott heard a voice from inside.

'It was the voice of an Englishman,' said Kamal. 'He was calling your father by his first name.'

Sam and Eleanor exchanged puzzled looks.

Kamal looked in the open doorway, where by now the men outside had relaxed, knowing that Scott was acquainted with the people inside. Kamal instantly recognised the owner of the voice. It was Philip Stirling, the Prime Minister.

'I knew your Prime Minister was in Marrakesh for talks,' said Kamal. 'We'd seen him on television. But I never dreamed I'd meet him.'

Stirling, who was enjoying his own tour of the medina – his care of the Moroccan Minister for Tourism – beckoned Scott in. Scott introduced Kamal to Stirling, which made Kamal's day, thanked him for the tour and Kamal returned to the Sofitel.

'Did you see him again?'

Kamal looked down. When his face rose again it was sombre.

'I was not on reception that evening when your father left for his dinner engagement. I believe he was joining Mr Stirling and our Prime Minister at a restaurant here in the medina. The next time I saw him was the following morning, when he checked out.'

Sam wondered why Kamal suddenly seemed so serious. He was looking Eleanor in the eye now, as if he felt the need to express maximum sincerity. 'Your father was no longer the man I knew. He was – how can I describe it? – grey. Like a ghost. I wished him bon voyage but all he could manage in response was a weak smile.'

Sam watched Eleanor's face, wondering how she was taking this story. Something dreadful had clearly happened to Scott between leaving Kamal at the antiques shop and the following morning.

Kamal glanced at his watch. 'I should get back to the hotel.'

He stood, dipping his head again in Eleanor's direction. 'I am so sorry for your loss, Miss Scott. And I am sorry if I have added to your sadness with my story.'

Eleanor stood, taking Kamal's hand in her own. 'Not at all, Kamal,' she said. 'It's been comforting to know how fondly you remember him.'

And with that, Kamal was gone.

'You OK?' Sam asked.

Eleanor had sat down, clearly a little shell-shocked. 'These new glimpses of my Dad slightly freak me out. But yes, I'm fine. I want to find out what happened that night.'

'I reckon our next move is to retrace your father's footsteps as best we can,' said Sam, sensing that support, not sympathy, was what was required. 'At some point in the hours between when he left Kamal and when he saw him the next morning, we'll find the event that unlocks this whole business.'

Eleanor nodded. Then she looked up, right into Sam's eyes.

'How about you?' she asked.

'I'm OK,' he said, unnerved by the penetrating stare.

'You didn't look that great in the barber's shop.'

'Just a bit out of shape,' Sam said with a shrug. 'And shit-scared.'

'Something else was happening,' Eleanor said. 'I saw that look on your face as you were about to get in the lift at the hospital. Ashen white. Chest rising and falling too quickly. You're claustrophobic, aren't you?'

Sam felt his body break into a cold sweat as a wall he'd carefully constructed in his head came tumbling down. He was completely unused to such direct questioning. Even his Jungian psychoanalyst, who could on occasion directly challenge, would never have been so blunt. But there was something about their situation – so far from the safe and, out here, somehow irrelevant, boundaries of therapeutic practice – that made him want to answer.

'When I get extremely stressed and anxious – and these past few days have given plenty of opportunity for that – and I find myself in a confined space, the claustrophobia can be quite pronounced.'

Eleanor placed her hands on the white tablecloth. 'What's that about?'

Her approach was so different to the delicate therapeutic dances around pain he often found himself engaging in. She was attacking the issue with a lance – and Sam realised he didn't want her to stop.

'Without going into too much detail – it's probably not wise right now; you don't want me descending into self-pity – small spaces tend to remind me of a rather unhappy period of my life.'

'I don't understand.'

'My mother,' he said, the two words catching in his throat, 'was a rather complex person.' He let out a short, mirthless laugh, aware of other, less generous phrases he'd used in the past to describe the woman. 'Her approach to parenting was a mix of harsh discipline and cold detachment.' Sam could hardly believe he was revealing this information – and so easily. 'The claustrophobia stems from when I was a toddler. I spent a great deal of it locked in a cupboard under the stairs. It was one of my mother's favourite punishments.'

He shook his head, attempted a smile, as if to say, 'it's nothing'. The throwaway description of those moments was, Sam knew, quite at odds with the intensity of his experience at the time; the knowledge, even at a very young age, that his mother's only feelings for him were, at best, displeasure and indifference, at worst, intense anger.

But Sam was also aware that while those early experiences had been hugely damaging to him, they paled when compared with her other legacy, a fear that had surfaced towards the end of his psychoanalysis. He'd ignored it then, but as with any part of a person's subconscious, it had a habit of returning – in his case, as part of the recurring nightmare that would wrench him from sleep into wakefulness, leaving him drenched in sweat, his heart pounding. There was, he knew, only so long that he could continue to disregard such a significant part of his emotional DNA.

Eleanor placed a hand over both of Sam's, which had knotted together. 'I'm sorry I pried. That was clumsy of me.'

Sam felt a strange sensation come over him, one he had never felt with Kate. He wasn't sure whether it was the circumstances he and Eleanor were in – their relationship being baptised in such a fiery way – but he realised that he trusted her. And the fact that he trusted anyone was a completely novel sensation.

Chapter 42

Downing Street

The inexplicable news Frears had relayed – via a mix of BlackBerry 'code' and a hurried conversation at Number 10 – was the worst possible.

One of his team had tapped an old colleague at the Border Agency to see if Keddie and Eleanor had, by chance, left the country. As it turned out, they were in Marrakesh.

The news felt like a winding blow to the stomach. And the fact that they'd only just discovered it, a full day after the two of them had arrived there, hurt almost as much. Here he was, the most powerful man in the UK, receiving scraps of information from the very departments he was in overall charge of. But this was the nature of his grubby little operation, one in which he could not afford to involve anyone else.

Stirling had spent the day at an academy school in Kent, gurning at teachers, pupils and parents while inside, his stomach did somersaults.

What had he been thinking? He should have fessed up right at the beginning. It would of course have been a cataclysmic story and his premiership would have died there and then. But at least he'd have exited with some grace, perhaps even with the sympathy of the nation. Now he'd be vilified.

It was simply a case of waiting. He'd stand on the beach, awaiting the tsunami that would sweep him away.

But at a certain moment in the afternoon, sitting in the assembly hall listening to the school choir annihilating a Beatles song, he perked up. Christ knows, he'd survived scraps before. The hopeless briefs he'd won as a barrister, armed only with guile and intellect. The rivals he'd beaten with a mix of bloody-mindedness, luck and determination to win the party leadership. And the biggest fight of all, the battle for Number 10. He wasn't out yet.

What would Keddie and Eleanor Scott realistically find in Marrakesh? There was no smoking gun. No piece of evidence that would conveniently drop into their lap. This wasn't a Hercules Poirot mystery. They were two British people in a very foreign city who in all likelihood didn't even know what they were looking for.

And even if they did strike lucky, surely there was something Frears could do, something pre-emptive. He thought of the turning point he'd made days before, when he'd more or less directly asked Frears to eliminate Scott and Keddie. He'd already crossed the line. Now it was time to finish the job.

Across the apartment's kitchen table, Frears looked the PM hard in the eye.

'So you want someone to go in. A specialist.' The Guardsman's voice was barely a whisper, but the note of derision was still evident.

'Yes,' hissed the PM.

There was another bottle of single malt on the table, but only one glass. Philip Stirling hadn't offered the Guardsman a drink. Frears was not a colleague, and certainly not a friend.

The sounds of the apartment leaked through the closed door: Newsnight on in the living room, some junior minister being slowly eviscerated. Further away, a lavatory flushed. Aidan getting ready for bed.

Frears was dressed, as usual, in suit and tie, a flash of red brace visible beneath his jacket. 'As I'm sure you know, these things require meticulous planning. Adequately prepping a man for Marrakesh would be impossible, given our resources. We can't ask the embassy to carry out surveillance on our behalf.'

Stirling, his head down, both hands lost in the thick locks of his hair, looked up.

'Well, that's not strictly speaking true.'

'I thought this was a tight-knit op,' Frears said. 'The secret we're protecting,' he looked briefly at the closed kitchen door as if he suspected someone was listening on the other side, then lowered his plummy voice even further, 'would, if out, ruin you.'

He said those last words, Stirling noted, without a huge amount of emotion in his voice, as if the prospect of his premiership going tits up were merely inconvenient.

'It was a tight-knit op,' said Stirling. 'But the members of the small team you assembled have not proved capable. Anyway, calm down. All I'm planning is a by-product of what we've been doing there anyway. The Foreign Office has, with the help of the embassy in Rabat, been compiling the names of every British national in Morocco, just in case the riots turn nasty and our people need to be rapidly pulled out. They will know where Keddie and Scott are staying. I can find an excuse to attend one of their contingency meetings and easily get my hands on the information we need.'

'The name of their hotel is just the start,' said Frears.

Stirling glared at the soldier. His obstructive comments were becoming very tiresome. 'Do I need to come up with every single solution? That's what I pay you for, isn't it?'

Stirling watched as the Guardsman clenched his hands on the table before him. The PM swilled the whisky in his glass and downed it. He was, increasingly, waking every morning with a hangover – a thick, pounding head and a stomach that swam with acid.

Frears seemed to calm. 'I've got an idea,' he said. 'I'll get on to the company database. I'm pretty sure we've got someone in Tunisia, a local. Just get me the hotel name. I'll look after the rest.'

Stirling's shoulders dropped slightly. This was better. 'I acknowledge that this is way beyond your original brief,' he conceded. 'But we don't have a choice, do we? The alternative is to sit and wait to be screwed every which way imaginable. And I've put way too much into this –'

At that moment, the kitchen door opened and Charlotte Stirling stepped into the room. With a look that the PM felt was worthy of the most wooden member of an amateur dramatics society, she froze in an attempt at surprise.

'Oh,' she said, with a smile that could have sunk the economy, 'I didn't realise you were still chatting.'

'We're not,' said Stirling. 'Frears is just going.'

The Guardsman rose from the table, muttered goodnight to them both, and headed out of the kitchen, turning left to the lift.

Charlotte dropped into his seat, taking the whisky bottle and pouring a large glass.

'I hardly think that's wise,' said Stirling.

'It's not for me,' she said, lifting the glass to her nose and inhaling deeply before placing it on the table before him. 'It's for you. You look like you could use it.'

Stirling didn't argue with her, taking another deep glug from the proffered glass.

'I want to thank you,' said Charlotte.

Christ, thought Stirling. This sounds ominous.

'You're sticking with this, aren't you?' She leaned across the table, fixing him with her eyes.

Once, a long time ago, Stirling had found those dark pupils, set off against the pale skin, rather attractive. But what had really drawn him to Charlotte Bowlby was her family wealth, money accrued from the vast tracts of Scotland her aristocratic parents owned. Dosh that had supported him on his long journey to the top.

'I am,' he said, hardly needing to spell out the implications of him not doing so.

'Good,' she said, matter-of-factly.

Despite the death of their marriage, which had foundered when Philip was still practising at the Bar, the Stirlings had remained together because their overriding individual needs found succour in the relationship. At first it had been a mix of Charlotte's vulnerability and Philip's reliance on the Bowlby fortune that had done the job. But these days, the marital glue was made of different stuff. She was, at least ostensibly, much stronger, no longer so desperate for the crumbs of support he offered. The self-harm, pills and booze had been replaced by a steely façade acquired through years of therapy. He'd noticed another trait too. She actually liked being the Prime Minister's wife. He could tell she got off on it. She had charities begging her to be their patron, organisations asking her to give speeches, magazines who craved interviews. She was wanted, if only after a fashion.

And of course one other thing bonded them together. Something both of them shared and neither of them ever wanted exposed. A poisonous family secret that had, in recent days, like a powerful virus, mutated in a deadly new direction.

This evening's exchange had been unusual. Usually the dark secret was the source of blazing rows in which Charlotte, with tedious predictability, always sided with Aidan. Tonight seemed to suggest to Stirling that she was moving on, appreciating his efforts. Or possibly, he thought, she was simply aware of the very precarious situation the family found themselves in. They were staring into the abyss, a Tunisian assassin all that stood between them and a very long fall.

Chapter 43

Marrakesh, Morocco

They stayed in the riad, ordering more tea. Little was said. It wasn't just that they were both tired. Sam could feel himself processing their recent exchange, his head, despite the danger of their continued quest, noticeably calming.

As they paid their bill they asked the waiter if he'd heard of Marcel Hadad's antique shop. The man sucked his teeth before finally giving in and scribbling a small map on the back of a napkin.

On finally locating the shop after a circuitous walk through more alleyways, they discovered it closed. In the end, there was nothing to do but head back to the hotel.

Once in the room, Eleanor headed into the bathroom for a shower, emerging a little later with a towel wrapped around her. Sam, who was watching a local news channel completely devoted to the continued tensions in the city – with excitable commentary in Arabic and images of small skirmishes between police and youths wearing balaclavas – tried to respect her privacy. But when her back was turned, he couldn't help but take in the graceful lines of her shoulder blades, the dark wet hair clinging to her back. At that moment Eleanor turned, catching him right at it. Sam smiled awkwardly, then hastily made for the bathroom to take a shower.

When they headed downstairs later, Kamal was on reception. Sam asked him if he knew the name of the restaurant where Charles Scott had dined on his last evening in Marrakesh.

'I'd like to go,' said Eleanor, noticing the doubt on Kamal's face. 'See the places he visited.'

Kamal reluctantly gave them the name of a place in the medina, but urged caution and insisted they took a cab.

It was dark as they left the hotel, a scattering of taxis and two slowly cruising police cars the only vehicles they passed.

They were dropped at Bab Laksour, an old gate north-west of the Djemma el Fna. Passing under a stone arch they moved down an ill-lit, near-empty street, the few people out walking at a pace, as if there were a curfew that Sam and Eleanor hadn't been told of. They passed a pile of rubbish bags that had been ripped open by an animal, the smell of festering food waste filling the warm air. A door slammed shut behind them, making Sam flinch.

As his eyes slowly adjusted to the gloom, Sam noticed that the walls were covered with the posters he'd seen earlier, of the young woman. He looked again at the angry red message below her. The characters – a mix of simple loops, hard angles and what looked like symbols – had an ancient feel to them. Sam could easily imagine them on a cave wall, carved thousands of years ago.

At the restaurant, the atmosphere in the alleyways was banished in an instant. They were greeted warmly by a maitre d' in a dinner jacket – a man clearly on a mission to dispel the atmosphere in the city – and led into a courtyard. Eleanor gasped at the sight before her. It was entirely lit by candles and enclosed by deep red walls. Underfoot were thick patterned carpets while the white table cloths were sprinkled with rose petals. Somewhere out of sight, possibly on the floor above, musicians were playing a haunting tune that somehow combined blues with a distinctly North African sound.

Sam guessed that most of the restaurant's guests, although foreign, were not tourists. In the midst of rising turmoil in the city, they seemed too calm, chatting in hushed tones. Sam made out French, Dutch and German voices.

An hour or so later, after courses of pigeon bstilla and lamb tagine, washed down with a bottle of French red, Sam realised he was staring at Eleanor again, and she was staring right back at him.

'Do you know,' she said, as if she suddenly felt the need to break the spell, 'this is the most relaxed I've felt in days. There may be riots breaking out everywhere, but I feel safe here, miles from the UK.'

When their waiter returned, they ordered tea and, inspired by the restaurant's other guests, a shisha pipe. Before the waiter departed, Sam asked him if he remembered a dinner given for the British PM. The waiter beamed and gestured to Sam to follow him back to the passage that led into the courtyard. There, on the wall, was a series of framed photographs that neither of them had noticed when they'd arrived. In each, the cheery maitre d' was seen shaking hands with some dignitary. Some Sam did not know – North African politicians or celebrities, he guessed – but others were instantly recognisable. There were faded photos of Chirac and Boris Yeltsin. Clearer ones of Blair, Clinton, Sarkozy and Angela Merkel. Then below, a photo of the night in question. It showed the grinning maitre d' flanked on one side by a man who had to be the Moroccan Prime Minister, his wife and a boy, possibly aged about ten, and on the other, by Philip and Charlotte Stirling. Sam darted back into the courtyard and gestured to Eleanor to come and look.

'Charlotte Stirling,' said Eleanor, looking at the picture. 'I remember her well. We used to go on holiday with them when I was a teenager. Most of the time she was drinking on the quiet, or in her room crying.'

'I wonder who that is?' asked Sam, pointing to the figure next to Stirling. The PM had an arm around the shoulders of another man, who was taller. There was a slight distance between the men as if, possibly, they weren't as chummy as the gesture suggested.

'Looks an unusually relaxed pose for a Prime Minister,' said Eleanor. 'Could be my father, I guess.' She looked a little closer. 'It's a bit out of focus at the edge. You can only see a corner of the head. The hair looks quite long, or is that a shadow? It's so hard to tell.'

The maitre d' passed by as they were studying the photo.

'Ah,' he gushed. 'Prime Minister Stirling. A charming man. And the beautiful Mrs Stirling.'

Sam realised that they had little hope of gaining any objective information from him.

'Can you remember who else was here that evening?' he ventured.

The maitre d' shrugged his shoulders, sweeping an arm across the gallery of photos.

They returned to the table for their tea and pipe. Eleanor was the first to take a hit, the smoke drawn through water from a small bowl in which coals gently glowed. She exhaled, the air around their table suddenly dense with fruity smoke. She passed the pipe to Sam, who drew on it. The smoke was cool, soothing. He could feel his head lighten.

In the cab back to the hotel, Eleanor sat close, her knee touching Sam's. She did not remove it for the duration of the journey, leaving Sam with the sensation of a small electric current flowing upwards from his leg.

In the hotel reception, a group of guests had gathered round a widescreen television. There seemed to be some heated discussion. Sam and Eleanor approached and saw, over someone's shoulder, a man in a suit on the television giving a stilted address. Below him, Arabic words ran along the bottom of the screen.

'What's happening?' Eleanor asked a woman next to her.

The woman, who was wearing a hijab and a smart tailored suit, turned to Eleanor with a grim look on her face. 'The man on the television is a government official,' she said. 'He is asking everyone to stay at home tomorrow. A lot of people are coming to march, people from outside the city. It will not end well.'

Chapter 44

Marrakesh, Morocco

Traffic in the district around the Sofitel was virtually non-existent. Clad in flak jackets, helmets and protective visors, riot police were out in force, groups of them standing at regular intervals along the avenues Sam and Eleanor's cab passed down. Their belts were heavy with crowd controlling gear – truncheons and canisters of what Sam guessed was tear gas. Others wore machine guns slung over their shoulders. Barricades had been erected to keep the crowds contained.

Down one side street Sam noticed a convoy of armoured vehicles, water cannons mounted on the drivers' compartments. He heard the buzz of a helicopter and looked up to see one hovering overhead. The State was watching and waiting, preparing to react with force if the day's march got out of control.

The cab driver dropped them before the Djemma el Fna, pointing ahead to explain why he was not going any further. At the edge of Place Foucauld, the tips of palm trees were just visible above a street-level cloud of dust and diesel fumes. Dozens of old coaches, their battered and dirty state suggesting they'd come some distance, were disgorging hundreds of passengers.

Sam and Eleanor paid up and got out of the cab, pausing for a moment to take in the scene before them. It was as if the clock had been turned back and the modern Morocco of broad avenues, sleek cars and men dressed in business suits had been forgotten. The crowd that had assembled were dressed in altogether more timeless garb: turbans and djellaba for the men, ornate, highly coloured kaftans heavy with jewellery for the women.

For now, there was a calm atmosphere, families and small groups sharing picnic breakfasts on the pavement. But Sam sensed that a protest this size, if pushed, could easily turn.

Eleanor consulted their street map, aware that approaching the souk through the Djemma el Fna was going to be impossible. She pointed out a route to Sam and they turned and headed south west, before cutting into the medina via a broad street.

After a few wrong turns, they were winding their way down a familiar alley towards the antique shop. Every door was closed and window shuttered. Down one side alley they saw a small boy kicking a football around, but within seconds he was scooped up by his father and pulled inside.

Unsurprisingly, the shop was closed, a wall of steel shutter drawn down. Sam pounded in frustration on the metal. Given what they'd seen so far in the city, he knew it was fruitless. Hadad had locked up, and probably left the city.

'Shit,' said Sam. Through small gaps in the metal shutters, they could see inside the shop. It was like an Aladdin's cave, clearly supplying a great deal more than just antiques. Walls were stacked with carved screens or hung with kilims, shelves piled high with clothing and scarves.

Sam hammered one more time on the shutters, more in frustration than with any hope that it would result in Hadad's miraculous arrival. He turned to see Eleanor shaking her head.

But just as they were turning away, they heard the sound of a lock turning. From inside the shop, an angry voice shouted out in Arabic.

Sam and Eleanor rushed back to the shutters. Inside, standing by an open door but with the metal shutters still firmly closed, was a rotund man with a moustache and small round spectacles.

'Mr Hadad,' said Sam. 'We urgently need to talk to you.'

'Who are you?'

'My father came here about two weeks ago with the British Prime Minister,' said Eleanor.

From behind the shutters a clearly irritated Marcel Hadad was struggling to make sense of what they wanted.

'It's complicated, Mr Hadad,' said Eleanor. She sighed. 'My father killed himself. And I am trying to piece together his last weeks, find out why he did what he did.'

Sam watched Hadad. He was looking at Eleanor, weighing up this strange piece of candour – and how it might relate to him.

But then, from inside the shop, they could hear another lock being turned and a moment later, the shutters were flung upwards. Hadad gestured for them to step inside. Now the full glory of the shop was revealed. Inlaid cabinets, tables and chairs, intricately patterned metal lanterns, a corridor narrowed by roll upon roll of rugs. Elsewhere, a wall dominated by a display of silver bracelets and necklaces, another with daggers and knives. The air was thick with the smell of cedarwood, metal and mothballs.

'I am sorry to hear about your father,' said Hadad. 'What was his name? We had a lot of visitors while Mr Stirling was here in Marrakesh.'

'Charles Scott,' said Eleanor.

'I remember him,' said Hadad. 'He seemed a good man. I am so sorry for your loss.'

He removed his glasses and rubbed his eyes. 'You will have to forgive me though. I still do not understand how I can help.'

'It's a really simple request,' said Eleanor. 'Can you tell me what happened at your shop?'

Hadad scratched his head. 'The Minister for Tourism called to ask if he could bring the British Prime Minister to my shop. Naturally I said yes. They arrived some time in the afternoon – I can find the exact date if you wish – a whole group of them. They browsed the shop for an hour or so. We had tea. Then your father arrived with another man, a Moroccan.'

'What was the atmosphere like?'

Hadad gave them another puzzled look. 'It was good. Your father and Stirling seemed to be friends. They were both in good spirits, almost as if they were celebrating.'

'And did they buy anything?' Sam asked. It was hardly likely to shed any light on matters, but in the absence of any other questions, Sam thought it worth asking

This prompted the most incredulous look so far. 'Do you really think I would allow people to leave my shop after such a long period empty-handed? They bought – or tried to buy – a long list of items.'

'"Tried to buy"?' asked Sam.

'The Minister for Tourism insisted on purchasing them. He said it was a gift from the State.'

'And can you remember what was bought?'

Hadad moved to a till in the middle of the shop, behind a pale marble fountain.

'I keep my receipts under here. It should not be hard to find.' He pulled a lever-arched file from some shelves beneath the till, gesturing for Sam and Eleanor to sit at a large table inlaid with small pieces of paler wood and mother-of-pearl.

Hadad took off his glasses, gave them a rub on his shirt and then placed them back on. He started leafing through the file.

'Here we are,' he said finally. He sucked his teeth. 'It was a good afternoon. Your father and the Prime Minister left with many things. Scarves, wooden boxes, tilework like this,'

Hadad gestured to a set of tiles decorated with a star motif that was mounted on a small easel above the till, 'a watercolour of the medina by an English Victorian painter.'

At that moment a gang of men ran down the street, chanting angrily. Hadad looked up nervously.

'Mr Hadad,' said Sam. 'Is there any way we can take a copy of the list with us? I'm sure you're keen to shut up your shop.'

'Take this,' said Hadad, handing them the piece of paper.

At the doorway, Hadad looked anxiously up and down the alley. He then shook their hands. 'Miss Scott. I hope I have been of some assistance. Now, if you'll forgive me.'

The cab driver took them a circuitous route round the city, apologising, in bad English, for the long journey.

'Many street closed,' he said.

In the back, Sam and Eleanor sat together, poring over the receipt Hadad had given them. There was a great deal more than he had mentioned: pieces of jewellery, ceramics, a knotted carpet, something called a koumyya, several sets of necklaces, kaftans, a chess set.

Sam felt Eleanor's hand reach for his and a warm memory flooded his mind. He turned and smiled at her. That morning, mindful of the rising tensions in the city, they'd got up in a hurry and rushed to Hadad's shop. There had been no chance to acknowledge what had been evident to both of them in the restaurant – the slow build of sexual tension – before the woman's comments in the hotel foyer had acted like a bucket of cold water. They had shared the bed again, but only to cling to each other as cold fear took a hold.

'You OK?' he asked.

'I'm fine,' she said. She smiled, squeezing his hand.

The cab had stopped at some red lights. By the side of the road, an old man, seemingly immune to the rising hysteria in the city, ambled across their path leading a tired-looking donkey. Sam watched him pass before his eye was caught by a poster plastered to the side of a building. It was another image of the girl. The same angry red writing beneath.

He leaned forward to catch the driver's attention. 'Excuse me,' he said. 'I keep seeing these pictures everywhere.' He gestured to the poster. 'Who is she?'

The driver turned, the dark look on his face suggesting to Sam that he'd made a terrible mistake. But then he seemed to soften, as if he knew Sam could not be blamed for his ignorance.

'She is Lalla, a Berber girl from the Atlas Mountains. She was killed about three week before. The police say a Berber man kill her. But her family do not believe this. Now it is big mess.'

The lights turned green and the cab sped off, with an impatient and noisy surge of acceleration.

'I think the police are right,' continued the cabbie. 'A man from her village kill her. Her lover. But these people cannot see this. They just shout: "Justice for Lalla! Justice for Berbers!" Pah!' This was accompanied by a dismissive wave of his hand.

'Where did this killing happen?' asked Sam, feeling a knot tighten in his stomach.

Just then one of the few other vehicles on the road, a dusty looking estate car crammed with sullen men, swerved across their path. The cabbie slammed on his brake and horn, shouting obscenities in the car's direction.

'The girl was killed in the medina,' the man said. 'Souk Sebbaghine'.

'Souk Sebbaghine,' repeated Sam, almost to himself.

The driver's eyes shot Sam a look from the rearview mirror, one that seemed to convey impatience. 'Sebbaghine, the dyers' souk,' said the man, with irritation. This was clearly hardly the point. He slammed the dashboard in anger. 'It is terrible thing for Marrakesh. Terrible thing for Morocco.'

But Sam wasn't listening any more. The hairs on the back of his neck had gone up.

'Your hand has gone cold and clammy, Sam,' said Eleanor. 'What is it?'

But her voice suggested that she already knew what he was thinking.

The cab came to a sudden halt. They had rounded a corner and come face to face with a wall of people moving across the junction in front of them. The driver pounded the steering wheel with the palm of his hand and barked more angry words. He then turned to Sam and Eleanor.

'No good,' he said. 'You must walk.'

Sam paid the cabbie and they stepped into the street. The noise of the crowds, audible from inside the cab, was deafening outside, a wave of voices chanting in unison. The protest was moving like a huge animal, its leisurely pace at odds with the heightened emotions on display. Clutching placards all featuring the girl's image and the same red message, they punched the air with their fists, faces filled with a mixture of anger, sadness and fear. One of their own had been killed. And this seemed to have spoken to them at a deep level.

Sam watched the crowd slowly edge by. He looked at the street they were moving down, and the direction they'd come from. Both were jammed with people. There were, he guessed, thousands out protesting. Despite the show of Moroccan State force Sam and Eleanor had seen earlier, this was a group who would not give up easily. A confrontation was all but inevitable.

By Sam's reckoning the crowd was heading towards the hotel district – the very area they needed to get to. Despite the prospect of being hemmed in – and the very thought made his throat constrict – Sam knew they had no choice. They would have to join the protest, at least for a while, until they found another route to their hotel. Sam hoped the police he'd seen earlier allowed them through the barricades.

'We have to join the crowd,' said Sam. 'It's the only way we can get back to the hotel.'

'Couldn't we wait until later?' said Eleanor, her voice hesitant.

'I don't want to be out on the streets later,' said Sam.

Eleanor paused, weighing up what he'd said, then nodded in agreement.

They entered the crowd, Sam gripping Eleanor's hand tightly.

As he attempted to lead her through the dense mass of people, the thoughts layered themselves over each other with increasing weight. Was this the secret that Charles Scott had been referring to in that second session? And if so, what was his involvement?

Before long, his thinking was drowned out by a roar that seemed to reverberate, not just in his ears, but throughout his body. The people on the streets had generated a fierce collective energy, as if the march itself were a simmering beast.

The protestors that they moved past, who were dressed, like the crowds at Place Foucauld, in traditional Berber clothes, paid the Europeans in their midst little attention. Still holding Eleanor's hand tightly, Sam moved past a group of women screaming their lungs out; a couple, the man's arm protectively around the shoulder of his young wife, a red headscarf over her dark eyes; an old man in a turban walking with a stick. But while Sam and Eleanor's presence was barely noted, their progress was seriously impeded by the sheer density of the crowd.

Marchers had spread right across the street, meaning that crossing the protest – effectively moving against the flow – was going to take some time. For now, the only option possible was to slowly edge sideways, hoping that, when they got to the other side, an opportunity to escape would eventually present itself.

Chapter 45

Marrakesh, Morocco

Several metres behind them, a broad, unshaven man was making slightly better progress as he kept Eleanor and Sam firmly in his sights. Not afraid to push his way through the crowds, he was slowly gaining on them.

He moved diagonally across the protestors, angry chants ringing in his ears. Slipping his right hand inside his jacket, he felt for the hard rubber of the knife's handle. The blade beneath was razor sharp, with a thin point that he could, with little effort, slide into the backs of both his victims, moving from the girl to the man within seconds.

He'd followed them from their hotel that morning, waiting for a discreet place to act. This was perfect. Two foolish Europeans caught up in the fervour of the day, stabbed by a petty criminal. He'd simply slip away, evaporating into the march.

The crowd around him felt like a river, one with currents that could easily pull him off-course. Like the group of older men that had now moved to block his diagonal path. He slowed, allowing them to move forward, before cutting across the direction of the marchers. He looked up, then cursed under his breath. His targets had disappeared. But they couldn't have been more than a few metres away.

He pushed on, stepping on a man's foot. The man turned to swear at him and he apologised profusely. In any other situation he'd have taken him on, shown him in no uncertain terms what he thought of such disrespect. But today he had an overriding agenda. His hand tightened around the knife's handle.

There they were again. The woman's hair gave their position away. Hers was one of the few female heads that wasn't covered – thick hair, cut in a Western style.

He pressed on, edging closer. How odd, he thought, that it was taking so long to reach them, when the final moment would be a matter of seconds.

He was now little under a metre from the girl. It was a shame. From what he could see of her, she had a nice body. He pulled the knife from his jacket, lowering the blade so that it pointed to the ground, ready to be lifted up and quickly plunged into her lower back.

He was now inches from her. He began to raise the knife, drawing back his hand ready to press the blade forward.

It was then that he felt his wrist being gripped hard by a hand. Another grabbed his other arm, wrenching it, in one swift and very painful move, behind his back. The hand holding the blade was being twisted and he felt the knife slip from his fingers to the ground. He struggled against those holding him, but this only increased the angle his arm was pushed up his back. He tried one last time to pull free, then felt the impact of a blunt-ended object to the back of his head – and everything go black.

Chapter 46

Marrakesh, Morocco

Out of the corner of his eye, Sam had noticed a brief commotion behind him. A man appeared to have been dragged backwards. Sam turned only to see him consumed by the advancing crowds.

He could feel his throat tighten again. The idea of thousands of people pressing in on him would, combined with the right level of anxiety, give him a huge panic attack. He had to concentrate. It was down to him to get them both out of here.

They were now about two-thirds of the way across the march, the side of the street – the pavements sealed off with barricades – now visible. Two policemen stood scanning the crowds from behind their visors.

Sam guessed that the march was heading down the city's main artery towards the Ville Nouvelle. Ahead he could see the minaret of the Koutoubia Mosque, its pinky red stone soaring above the heads and placards of the crowd. If they could just peel off and get through the barricades, it was a short walk west to the Sofitel and safety – at least for now.

Just then, above the din of the protestors, they heard the amplified voice of a man. The crowd was being addressed. A moment later, Sam saw the source of the noise, a police officer standing on the roof of an armoured vehicle clutching a megaphone to his mouth. Neither of them understood a word of what the man was saying but the sentiment of the message was obvious. They were all being warned.

They were now feet from the barricade and Sam made a last push for the pavement. But no sooner had they reached it when a policeman arrived at the spot and started barking at them.

Behind Sam and Eleanor, crowds were jostling their backs, threatening to pull them back into the flow of the march.

Eleanor began pleading. The policeman could clearly understand the substance of her words, even if he was standing firm. But then another officer came over, cupped his hand to his colleague's ear, and muttered something. A second later, the barricade was disengaged and pulled open like a gate, and Sam and Eleanor were free.

As they walked away, Sam looked back. The barricade was back in place, and the police had maintained their vigilant scrutiny of the marchers. All, that is, except the officer who'd intervened, who was watching them as they walked away.

'You think he —'

'I don't know what to think,' said Sam, cutting her off.

Eleanor's eyes were blazing, her face flushed and covered in a film of sweat.

They were both fired up – struggling to calm down after the turmoil of the march, and with the implications of a new and poisonous knowledge.

'I knew what you were thinking as soon as the cab driver started talking about that girl,' she said, her voice raised. And with that, she collapsed on to the bed, her head in her hands.

Sam remained standing. 'Eleanor,' he said, his voice more soothing. 'We don't even know the murder occurred the evening of their dinner.'

Even though their window was closed, they could hear the protestors. A muffled noise that still conveyed the anger of thousands of people. Sam could scarcely believe that all of it stemmed from a single act. He moved to the closed windows, as if drawn to the crowds they'd so recently escaped.

'I need to know, one way or another,' said Eleanor. She paused. 'What did my father say in his notes about what he'd done?'

'Something terrible; something that haunted him day and night,' Sam reluctantly replied.

'Oh God.'

Sam was standing at the closed window staring out at the rooftops of the city. From here you might have imagined the place was peaceful. But then another chant went up.

He turned to Eleanor, who was still sitting on the bed, a finger to her mouth as she bit furiously at its tip.

'We need to speak to Kamal.'

Chapter 47

Marrakesh, Morocco

Sam called reception, asking if Kamal was available. He was told that the deputy manager would be up in a matter of minutes. Sam was surprised that he was able to drop everything – particularly on a day like this – to see them.

Sitting on the bed waiting for him to arrive, they discussed what to reveal if Kamal asked. In the end, they decided that the entire truth was needed. It was simply too complicated – and, by now, too pointless – to edit. They would give him the facts, from the moment Charles Scott first walked into Sam's house.

Kamal arrived and sat at the desk. Sam thanked him for coming so quickly and then came straight out with the question that had been sitting in the room between them, poisoning the air like some malevolent spirit.

'Kamal,' Sam said, 'when did Lalla's murder happen?'

Kamal gave them a puzzled look. 'Why do you need to know this?'

'We will explain but please, if you can...'

Kamal looked down, clearly uncomfortable with what he was about to talk about.

'The media is moderately free here,' he said, 'but journalism that is perceived to be challenging certain areas – the monarchy or Islam, for example – is not permitted. This kind of censorship is sometimes true of sensitive news. So it took a little time for the truth to come out. People only began talking about it some days after it had happened. What I began to hear was that a young Berber girl had been stabbed on the 9th September. The date has now taken on a mythical status. Berbers in the city refer to it as their day of awakening.'

'And can you tell us when my father stayed here?' asked Eleanor, her voice laden with dread.

'It will take me a moment,' said Kamal. He reached for the phone on the desk behind him and called reception. He spoke some words of Arabic and then waited as the person at the other end searched for the information. A moment later, he said 'shokran' and put the phone down. His face had paled.

'Your father last stayed here between the 8th and 10th September. His dinner in the medina was on the last night – the 9th.'

'Oh no.' Eleanor buried her head in her hands again. Sam heard her wail softly. He pulled her into him, feeling her trembling body against his.

'Please,' said Kamal, 'I don't understand.'

With Eleanor still clasped close to him, Sam began to explain. It took him about half-an-hour to tell the story fully, during which time the deputy manager's eyes slowly widened in shock.

Once the story was complete, the three of them sat in silence for a minute or so. Eleanor had calmed and was now looking at Kamal expectantly, as if hoping he might be able to make this whole thing go away.

'So,' said Kamal finally, 'this is why you were so determined to visit the medina and the antique shop.'

'We had to try and piece things together,' said Eleanor. Her eyes were red and her cheeks streaked with tears.

Kamal shook his head. 'I cannot accept that your father would do this,' he said. 'I do not claim to know him as well as you, Miss Scott, but the man I became acquainted with was cultured and civilised. The murder that took place in the medina was brutal and inhuman.'

'Kamal,' said Sam, jumping in to spare Eleanor a chance to dwell on Kamal's last words. 'To prove, beyond any doubt, that Charles Scott did not kill that girl, we need to find out as much about what happened as possible.'

Kamal looked reluctant to speak again.

'Please,' said Eleanor, 'don't worry about me. I'm beyond shocking now.'

Kamal took a deep breath and began. 'It happened in a place called Souk Sebbaghine. It's where wool and skins are dyed and hung out to dry.'

Sam remembered the cab driver's words, but these were then eclipsed by what Kamal said next.

'The girl was stabbed with a koumyya.'

At the sound of this last word, Sam felt his body break out in a cold sweat.

'I'm sorry, what did you say?'

'A koumyya,' said Kamal. 'It's a traditional dagger.'

'Oh God,' said Eleanor.

'What is it?' asked Kamal.

Sam stood to root in his pockets for the receipt that Marcel Hadad had given them. Retrieving it, he then spread the page out on the desk before Kamal.

'One of the items Philip Stirling and Eleanor's father left Marcel Hadad's shop with was a koumyya,' he said.

Kamal looked at the list and then the three of them sat in silence. If, thought Sam, the point of their conversation with Kamal had been to build a case for Charles Scott's innocence, they were doing a bloody bad job.

'OK,' said Sam. 'We don't yet know what that proves, if anything. Please finish what you were saying, Kamal.'

Kamal began hesitantly, as if aware that, with every word, he was making things worse for Eleanor.

'The conclusion the police came to,' he said, 'was that this was a crime of passion committed by another Berber, the girl's lover.' He paused, clearly choosing his next words carefully. 'The Berbers are now very angry. They are angry because one of their own has been murdered – and because of the way this case has been handled. They do not believe this man – who was to marry Lalla – did this. I think they are also angry because they are poor, on the fringes of society, struggling to keep their language and culture alive. I believe this terrible business has convinced them that modern Morocco no longer cares.'

Sam had the distinct impression that Kamal was struggling to maintain a measured, calm appearance.

Just then, another wave of chanting went up.

'Justice for Lalla. Justice for Berbers,' said Sam softly, now acutely aware of the words' significance.

'I fear this will be a bad day,' said Kamal. 'We've seen protests before in Morocco, but nothing on this scale. If they step out of line, there will be bloodshed.'

A horrible image appeared in Sam's head. Hundreds – possibly thousands – of bodies lying in the street.

'We need to tell the authorities,' Eleanor said.

'Tell them what?' said Sam, seeing the sudden look of purpose on her face.

'That my father may have killed the girl.'

Sam had seen this kind of anger before. Countless clients who had struggled to come to terms with a childhood experience of neglectful or abusive parenting and who, after finally acknowledging what had happened, moved into a period of rage. Eleanor was mad with her father for leaving her – and this was merely another reason to reject the man who had, she believed, rejected her.

Eleanor was on a roll, the words spilling out of her with indignation. 'We cannot stand by knowing that thousands of people are potentially putting themselves in harm's way when the truth might protect them. If Kamal's prediction of violence is true – and everything we've seen in the streets suggests that the State is ready to act with force – we will have corpses on our conscience. We have to act to protect those people. We have to tell the authorities.'

'But we don't know all the facts,' said Sam. He was now pleading with her, desperately trying to prevent her going down a path that might destroy a once-cherished figure in her mind. 'We can't be sure the knife was in your father's possession. Besides, remember the other phrase he used during therapy – that something had happened and he'd done nothing to stop it. If anything, that suggests a bystander, not a perpetrator.'

'Even if we don't know the complete truth,' said Eleanor, 'we must tell them.'

'You need to be careful, Eleanor.' Sam's voice was frantic.

'Time could be running out for those people, Sam,' she said. She paused, seeing the look on his face. 'You're worried about me, aren't you?'

'Of course I am,' he said. He was suddenly aware that Kamal was scrutinising them both with great interest. Sam sat down by Eleanor again, gripping her shoulders with his hands. He wanted to shake her.

'You have to remember,' he said, 'that there were others dining there that night. Other members of the British team. It could have been any one of them. Once we tell the authorities, that's it. They are not going to be able to begin a lengthy investigation on British soil. They will want a suspect, fast. Your father will be condemned.'

He could see the doubts suddenly in Eleanor's eyes.

'That's not true,' said a voice behind them.

Sam turned to see Kamal standing, the look on his face one of deadly seriousness.

'I don't understand,' said Sam.

'The authorities will look at this properly. You have my word.'

Sam and Eleanor exchanged puzzled glances.

'I am from the Direction Générale de la Surveillance du Territoire,' said Kamal. Then, seeing their expressions, he added: 'State security. You must come with me.'

Chapter 48

Marrakesh, Morocco

Outside, the marchers slowly progressed towards the Ville Nouvelle. They were inching down Avenue Mohammed V, the broad spine of Marrakesh that connects the old city and the new. From the police helicopters in the air, they appeared like a slow-moving army of ants.

The media – both national and international – had been restricted from recording the protest. But that didn't stop protestors holding their mobile phones aloft or people in the buildings overlooking the march from recording the event on theirs.

The street ran alongside the Sidi Ali Belkacem cemetery and the Arsat Moulay Abdeslam Park, its peaceful acres of palms, olive trees and oleanders shattered by the noise of the protesters.

Beyond was Place 16 Novembre, where a company of soldiers was positioned. Their orders were simple: to ensure the protestors were halted.

Chapter 49

Marrakesh, Morocco

They exited the hotel by a service staircase. In contrast to the rest of the building, this was an austere area of plain concrete walls and steps, one they'd only have used in an emergency. They were certainly no longer being treated as guests. The man they'd thought was the deputy manager, who was now hurrying them down the stairs, had effectively arrested them.

Sam had contemplated refusing to go, but he sensed that Kamal could have easily summoned assistance. They had no choice. They were, Sam assumed, now helping the Moroccans with a murder enquiry. Obstructing an investigation in a country like Morocco – what they'd be doing if they resisted – was not worth contemplating.

At the bottom of the stairs was a set of metal double doors. Kamal pressed down on a long bar to release them and stepped on to a platform just above the back entrance to the hotel. Against one wall was a line of large metal bins. A skinny mongrel was picking at scraps that had fallen from one. A handful of cars were parked opposite while an open gate led into the street. The door closed behind them with a loud clank, startling Sam and Eleanor.

Kamal directed them down a few steps and towards the vehicles. As they approached the cars he reached into his pocket. Retrieving some keys, he pressed the fob and the lights on the side of a large black 4x4 flashed in response.

'Please,' he said, gesturing for them to get in the back.

The 4x4 was soon speeding out of the hotel backyard. It turned left and then right down a street bordered by a stretch of the medina wall. They then veered left, passing into a commercial district. Out of tinted windows Sam and Eleanor watched a ghost town pass by, with shops, banks and cafés all shut. A solitary figure, a bar owner padlocking his closed shutters, looked up at the passing vehicle, his face full of fear.

'Where are you taking us?' asked Eleanor.

Kamal raised a hand in response, whether to calm Eleanor or silence her, Sam couldn't fathom.

Sam reached for Eleanor's hand and squeezed it. He meant the gesture as both a reassurance and light warning. There was little point attempting to communicate with Kamal. It was clear all would be revealed and Sam saw no reason to aggravate a member of the security services.

He thought of how they'd been duped. How they'd accepted the charming deputy manager as genuinely concerned for the wellbeing of his dead friend's daughter. How quickly they'd dismissed the idea that this man could be anything to the contrary.

Sam knew little of Morocco's security services but somehow wasn't surprised that they placed officers in the kind of large hotels where senior British politicians stayed. And what officer wouldn't be curious about the sudden arrival of a Cabinet member's daughter – particularly in the midst of unrest in the city? Now Kamal, thanks to a mix of charm and guile, had managed to extract every last finding of their investigation to date. Sam's fear, that they wouldn't look too hard beyond the most promising suspect, Charles Scott, was now growing. He'd persuaded Eleanor to join his hunt. But now, if it destroyed her father and his reputation, what had he achieved?

After about twenty minutes, during which time the car appeared to circuit around the east of the medina, the vehicle began climbing a gentle gradient then, minutes later, took a sharp left. They had now entered a distinctly different district. The banks and offices had given way to a residential area. Large gleaming BMWs and Mercedes sat in the shade of trees. Behind the foliage Sam could see smart new apartment blocks clad in the same soft pink as the medina's old buildings.

He began to notice men regularly positioned along the pavements. One waved casually at the 4x4 as it passed. As he did, his jacket opened to reveal the unmistakable grip and trigger mechanism of a handgun.

Ahead were the flags of a number of consulates – France, Finland and then the UK. The last flag should have signalled a haven for two nationals caught up with the security services of another country, but Sam knew it was the last place they'd go to, even if they could escape the vehicle.

A little later, the car turned left down another, narrower street, then right through a large opening, two men with machine guns over their shoulders holding the gates open and waving nonchalantly to the driver.

They were now in a courtyard, a functional place far removed from the grandeur of the buildings in the street outside. A Moroccan flag hung over the entrance. As the gates closed shut behind them with a loud clang, Sam shuddered.

He couldn't help but conclude that the faceless place before him was the kind Amnesty International wrote about, one of a number of security buildings dotted around the Middle East and North Africa. Places where people were taken for interrogation, often never to return.

Chapter 50

Marrakesh, Morocco

The room was, like the outside of the building, austere and devoid of any decoration save for a large framed photograph of the King that hung in the middle of a wall, his rounded, genial face adding the proceedings an extra element of menace. Two windows, thick with dust, let in a weak light from the courtyard outside. Another window, higher up an adjacent wall, offered a glimpse of a roofline and the sky beyond. A rattling fan hung from the ceiling, gently stirring the syrupy air. In the background, they could hear the distant sound of chanting, the muffled roar of an angry mass.

Kamal had now left them and closed the door. They were seated one side of a plain wooden table. Sam noticed there were scratch marks across its surface, about the width of fingernails. He dreaded to think who had made them, and under what circumstances.

In the hallway outside, he heard the banter of colleagues, men joshing with each other, followed by raucous laughter. Sam locked on to that noise, convincing himself, momentarily, that they were just visiting a regular office, rather than a building belonging to the Moroccan state security service. The reality came crashing back with a brief memory of the building's exterior. There had been no plaques outside announcing its identity or purpose. It was, in effect, faceless and invisible. What went on here was beyond the law.

Eleanor's face had taken on that determined look Sam was now so used to. But the question she asked suggested it was all front. 'What's going to happen?' she said, her voice quivering. 'Why have they brought us here?'

Sam could have given her his more paranoid reading of the situation – that they were about to be interrogated by people who, by all accounts, tortured those in their custody. But mindful of her already fragile state, he chose to comfort.

'We're helping them with their enquiries,' he said, hoping he sounded confident. 'They don't want riots on their streets, particularly when there's a chance we can help them solve the crime that's led to those marches.'

Eleanor nodded, her eyes briefly widening with fear and uncertainty. In the distance, another cry from the marchers went up.

Just then the door opened and they turned to see a man walk into the room, clutching a manila folder. He was tall and broad, and wore a white shirt that strained against the bulk of his torso. The man sat down opposite them, the chair creaking under his weight. He dropped the file on the desk and exhaled noisily. He then cleared his throat – a guttural sound that suggested a history of cigarettes or shisha pipes – and looked up.

His features seemed crammed into the middle of his wide face beneath the thick folds of skin that made up his forehead. There was a deadness to his eyes, as if emotion didn't really figure in his DNA. Sam had seen eyes like that in his consulting room. Their owners tended to make the worst clients. Men, more often than not, who simply couldn't make a connection with others because of a total lack of empathy.

'My name is Maalouf,' the man said.

For a brief moment, Sam found this strangely comforting. The security services officer who was happy to be identified suggested that this was more of a chat, rather than the beginning of some gruesome interrogation at the hands of an anonymous operative. Sam shook the thought from his head. It could of course mean the exact opposite; the interrogator who started soft, before becoming increasingly aggressive.

'You think a British man may have killed the Berber girl on the 9th September?'

Sam and Eleanor nodded, both knowing that asking Maalouf why they were here was pointless. The questioning was already underway, and they had no choice but to fully participate. Besides, they couldn't insist on the British consulate being called, a representative being present. They were, at least for now, stateless.

Sam then quickly spoke up, worried that, if he let Eleanor speak, the confused, angry feelings she felt for her father would start to cloud things. 'Everything we have learnt so far suggests the British government is trying to cover something up. Certain members of it were dining in the medina the night of the killing and a knife similar to the murder weapon was purchased that day.'

As the words poured out, Sam realised what he was saying. He was accusing his country of a crime.

He was no die-hard, flag-waving patriot, no rabid royalist and, God knows, there was plenty about Britain to gripe about. But until now, he'd believed it was still fundamentally a decent country, not least when compared with others in the world. But loyalty, as he frequently told his clients, was an overrated quality. Why stay loyal, for example, to the husband who drinks and beats you? And why, in their case, stay loyal to the country that's tried to assassinate you?

'We have the knife,' Maalouf said, his face barely registering expression. 'It has fingerprints on it.'

Sam and Eleanor exchanged glances.

'We also have a man in custody,' continued Maalouf, coughing again. 'I would like you to meet him.'

Chapter 51

Marrakesh, Morocco

The head of the march had now reached Place 16 Novembre and a barricade erected by the company of soldiers. Behind the protestors at the front, thousands began slowing to a halt. Lining Avenue Mohammed V were police with their batons, tear gas and water cannons.

The people who'd made it to the Place first were the youngest, fittest and most vociferous. Still clutching their placards emblazoned with Lalla's image, they shouted angrily at the soldiers standing by their armoured cars.

The guards' weapons were – for now – still slung over shoulders, a deliberate signal designed to say that this was not an impending conflict, merely a full stop. The marchers would not be allowed to continue.

To many of the protestors, these soldiers were part of the problem, symbols of a State that had turned its back on them. The volume of their chants began to grow.

The sun beat down on the two opposing sides. It was stalemate.

Chapter 52

Marrakesh, Morocco

Maalouf insisted that Sam alone accompany him to meet the suspect. Eleanor objected, telling Maalouf that this was about her father and that she'd been part of the investigation from the start.

Maalouf held up his hand to halt her. 'This is not for a woman.'

Eleanor was silenced. Looking at her apprehensive face, Sam knew what she was thinking. It wasn't that she'd been denied involvement because of her gender, but what was inferred by Maalouf's comment – that the suspect was clearly in a bad way, most likely beaten or tortured. What did that say about what might happen to them?

Sam followed Maalouf from the room. They walked down the corridor past a series of doors, all closed bar one which revealed a room full of women typing away at computers, before they moved through a set of doors to a stairwell. The stairs were lit by strip lighting which barely illuminated the steps. Sam passed under one light that was blinking on and off, as if the area they were heading towards was a forgotten corner that was rarely visited. At one stage they passed a window that looked out on to the courtyard at ground height, the exhaust pipe of a car visible. They were now below ground, heading to what Sam was sure was the dark heart of the building. A deep sense of dread had enveloped him, adding to the breath-constricting terror that grew with every step he took.

Finally they reached the base of the stairs and, as Sam struggled to adjust to the dim lighting, they moved through another set of doors. The corridor ahead of them, though better lit, made the utilitarian feel of the upper floors look positively upbeat. The walls were rough, unfinished brick work, off which were heavy steel doors with small peepholes at eye level.

Maalouf stopped before one at the end of the corridor and pounded on it with a chunky fist. It was opened by a man in a t-shirt, his face glowing with a sheen of sweat.

With his body now rigid with fear, Sam followed Maalouf inside. The room was windowless but lit with a blue-white overhead light, giving it a bleached, unearthly feel. On the floor in one corner was a man whose torso and arms were held within a car tyre. One of the man's eyes was fat and bruised, barely a slit. There were cuts to his face, the bottom lip was split and bleeding. A flex, copper wiring exposed at one end, snaked across the room. Sam followed the wire and saw, to his horror, a car battery tucked beneath a table at the other end of the room.

Maalouf exchanged a few words with the man in the t-shirt, then turned to Sam.

'Do you know this man?'

Sam was struggling to control his thoughts and emotions. Disgust, at what Maalouf and his man had done, complete terror as he tried to communicate lucidly with such people, as well as the knowledge that, were he or Eleanor to put a foot wrong, they would be treated in a similar way.

Sam shook his head.

'He seems to know you,' said Maalouf.

He said a few words of Arabic to the man in the t-shirt, who fetched a piece of paper from the table and handed it to Maalouf. Maalouf looked at it briefly, then gave it to Sam.

'He had this on him,' said Maalouf.

Sam glanced at the paper and saw two grainy black and white images – one of him, one of Eleanor. They looked as if they'd been taken from a distance, but God knows where.

'I don't understand,' Sam said, the words faltering in his mouth. 'I thought you said you had a suspect in the murder of the Berber girl.'

Maalouf muttered a few words of Arabic to his colleague who grunted in response. Then Maalouf turned to Sam.

'This man is a suspect, but not in that case. He was trying to kill you and your friend.'

Chapter 53

Marrakesh, Morocco

'I don't understand,' said Sam.

They were back in the room with Eleanor, to whom Maalouf had briefly repeated the explanation he'd given Sam in the basement cell, of the assassin's attempt on their lives in the midst of the protest. Sam's mind was reeling with questions.

'How did you know he was following us, let alone trying to kill us?' he asked

Maalouf shrugged. 'We were following you.'

Of course, thought Sam. After Kamal had spoken to them in the medina that first time, explaining his surveillance of them as concern for his old friend's daughter, Sam hadn't expected – or bothered to look for – any further tails. How would they have known there were other men watching them?

Eleanor, who'd seen the pale look on Sam's face on his return, was subdued, taking a back seat as more and more confusing and distressing information was revealed.

'We'd seen the man pursue you in his car to the medina that morning, then watched him as he followed you into the crowd. We knew that he wasn't here to protest. He was not a Berber and he was also moving with too much...' Maalouf seemed to struggle looking for the right word.

'Intent?' suggested Eleanor flatly.

Maalouf nodded. 'We may have been suspicious of your actions, but we didn't want you killed. The repercussions of the daughter of a British Cabinet minister being murdered in Marrakesh would have been a headache to resolve.'

Eleanor laughed dryly, Maalouf's cold analysis of their near-miss with an assassin clearly adding to the absurdity of the situation they found themselves in.

'Given what you have said about the attempts made on your life in Britain,' said Maalouf, 'we must conclude that this man – a Tunisian, it turns out – was hired by the British Government, or select elements within it, to kill you.'

Eleanor let out an enormous breath, the air escaping with an audible tremor. Suddenly, it had been spelt out. Even out here, in North Africa, they were still trying to kill them.

'You have rattled them,' said Maalouf, 'which means you are close to the truth.'

Sam, who had been struggling with the idea of helping – for this was clearly what Maalouf required of them – a man who could oversee a brutal torture like the one that had just been meted out in the basement of the very building they were sitting in, now realised that they had little choice. Maalouf was their new ally. They had to work with him. But the prospect revolted Sam.

It was as if Maalouf could read his mind. 'You do not approve, do you?'

Sam shook his head.

'What you saw in the basement is what your Government has frequently asked other countries to do on your behalf since 9/11 and your invasion of Iraq. You may choose to be disgusted, but you are complicit.'

He leaned across the table, his bulk blocking some of the feeble light coming through the window. 'The march going on today – I imagine you think I'd like to crush them. This is not true. The people out there have a right to justice. One of their own was murdered. Unfortunately the police have mishandled this by arresting the wrong man. So now we have a bigger problem. The Berbers mistrust us. The next man we arrest must be the right one.' He paused, clearing his throat again. 'For now we must contain their anger – but with restraint.'

He leaned back in his chair, stretching out his burly arms to reveal damp patches under his armpits.

Sam closed his eyes. He heard the ceiling fan's rattle, another far-off cry for justice from the marchers.

He didn't buy Maalouf's talk of the crowd's legitimacy. He suspected the man would, if he had the chance, pound every last protestor into the ground. This wasn't about justice, but about maintaining order.

'OK,' said Eleanor.

Sam looked at her. She nodded back. She'd clearly been on her own journey, weighing up the moral difficulties of working with Maalouf, and had come out the same place as Sam.

'So, if you're right,' she said, 'and we are close, how do we finish this?'

Maalouf cleared his throat again. 'Fingerprints.'

Chapter 54

Marrakesh, Morocco

Maalouf held up a finger, pausing proceedings, and made a quick phone call. A moment later, the door opened and a small, slight man with bulging eyes and pock-marked skin entered the room. He hastily pulled up a chair and sat down next to Maalouf, letting out a noisy sigh, as if this meeting were something he was trying to cram into an already busy day.

'This is Badaoui,' said Maalouf.

The smaller man nodded at Sam and Eleanor.

There then followed a brief discussion between Maalouf and Badaoui in Arabic, during which it was clear the larger man was bringing his colleague up to speed.

The conversation was over and Badaoui opened a manila file on the table before them and began lifting out various documents. The first was a colour photograph of the knife. There was a sharp intake of breath from Eleanor when she saw the weapon. Sam leaned in to examine the picture and saw immediately why Eleanor had reacted the way she had. The blade, a long, curved piece of tapering metal, was almost entirely covered in blood.

Sam swallowed hard. Above the blade, the dark handle appeared to be made of hardwood. It was smooth and bulged at the far end where it was clad in engraved silverwork. Sam stared hard at the wood, imagining the secrets its surface contained. Who had last used it?

He turned to see Eleanor giving the photo the same scrutiny, a frown now replacing the initial horror she'd expressed.

'The fingerprints are good,' said Badaoui, his voice deep, with a hint of a French accent. 'We just need to find a match.'

'What do we know about the attendees at the dinner that night?' asked Maalouf.

Badaoui sifted through the documents he'd pulled from the file and placed a sheet typed with what appeared to be a list of names in Arabic over the photo of the knife. He and Maalouf then studied the list. They weren't quite putting their arms in front of the list, as a child might to avoid someone copying their work, but there was a sense that this part of the investigation was for their eyes only.

Badaoui muttered something to Maalouf. The large man grunted in response and then looked up.

'It seems your Prime Minister is in the clear,' he said.

'Philip Stirling could not have killed her,' said Badaoui hastily, as if Maalouf was stealing his thunder. 'The Prime Minister was in the restaurant all evening.'

'What about the other guests?' asked Eleanor, her voice anxious. 'Did any of them leave?'

Badaoui sighed. 'All evening there were people coming in and out. It was an informal dinner and the business of Government – on both sides – continued all night. People got up to answer their phones or go outside into the alleyway to have mini meetings. There were numerous small details to be tied up after the intense discussions of the last few days – '

At this point, Maalouf interrupted Badaoui with a few short, terse words in Arabic.

'Can we look at the list?' asked Sam, at the same time wondering why Maalouf had cut short Badaoui so irately. 'See if any of the names seem significant?'

Badaoui looked at Maalouf, who had paused to consider this request, rubbing his jaw with one of his outsized hands. The larger man nodded.

Badaoui reached into his file and pulled out a sheet of paper – another list, this one in English – then placed it on the table before Sam and Eleanor, who began poring over the names. Maalouf then gestured to Badaoui and the two men got up, went over to the window and began a conversation in hushed tones.

Sam watched the two men for a moment, wondering what they could be discussing. In all likelihood, it was the amount of information that could be revealed to two British nationals. What was happening, Sam suspected, was as unusual for the Moroccans as it was for them.

'God,' whispered Eleanor suddenly, 'there's a blast from the past.'

'Who?' said Sam.

'Him,' she said, her finger pointing to a name on the list.

'Aidan Stirling,' said Sam.

'You remember those family holidays I mentioned when we were in that restaurant?'

Sam nodded, happy to give Eleanor something else to think about.

'Well in addition to Charlotte Stirling hitting the bottle in spectacular fashion, the other strong memory I have is of Aidan Stirling. We had about three, maybe four, holidays with them in Cornwall before my Mum cracked and said enough was enough – she and Charlotte didn't really get on.'

Eleanor's eyes drifted as she was momentarily lost in recollection.

'I quite enjoyed the holidays. A big gang of families took cottages in the same village, so it was quite good fun. But the first year was different. It was just us and them, so Aidan and I were the only children. It was a typical British summer, pissing down non-stop. I must have been about 15 then, Aidan around five, and we were kind of flung together. We used to play games to keep the boredom at bay. I liked him. The thing was, he seemed overjoyed, as if no-one had ever given him that kind of attention before. Poor guy, on the day we left, he got incredibly upset. It was as if I was leaving him forever – when all I was doing was going home. I remember Philip and Charlotte Stirling had to hold him back while we got in the car. Otherwise he'd have jumped in and come home with us.'

'Clearly not a fan of his own family,' said Sam, who felt an instant kinship with Aidan Stirling. 'What was he doing at the dinner?'

'It was a celebration to which our Prime Minister had invited both his family and Philip Stirling's,' said Maalouf, who had clearly overheard their conversation – or certainly the latter part of it. 'Should we view him as a suspect?'

Eleanor took a sharp intake of breath, suggesting horror that she could have fingered someone so easily in Maalouf's eyes.

'For now,' said Sam, keen to diffuse her concern, 'surely everyone on this list, except Stirling, is a suspect until proven otherwise.'

Badaoui suddenly clapped his hands together. 'The table at the ministry!' he cried.

For once, Eleanor, Sam and Maalouf were united in their expressions, all turning to Badaoui with bewildered looks.

'Most of the people at the restaurant that night also came to the ministry for the final meeting,' said Badaoui, his voice filled with excitement. 'The table they sat at will be covered in their fingerprints.'

'But hasn't the table been used since – or cleaned?' asked Maalouf.

'It has been used once,' said Badaoui. 'A short meeting – a formality more than anything – to welcome the new Iranian consul. But it was only a handful of people and it has not been used since. Of course the room has been cleaned. How well, who knows? It is certainly worth a try. We have a table plan which will give us the exact seating position of all the British delegates. If we can retrieve any fingerprints from its surface, we can then compare them with those on the murder weapon.'

Maalouf looked unconvinced, but nodded at Badaoui. 'Get on to it now. We need answers. Quickly.'

As he watched Badaoui rush from the room, Sam felt oddly relieved that Maalouf was actively pursuing this. It would have been only too easy to nail Scott at this point – to implicate a man who was already dead, someone who could easily be disowned by the country he'd once served.

He glanced at Eleanor – saw her eyes sweeping the table's surface, her brain clearly working through a series of similar outcomes – and hoped to God that her father, who she already felt had abandoned her, wasn't about to be destroyed in the cruellest way imaginable.

Chapter 55

Marrakesh, Morocco

Sunlight was now pouring through the dust-covered window panes. The weak ceiling fan did little to prevent the air slowly cooking, bringing the room's stale aroma to life. Sam could smell Maalouf's body odour, cigarette smoke and a distant hint of acrid cleaning fluid. God knows what it had been used to clean up.

Maalouf had moved to the window and was staring through the dusty panes into the courtyard below. He clearly had no intention of speaking, at least for now. The fan continued to circle noisily, never quite managing to drown out the muted din of the protestors.

'Can I get some water?' asked Eleanor.

Maalouf turned in her direction but his response was interrupted by his mobile phone ringing. He answered with a grunt.

Sam and Eleanor watched Maalouf's face slowly lose colour as he listened to the voice at the other end, a breathless avalanche of Arabic loud enough for them to hear. The large man intermittently muttered a few words, catching brief moments in the rant to respond. Seconds later he had a chance to speak at greater length and used it to bark down the phone. Ending the call, he then dragged a chair to the wall.

Maalouf had positioned himself beneath the solitary window and now stood, the chair groaning beneath him, as he took in the view. When he got down moments later, his face was ashen.

'I must go,' he said.

He then stormed from the room, the door slamming behind him.

Chapter 56

With the door closed, Sam wasted no time, mounting Maalouf's chair to see what had turned the giant so pale. Unlike the other dusty windows, this one was clear, and Sam knew in an instant what he was watching. Below was a section of broad avenue, seen between two buildings. The street was thronged with the same marchers they'd left earlier that day. They were visibly angrier, chanting, fists raised in unison.

Sam wondered why, given the protest's proximity, they hadn't heard the noise more clearly. And then he understood. The windows were sealed tight, the room's dark business not for others to hear.

'It's the march,' Sam said. 'Looks like it's getting nasty.'

'Oh Christ,' he said, his voice hushed.

Eleanor had dragged another chair over and joined him at the small window. Seconds later, they watched as cannisters flew through the air, landing in the crowd.

'Tear gas,' muttered Sam.

Thick plumes of white smoke poured from the disturbed canisters, diffusing lazily into the still, humid air.

The effects of the gas were soon terrifyingly evident. There was a sudden surge, as those affected by the fumes pushed backwards away from the source of the smoke. Sam and Eleanor watched in horror as the people behind them began to compress with this surge. It was clear that the sheer weight of their number meant there was little room to accommodate the new movement.

'Someone's going to be crushed,' said Eleanor.

Whichever force had shot tear gas into the crowd, now engaged water cannons. High-pressure jets hit the protestors, knocking already panicked and disorientated people to the ground, as if the intention was simply to scrub the streets clean of dissent.

'But they've got nowhere to go,' said Eleanor, her voice choked with emotion.

They heard a muffled screaming as chaos took hold. Those at the front were continuing to drive backwards away from the tear gas and water cannons.

Soon more people lost their footing. Sam and Eleanor saw an elderly man, distinct in his white robes, drop down and then a wave of people move over where he'd fallen. A woman fell too, only to be pulled up again by two men.

Despite the insulation of the room, a dull cracking sound penetrated its windows, sending a shudder through Sam and Eleanor. It was the unmistakable noise of gunfire.

Chapter 57

Sam and Eleanor stood frozen at the small window, convinced they'd see bodies fall to the ground. But it appeared the shots were either fired over heads, or rubber bullets.

Some easing of the crowd behind meant that the fleeing protestors moved more quickly. But what was left in their wake made Eleanor sharply intake breath, a hand cupping her mouth in horror.

Sam counted about twenty bodies. There was the old man in his now dirtied white robes; a woman, perhaps in her thirties, her neck twisted at an unnatural angle. The rest seemed to be young men. Faces bloodied.

Among the bodies were scores of discarded placards. Sam strained his eyes at them, then drew back as he recognised the all-too-familiar image. The Berber girl, lying with those who'd marched in her name.

Eleanor stepped off the chair, stumbling as her feet touched the floor. She slumped to the ground, her back to the wall, knees drawn into her chest. Sam dropped down beside Eleanor, pulling her to him and wrapping his arm around her shoulder.

Chapter 58

Marrakesh, Morocco

Hours passed. At one point, the door opened and an unshaven man with thick eyebrows that met above his nose brought food and two glasses of water on a tray. Sam saw the man scan the room in mild alarm, before he noticed them on the ground.

They downed the water but couldn't face the food, a plate of stale pitta breads and an indecipherable dip with a hard, dark skin on the top.

The sun moved round the side of the building, the room taking on a gloomy pall. Neither of them spoke, the images they'd witnessed replaying in their minds.

Just after 6pm – Sam had just checked his watch – the door opened and Maalouf returned.

He dragged the seats from under the window, urging them to sit down. Sam and Eleanor eased themselves off the floor, then sat. Opposite them, Maalouf rubbed his face with his hands. When he looked up, he seemed to have visibly aged, the plump bags under his small eyes were swollen, the lines between the meaty creases of his forehead furrowed and dark.

'You saw what happened,' he said. 'The march got out of hand. People have died.'

Eleanor and Sam stared at the large man, too numb to speak

'Believe me, it was not as bad as it could have been,' said Maalouf. 'But unless this can be resolved, they will be back, angrier than ever. And more will join them. Whatever you think of the Government of my country, you can see that this benefits no one.'

The door opened again and Badaoui stepped into the room. Unlike his colleague, the slight man seemed to have been invigorated by the time that had passed. Sitting next to Maalouf, his eyes were bright and he seemed bursting to impart his new knowledge.

They briefly conferred in Arabic, Badaoui's excitable voice dominating the exchange. At one point Badaoui gestured towards Sam and Eleanor and muttered a question. Maalouf dismissed the query with an irritated swat of one of his substantial hands.

The matter – Sam suspected it was about sharing this new information with them – was settled and Badaoui turned to face them.

'We now know,' he said, 'that, in addition to Philip Stirling, his wife also remained in the restaurant all night, so we must eliminate them from our enquiries. We have analysed the prints we took from the conference table at the ministry. Of those in the restaurant that night, we have, as yet, no matches for the murder weapon.'

'"As yet"?' asked Maalouf, barely containing his impatience.

'Two sets of prints remain unaccounted for,' said Badaoui. He paused a beat, at which point Sam thought Maalouf would grab the man and fling him across the room like a rag doll.

'Two men,' said Badaoui finally. 'Charles Scott. And Aidan Stirling, the Prime Minister's son.'

Eleanor glanced at Sam, the look of trauma in her eyes now replaced by blind panic, as she came face-to-face with the prospect of her father being labelled a killer. Meanwhile, Maalouf's face barely registered a jot. The prospect of either men – even the British Prime Minister's son – being guilty was not even worthy of a raised eyebrow.

Badaoui was now explaining in laborious detail how, in all likelihood, Scott's fingerprints had probably been wiped clean from the conference table while Aidan of course had not attended any of the meetings. Maalouf was barely listening.

Sam felt Eleanor's pain, but he was also stunned at the new name in the frame. Save for Eleanor's memories, he knew little of the PM's son. Aidan Stirling seemed to live a quiet life out of the public eye. He was, Sam seemed to remember, a designer, or perhaps an architect.

Maalouf's voice interrupted his thoughts. 'If we are to pursue this line of enquiry to its logical end and, God willing, find our man, we must have those two sets of prints.'

He cleared his throat. 'You can get us evidence of your father's prints?'

Eleanor nodded imperceptibly, Sam unsure whether she'd actually agreed. Despite Maalouf's plea for both sets of prints, Sam wondered whether her cooperation was even really necessary. The prospect of a dead killer was, again, all too convenient, particularly when the alternative was Stirling's son.

'What about Aidan Stirling?' said Badaoui.

Maalouf's silence said it all. For Moroccan secret service, such a figure would be impossible to gain access to.

'Leave that to me,' said Eleanor.

Sam looked over at her. Eleanor's face had reddened, the eyes were blazing. She might have had fond memories of Aidan, but she was going to give her father a fair hearing, with all the evidence available.

'You said you knew him?' said Maalouf.

'That's right.' Eleanor's face was tightly set.

'Then we leave this with you. Get the prints to the Moroccan embassy in London. Leave the rest to us.'

Sam was suddenly aware of the gear shift, their virtual imprisonment now about to end.

'You look concerned, Mr Keddie,' said Maalouf. Sam noticed the gap between what had been said and the tone of voice that had accompanied it, one wholly lacking in any empathy.

'I'm a little worried about our safety in the UK.'

'Get this done swiftly and you'll soon be safe,' said Maalouf, virtually sneering at Sam's concern.

Sam was unconvinced.

'Think of the attempts on your life in the UK and here,' Maalouf said, a note of exasperation in his voice. 'They are discreet, deniable, meant to look like accidents or the work of a petty criminal. Few people involved. No questions. That's what they want.'

'But they know we're here. Do you think they'll just let us re-enter the UK?'

'The last thing they want is for you to be processed by the police,' said Maalouf. He paused for a moment, as if a thought had suddenly occurred to him.

'But just to be safe,' he said, 'we will get our Tunisian friend to contact his handlers. Tell them his job is done. And one other precaution may be necessary.'

Maalouf then turned to Badaoui and, in Arabic, started firing off what sounded like instructions. It was as if Sam and Eleanor were no longer in the room. Sam suddenly realised that, in one respect, they weren't. They were now simply pawns in a game.

Part III

Chapter 59

Downing Street

'Enchantée de faire votre connaissance, Madame,' stumbled Stirling, his French far from slick.

The French President's wife didn't seem to mind, giggling nervously and offering him a coy smile. In truth, she was not a patch on the previous incumbent, but with her slightly rounded behind and short legs, she was somehow far more human. And besides, Stirling was positively brimming with bonhomie, in love with life and indeed with everyone he spoke to.

The reception was in the Pillared State Room, its walls of cheery yellow matching his frothy mood. It was the first meeting between Stirling and his French counterpart, a deliberately light affair designed to confirm that, with their countries' long established friendships, the two leaders were already pals.

Stirling salivated at the prospect of the forthcoming lunch. The fact that his appetite had returned was a sure sign that life was back on track after the nightmare of the past days.

They were drinking a sparkling wine from the Camel Estuary in Cornwall with their canapés, before moving into the State Dining Room for a lunch of potted shrimp, rare Aberdeen Angus beef and new potatoes, finished off with a pudding of raspberries and cream.

Stirling was feeling as enthusiastic about the British food the chef was showcasing as he was about Britain itself. There really was no finer country to govern. Now that Keddie and Eleanor Scott were no longer in the way – as confirmed by Frears that morning – he could get on with the job he was elected to do. The negotiations with Morocco would, in all likelihood, come to nothing – the place was simply too volatile for the project they'd discussed – but maybe that was a lesson. Domestic issues were clearly where his energies should be directed.

They were being summoned to lunch. He watched Charlotte link arms with the President. The French leader was clearly charmed by this tall dark woman, a sharp contrast to his shorter, more rotund wife.

He marvelled at the journey Charlotte had made. Her current role would have been unthinkable just a few years back.

He studied her briefly as she exited the room, the straight line of glossy dark hair against the pale skin of her neck, her strong, broad back, firm athletic arse and long shapely legs. God, was he getting turned on by his wife again?

He followed Charlotte's example and linked arms with the President's wife. She giggled again. He'd watched her necking the sparkling wine and was fairly certain the woman was well on her way to being pissed. Marvellous, he thought. She was, like him, only human. How he'd beaten himself up about everything that had happened since that fateful night in Marrakesh. How unnecessary that had been. After all, we were all flawed in some way.

Chapter 60

Biggin Hill, London

The jet taxied to a standstill before a small terminal building. From the window, through a veil of drizzle, Sam saw Canary Wharf in the distance.

A moment later, a car sped towards them, the side of the vehicle emblazoned with the words 'HM Customs and Immigration'.

The steps of the jet were lowered and a member of the cabin crew met the vehicle, handing two passports to the driver.

Maalouf, who had accompanied Sam and Eleanor on the flight from Marrakesh, explained what was about to happen.

'As far as that man out there is concerned, you are a Moroccan diplomat and his wife. This means you are granted unimpeded entry into the UK. You will not be required to pass through the immigration building out there. Once those passports have been examined, a car will draw alongside the plane and you will be free to go.'

They'd heard this twice already. It was clear that Maalouf was now feeling anxious. In his airless interrogation room in Marrakesh, he was in charge and could talk with ease about a hypothetical operation on foreign soil. But now they were actually in the UK, Maalouf's discomfort, his obvious desire to extricate himself from any further involvement, was plain to see. Sam had no doubt that foreign powers did all sorts of things undercover in London, but getting caught up, however indirectly, in an operation that targeted the son of the British Prime Minister would be a diplomatic disaster. He and Eleanor were on their own from here on.

The HM Customs and Immigration vehicle was driving away and now a dark Mercedes was heading towards the plane. As the vehicle stopped alongside, Maalouf stood, offering his hand to both of them. His face had returned to normal – utterly devoid of emotion.

'Good luck,' he said.

Sam drew no comfort from the words. Christ, he thought, this man is the nearest thing we have to an ally. And he can't get away fast enough.

Eleanor was off the plane first. She wore a knee-length skirt and jacket, her thick hair contained in a hijab in case anyone happened to be watching too closely from the terminal building. Sam was down the steps next, wearing a black suit, his face covered with a dark baseball cap.

The door of the Mercedes closed with a soft but heavy thud. The car moved past a series of hangars – the huge doors of one open to reveal a black helicopter and the sleek white lines of a private jet not dissimilar to the one they'd arrived on – then a car park filled with high-end vehicles, before speeding out of the airport's exit.

There was no relief at their safe re-entry into the UK. All Sam could see was the challenge ahead, something he and Eleanor had run through on the flight back.

Eleanor planned to use her father as an excuse for getting in contact with Aidan Stirling. As Aidan's godfather, Charles Scott had seen him regularly over the years. Eleanor had concluded that it was perfectly logical to ask Aidan whether he could spare some time, maybe over a drink in a bar or pub, to reminisce. It was then a question of discreetly removing the glass he'd drunk from.

It was, as Sam had repeatedly said, an incredibly risky plan. What if Aidan Stirling was a killer? What if the people who'd so ruthlessly hounded them also minded him? What if, in contacting him, she alerted them?

But Eleanor's blood was up. Time after time on the plane she talked of what they'd seen from the interrogation room window.

'People died,' she said. 'And unless we act, more will. I have to do this, Sam. Not just for the Moroccans, but for myself. I have to prove Dad wasn't a murderer. And all we need is a glass.'

A glass, thought Sam. But what if Eleanor was captured? And even if Sam did then manage to get the glass – and it provided proof of Aidan's guilt – would that be enough to guarantee Eleanor's release?

The Mercedes was slowing to a halt. Sam had asked to be taken to King's Cross so that they could book into the same anonymous bed & breakfast where he'd holed up when this nightmare had first erupted.

They stepped out on to the pavement, a chill wind hitting them both in the face. The drizzle that had greeted them at Biggin Hill was now a steady rain.

The car sped off with indifference, joining a busy stream of morning traffic on the Euston Road. People spilled by them, heads down to avoid the elements. Sam took Eleanor's hand and led her down a side street.

A little later, in a small, dark room that overlooked the pipework and windows of the back of another building, they stood just inside the door, holding each other tight. The weight of the task ahead had been momentarily suspended when the door closed and Eleanor dropped her bag, wrapping her arms around Sam. There was a pause and then she looked up at him. The eyes Sam had got to know so well in the past days – dark pools set in delicate, gently freckled skin still pale despite the intensity of the Moroccan sun –

bore into him. The previous night, exhausted after their ordeal with Maalouf and Badaoui, they had collapsed fully clothed on the hotel bed and not moved till morning. Now, as if a precious opportunity had presented itself, Eleanor kissed Sam. He felt her tongue in his mouth, her breasts pressed against his chest and would have loved nothing more than to cast aside the task ahead, and escape with her into the warm haven of the bed. But the job that needed to be done hung over the room like a black cloud and, a moment later, a tacit agreement passed between them, and they peeled apart.

Eleanor phoned home and spoke to Jill, Wendy's carer. In addition to passing on the message that she was now home from her trip and would be back by the weekend for her father's funeral – and at this, Sam tensed, hoping to God that Eleanor was right – she asked Jill to root out her father's address book in the study. In it, Eleanor said, Jill would find a mobile number for Aidan Stirling.

There was a pause, and then Jill returned to the phone. Sam watched Eleanor's long fingers, the nails gnawed to the core, as they scribbled down the number on a scrap of paper. She then thanked Jill, and hung up.

'Right,' she said, her voice tight and breathless. 'No time like the present.'

Her fingers were trembling as they pressed the keys of her mobile.

'Oh hi,' she suddenly said, 'this is Eleanor Scott, Charles's daughter.'

It was clear from her tone that she was leaving a message. Sam's shoulders dropped a fraction.

'I realise it's been a long, long time.' She laughed slightly at this, clearly as much from nerves as from the effort of sounding light and breezy, 'but I was wondering if we might get together for a drink. It's kind of hard to explain on the phone, but I guess I just want to talk to people who knew Dad. Anyhow, if you're free, and you can spare a bit of time to meet, it would be lovely to see you. Here's my number.'

She repeated the number for good measure, then hung up, collapsing on to the bed.

Ten minutes later, her phone began to ring.

Chapter 61

King's Cross, London

'He was a little taken aback at first,' said Eleanor, 'but then full of sympathy.'

Sam stood staring at the cheap brick of the building opposite, the windows with their bubbled, opaque glass, a stain of algae below a leaking pipe. Eleanor's description of the man she'd just spoken to – and his 'normal' reactions – did nothing to reassure him. Nor did the meet he'd suggested that very evening, in a pub in St James's. It all seemed too quick. Too convenient.

He turned and went over to the bed, where Eleanor was still sitting. 'You don't have to go through with this, you know.'

Eleanor looked into his eyes. 'I do, Sam,' she said. 'You know I do. And it will be fine, I promise. '

'Listen,' he said, 'I'll be in the pub. Any problems, I'll be right by your side.'

She nodded, her smile uncertain.

As a distraction, Sam suggested they plan their next steps.

Shortly after 5.30pm they'd take the Tube to St James's, giving them both a chance to check out the pub and layout of the streets around it before Aidan turned up at 6.30pm. Sam would then find himself a discreet place to sit, a little way from Eleanor. If, for whatever reason, Eleanor failed to remove the glass before she left the pub, then it was up to Sam.

It was, as plans went, flimsy as hell. But as Eleanor had said, all they needed was a glass. And as soon as Sam could deliver that to the Moroccan embassy, the dynamics would soon shift. He hoped to God she was right.

'I can't talk about this any more,' said Eleanor. She lay back on the bed, breathing out deeply.

Sam felt a hand on his back and turned to see Eleanor looking straight at him, her eyes beckoning. He lay down next to her. They kissed again, hands slowly exploring each others' bodies. He began to unbutton her shirt, reaching inside to touch her breasts, her hardened nipples. Eleanor sighed with pleasure.

Sam felt the moment take over, the dark thoughts that had occupied his brain for days, finally evaporate.

Chapter 62

St James's, London

The pub was a narrow building in a one-way street of Georgian townhouses that seemed, for the most part, to be divided into offices. Sam saw brass plaques for solicitors, recruitment consultants, accountancy firms and what appeared to be a private bank. There would be people around, and quite probably plenty of employees having an after-work drink in the pub. He couldn't decide whether this was a good thing or not.

Sam and Eleanor took a few minutes to explore the area immediately around the pub. The streets were laid out in grid fashion, giving them a quick sense of the neighbourhood.

In front of the pub itself, underneath hanging baskets overflowing with brightly coloured flowers, were a couple of tables for drinkers. Behind was a bay window of dark glass that afforded a murky view of the interior. Inside, the pub was long and narrow, with seating spread along both interior walls, and a small beer garden at the rear. Eleanor planned to sit near the front, Sam in the middle.

The pub was already busy, most of the tables occupied and people beginning to throng at the bar. A group of men with loosened ties stood at a gaming machine, laughing as a colleague clumsily attempted to steer a Formula One car round a course. Beneath the hubbub of voices, Sam could hear Paint It Black by the Rolling Stones. In the far corner, a music video – a rap star gesticulating with his hands as he sat on the bonnet of a Jeep, two busty women in swimsuits writhing around him – silently competed for attention. While all this commotion and activity seemed comforting to Eleanor, Sam couldn't help worrying that Aidan might suggest another, quieter venue, one that was beyond Sam's control.

They bought drinks, a mineral water for Sam and a gin & tonic for Eleanor, who'd admitted to raging nerves. By 6.15pm, they were seated in position, Sam getting one of the last tables in the middle of the pub.

A discarded newspaper lay on the table and Sam opened it, while keeping an eye on the door. Eleanor sat with her back to him. The pub was filling, people now frequently blocking Sam's view.

About ten minutes later, as Sam was about to go over to Eleanor and call the whole thing off because his view of her was getting too obstructed, he saw a solitary figure walk in.

Aidan Stirling wasn't a regular in the media, so Sam was unsure if it was him. But he watched the man slowly look round the room, lock on to the spot where Eleanor sat, smile, and walk over to her.

It was Aidan Stirling. Sam saw Eleanor stand and receive a kiss on the cheek.

It was too late. Their amateur operation was in motion.

Chapter 63

Downing Street

Frears had taken the call in the small first-floor office he used whenever he was in Downing Street. It was shared by a variety of advisers who could plug in their laptops and make it their temporary home. Today he was alone save for a new drugs adviser, an articulate ex-addict the PM had met on a visit to a community centre in Sheffield. The adviser called everyone 'man', including women and Frears.

The Guardsman had felt his body go cold as his surveillance man, based outside Downing Street to the west, relayed the news. He was now trying to process it, despite the best efforts of the old junkie next to him tapping away incredibly loudly at his keyboard. Aidan was un-medicated and with Eleanor Scott. It was like the perfect storm.

He thought of the basic tenets of his military training. How it was about following orders but also about using initiative when a situation demanded more flexible thinking. Christ, was this such a situation. Whatever happened now, it was, he knew, probably over for him. This could not end neatly.

He began to shut down his laptop, not out of any desire to protect the secrecy of his work – that hardly mattered given the nature of his extra-curricular activities – but to give him some extra time to think. He then got up and walked briskly out of the office.

'Later, man,' said the drugs adviser.

Chapter 64

St James's, London

Eleanor had almost finished her gin & tonic when Aidan strode into the pub.

A gap of almost twenty years might have passed since they'd last met but he was instantly recognisable. Despite the height he'd acquired in the intervening years, he still had the same round face and curly hair, now a mop that fell in front of his eyes. She watched him scan the room and then, when he spotted her, break into a broad grin.

She was acutely aware of her mission – of the need to stay focused – but for a moment it was all too easy to imagine that sweet but rather troubled little boy from Cornwall heading towards her.

He stood before her rather awkwardly. Eleanor got up and then Aidan leaned forward to plant a kiss on her cheek.

'I'm sorry about your dad,' he said, his voice raised against the din of the pub.

'Thank you,' she replied, realising that she too was talking loudly to be heard.

They sat down, Aidan brushing the hair from his face. 'Your dad was very kind to me,' he said. 'Fatherly,' he added.

Eleanor, despite her nerves, sensed that this was entirely sincere on Aidan's part.

'Listen,' he then said, 'do you want a drink?'

'Thank you,' said Eleanor. 'A gin & tonic would be great.'

Aidan moved towards the bar and stood waiting to be served. Eleanor knew that more alcohol probably wasn't the best idea but she felt it was the only way to calm her nerves. She watched Aidan's back as he leaned against the bar. There were about ten other people waiting to be served.

A tall man in a suit appeared at Aidan's side and leaned into him, whispering in his ear. Aidan turned and gave the man a look of utter contempt, spitting some words back at him. The man smiled slyly, and then said something else.

As Aidan looked back to the bar, as if trying to ignore the man, Eleanor heard a voice in her ear.

'Miss Scott.'

Eleanor turned round sharply and found a bald man leaning down towards her.

'Do I know you?' she said, although she had already guessed. As her heart leapt, her mind began rapidly processing her options. Could she run from here? Probably not. Could she start screaming?

'Before you do anything rash,' the man said, his voice quietly loaded with threat, 'I want you to know there's a man outside your mother's house in Sussex. If you become uncooperative, he will go inside and kill her.'

Eleanor turned away from the man to stare at the table top before her, its surface covered with pale, ghostly rings where wet glasses had stained the varnish. She felt her stomach drop, the blood drain from her face. She thought she was going to pass out.

'Now when Aidan gets back from the bar,' the voice continued, 'he's going to suggest a drink back in Downing Street. You're going to accept. Understood?'

Eleanor felt paralysed, numb from the tip of her head to her toes.

'Understood?' repeated the man, with more vehemence.

Eleanor managed a nod.

She then turned again. The man had disappeared.

She closed her eyes, grappling for something solid to hold on to. Could she text Sam? Of course not. She was still being watched. She thought of her Mum, vulnerable, unprotected. These people were monsters.

Aidan was coming back to the table. Had this been a trap all along? Was he in on it? The man's sudden appearance at his side suggested otherwise. As if this sudden change had been sprung on him as much as her. Aidan's expression seemed to confirm this. He looked rattled.

'Listen, Eleanor,' he said. 'I've been up at the bar for ages and I'm nowhere near being served. It's also getting really noisy in here.' It was as if he were reading from a script. 'So I had a thought. How about a drink back in Downing Street? Mum and Dad are out at some engagement. I could show you round.' He attempted a grin.

Eleanor thought of her mother at home. It was her suppertime. Jill would be feeding her right now. No doubt she would also be killed.

'OK,' she said, offering what she hoped was a reasonably enthusiastic smile.

She downed her gin & tonic then followed Aidan out of the pub.

'Hope you're OK walking,' said Aidan. 'It's only five minutes away.'

Eleanor shrugged. 'Sure.'

As they walked, Eleanor cast a look over her shoulder, worrying that, if Sam saw her, he would try to intervene, when she knew, with a certainty that sat like undigested poison in the pit of her stomach, that this would be a disaster. She had to comply with the request made of her.

There was no sign of Sam. Eleanor felt no relief, just a sense of utter desolation at the impossibility of her situation.

At the end of the road, they crossed Bird Cage Walk to the south-west corner of St James's Park. It was a sunny evening with a slight bite to the air, the sky a magnificent deep-blue backdrop for the leaves, which were just beginning to turn orange as autumn approached. As a couple jogged along the pavement past them – each lost in their own iPod soundtrack – Aidan and Eleanor turned left, walking up the east side of the park.

'So what are you up to these days?' asked Eleanor. It was all she could think of to maintain an air of normality. She also wanted to keep the man by her side calm, as well as her.

Aidan paused a moment, as if contemplating the right answer. 'Training to be an architect,' he said.

'That takes a while, doesn't it?'

'Seven or eight years,' Aidan said. 'But I'm totally committed. I'm going to open my own practice, build some really innovative stuff.'

Moments later, they crossed to a small green at Downing Street's western end, just south of Horse Guards Parade Ground. To their right was a set of tall black gates guarded by a couple of policemen clutching machine guns.

'You can drive a truck at them and they won't budge,' Aidan said, as if he'd been studying her gaze. He then explained how the gates had been installed in Mrs Thatcher's time, when the threat from the IRA was at its highest.

Eleanor smiled feebly, the street's impregnability hardly comforting. If getting in was this difficult, getting out would be just as hard.

She inhaled deeply. She wanted to encourage more conversation from Aidan. He seemed to enjoy the sound of his own voice.

Aidan approached the policemen who were standing at the gates and explained that Eleanor was with him. After her bag was checked and she was frisked, a small pedestrian entrance within the gates was opened. They then passed into Downing Street itself.

The tall building on their right – the Foreign Office, declared Aidan, when Eleanor asked – cast a long evening shadow over the houses opposite but even in the gathering gloom, the one they were heading for was instantly recognisable: the last in a terrace of dark brick houses, with an iconic, glossy black front door.

Eleanor could feel her heart hammering away.

'Nothing is what it seems here,' Aidan said.

Eleanor stiffened at the comment, unsure of his meaning.

'The bricks are yellow underneath,' he said, as if enjoying the momentary confusion he'd created in her, 'but when the house was renovated in the 50s, they discovered that soot and pollution had stained them this colour. After cleaning, they decided to paint them black to retain the look.'

'Guess what?' he then said. Eleanor sensed another of his little tour guide revelations on its way.

Aidan pointed to the famous door ahead of them. 'It's not wood, but solid steel.'

'Wow,' said Eleanor, now playing the role of fascinated guest, despite the rising panic she was trying to quell. 'I've always wondered how they know when to open it from the inside,' she said. 'You see people approaching it and then the door opens up like magic.'

They were now standing on the front porch.

'Look up,' said Aidan.

She saw a small CCTV camera tucked in beside the fanlight beneath the hood of the doorway. Her entry into Downing Street recorded. And surely anyone who entered Downing Street had to come out? But Eleanor then thought of the forces that had brought her here – and how powerless she now was – and her optimism swiftly faded.

As they waited for the door to open, she stole another quick glance at the man next to her, as if his face might offer some clue as to his make-up; some tell-tale sign, if not of psychosis, then at least his current motivations. He was, despite the years that had passed, still boyish looking, with a face that was, without worry or laughter lines, very hard to read.

At that moment the door was eased open by a policeman.

'Hi John,' said Aidan cheerfully.

'Hello Aidan,' said the policeman. 'And who's this?'

Aidan introduced Eleanor and the policeman shook her hand with a slight nod of his head, as if the mention of her name had prompted a small gesture of sympathy.

They were now in a large entrance hall, dominated by black and white floor tiles and, stretching upwards to their left, a staircase Eleanor had seen countless images of. Hanging on the yellow wall up the stairs were photos and, towards the top, engravings, of past Prime Ministers.

Aidan was talking about 'a ghastly architect' who'd helped rebuild the house in Macmillan's day, giving it all the fake antiquity that she saw today.

'It's all façade,' he said, with a real sense of disgust in his voice.

'But rather amazing, all the same.'

Aidan seemed to readjust his mood, smiling again. 'Yes,' he acknowledged. 'I suppose you're right.'

They moved on through one big room after another, Aidan's commentary now flowing over her as she tried simply to remain attentive. She noticed a vast Persian carpet in one room, a terracotta wall colouring in another, and then she was through a door and down a rather non-descript staircase and into a huge kitchen of brushed steel cookers and work surfaces sitting beneath a vaulted ceiling. A handful of staff were chopping vegetables and Aidan offered them a wave, which was reciprocated.

Finally, the tour was proclaimed over and Aidan moved to a lift just outside the kitchen.

'This takes us up to the apartment,' he said. 'It's actually above Number 11. Blair swapped with Brown when he lived here because this one is bigger. Every Prime Minister since has done that too. Mum still complains it's small though.'

They travelled upwards in silence, Eleanor now rigid with fear. At that moment the thought of the men who'd forced her here – and the man next to her and what he might have done in Marrakesh – gripped Eleanor with such ferocity that she had to lean back against the lift's wall to stop her knees buckling.

The lift opened into a small hallway. Aidan opened the door in front of them, ushering Eleanor inside. There was a large, modern kitchen off to her right, a spacious sitting room to her left. Attempting again to appear interested, she paused at the entrance to take it in. There was a mish-mash of unstuffy furniture, a huge flat-screen television, houseplants dotted around the room and a vase of roses on a dresser between two windows that looked out on to Downing Street.

The lived-in, homely look of the apartment reminded Eleanor suddenly of the farmhouse in Sussex. She felt her eyes well at the thought of her parents – her father dead, her mother lost in another way. She knew the tears were for herself too, her imminent death a possibility she couldn't shake from her head.

Aidan was moving down the corridor, pointing out rooms – his, a rather cramped single room with a poster of a Frank Lloyd Wright building on one wall; his parents' bedroom, a more expansive one with a huge double bed; his father's dressing room; a spare room with a bed that was, Eleanor noticed, still unmade from its last inhabitant.

'Would you like a drink?' asked Aidan, who was now heading back in the direction of the kitchen. 'I thought we could chat up here instead of downstairs. It's a bit cosier. We've got some white wine in the fridge.'

'Sounds good,' said Eleanor. What could be more normal, after all? Two childhood acquaintances reminiscing over a glass of wine. She felt her body tense again.

Aidan had never expected Eleanor Scott to get in touch. He'd not seen her in – what? – nearly twenty years. It had caught him unawares and before he'd had a chance to think things through, he'd agreed to meet. As the evening approached, he'd felt himself get more and more agitated.

But then he'd seen her and, for the first time in a very long period, he'd experienced a sense of calm in the presence of a woman. As if he'd been transported back to a more peaceful period. Before everything had gone wrong.

But that sense of calm – comparable to the stillness he felt contemplating the balance and simplicity of Falling Water – was then shattered with the arrival of one of his demons, summoning him home like a naughty child. At least the man hadn't humiliated him, but instead given him the chance to carry on the conversation with Eleanor back at Downing Street.

Since then he'd managed to calm down again. Being with Eleanor had helped. She seemed, despite her loss, to be happy in his company. She was interested in architecture – a real bonus – and was, more importantly, a clear communicator.

But as he uncorked the bottle, the noise of the air escaping with a pop, the anger simmering away within him seemed to burst to the surface. Aidan had his back to Eleanor – his hand reaching up to a cupboard for two wine glasses – which meant he could hide his grimace from her.

He tried to imagine Falling Water, but all he could picture instead was the blueprint of an incredibly complicated house he'd been helping to design at work, a building so packed with telecommunications, entertainment and security systems that Aidan was convinced it would, through a simple fault or trip, be brought to its knees.

Chapter 65

St James's, London

Sam couldn't see Eleanor, and it terrified him. There'd been regular obstructions to his view but now a group of drinkers had taken up a position between them. He glanced at his watch. Eleanor and Aidan had probably only been seated for about twenty minutes – and the last thing Sam wanted to do was to put Eleanor off by making his presence felt – but he had to see if she was OK.

He stood, then began nudging his way through the dense mass of drinkers. A moment later, he reached the table where he'd left Eleanor. At the sight that greeted him, Sam felt the hairs on the back of his neck rise. Another woman, with short blonde hair, was sitting in Eleanor's place.

Sam quickly scanned the room. He couldn't see her. Had they moved to a table in the street outside, or to the beer garden at the rear? If it was the latter, he'd certainly have seen them. They had to be at the front. He pushed his way forward, a white noise of laughter, shouted conversation and music invading his already frazzled head.

Outside, the pavement was thronged with drinkers. But Eleanor and Aidan Stirling weren't anywhere to be seen. Sam's heart was pounding.

Eleanor had gone, and he'd no idea where.

Chapter 66

Downing Street

Frears had gone on ahead of Aidan and Eleanor Scott, while one of his men followed them at a discreet distance to ensure they returned to Downing Street. He was fairly certain they would. After all, they both had good reason: Aidan to save face, Eleanor Scott to save her mother.

Getting them back to Number 10 had seemed the most sensible option. This way, they were quickly contained. And keen to avoid a scene, he hadn't told Aidan that Eleanor Scott was no doubt coming to trap him in some way.

He had to hand it to Keddie and Scott. They had a canny knack for avoiding death. Unfortunately this little idea of theirs had seriously backfired.

The Guardsman had planned to be up in the apartment to meet them. He was then going to contact Stirling, drag him out of the reception he was attending and await his return and instructions.

But as he headed for the lift, he heard a shrill voice behind him.

'Major Frears?'

He turned to see the diminutive figure of Gillian Mayer bearing down on him.

'Might I have a word?'

'I'm on my way to a meeting, Foreign Secretary. I haven't really –'

'It won't take a minute,' said Mayer, cutting off any further debate.

She leaned against the wall, signalling that the chat was happening here and now. Hopefully it really was to be a brief conversation. He dreaded to think what Aidan Stirling might do in the comfort of his own home.

'We have a spot of bother on an island off the coast of Equatorial Guinea,' said Mayer, raising her eyebrows. 'It seems Gabon have landed some soldiers there in an attempt to seize what they say is their territory. Ordinarily, that corner of Africa doesn't cause me much lost sleep. But the thing is, there are some British oil workers there. Don't want it turning into a shit storm. Any thoughts?'

Frears felt a bead of sweat escape an armpit and trickle down his side. 'What are we talking about here, Foreign Secretary? Extraction?'

'Well, we certainly don't plan to send a task force,' she said, with a snort of laughter. 'Why is it you military want a bloody skirmish all the time?'

'Extraction, as you know, is not that easy these days with our limited resources,' said Frears. 'We're talking 48 hours at the earliest – and you'll need a good team to ensure there's no unnecessary bloodshed. I'd need to go away and have a think.' He puffed out his chest and lifted his head, trying to command the situation. 'Now if you'll excuse me, I really must dash.'

'In a minute, Major, in a minute,' said Mayer, who was not to be intimidated. 'Just so we're clear, what sort of sized team are we talking about? And could we narrow the timeframe if we sourced men from inside Africa?'

Frears' toes strained inside his brogues. He had to get moving. Racking his brains for a suitable response, he remembered his ill-fated stint in Nigeria.

'There's probably a team at the consulate in Lagos that could be mobilised. Twenty men. Experienced guys.'

Mayer looked at him with her small, hawk-like eyes, then nodded. 'Very good, Major. I'll mull that one over. Might pick your brains again later, if that's OK.' She smiled sweetly, as if they'd just been discussing knitting patterns, then turned on her heel.

Frears rushed down the corridor towards the lift.

Chapter 67

Downing Street

Eleanor realised how little she'd eaten that day. The gin & tonic, and now the sip of wine she'd drunk simply to settle her rampant anxiety, had gone straight to her head. She was giddy, nauseous. Her head ached. She felt as if she were waiting for the executioner.

That this might be Aidan no longer seemed likely. She was no expert in psychosis, but the idea of him attacking her, when she visualised it in her head, seemed absurd. Whether he'd killed that girl or not, there was no anger right now, no whiff of madness about him. No, the threat she was convinced she faced was from the men in the pub. She shuddered, her body breaking out in goose bumps.

'Do you mind if I use the bathroom?' she asked.

'Of course not,' said Aidan. 'You know where it is – just down the hall.'

'Thanks,' she said.

The conversation had become stilted. Attempting to be chatty and normal was becoming an unbearable strain.

Locking the door behind her, she sat down on the closed toilet seat, took out her phone and began texting:

Forced to come to downg st with aidan. They threatened to kill my mother.

She felt the futility of the message even as she pressed 'send'. What could Sam do? But to feel even vaguely connected to him seemed somehow comforting. She leaned back against the toilet, scanning the room to distract herself. There was a large, free-standing bath, an antique table by it – Indian perhaps – covered in shampoos and conditioners. A shower enclosed in glass. A basin sitting beneath a mirror-fronted cabinet. What secrets would she find in there, Eleanor wondered? To the right of the basin, just before a window, was a large red push button at shoulder height. She'd seen a similar one in the kitchen.

Eleanor closed her eyes. She was acutely aware of her fears, and how they shaped the way she'd been all evening. Desperate not to upset Aidan in any way, to play to his interests. Her shoulders ached with tension.

She stood, flushing the toilet, and then unlocked the bathroom. As she walked back towards the kitchen, the front door of the apartment opened.

Chapter 68

St James's, London

Sam was walking north away from St James's – his mobile gripped tightly in his hand as he debated the pros and cons of dialling Eleanor's number – when he received her text. The stomach-churning theory that had been building since she'd disappeared was now confirmed. Eleanor was in Downing Street.

Sam froze for a moment, the air around him suddenly cold. How could they have been so naive?

He looked around him. There was a man at a stall selling hotdogs, the whiff of onions and sausage fat nauseating. An old woman feeding pigeons by a lake in the park. Moving towards him, a group of schoolchildren shepherded by a teacher.

He'd never been more alone.

Chapter 69

Downing Street

Eleanor recognised the tall man immediately from the pub. He was still wearing a suit but had removed his tie. He seemed to be rapidly assessing the situation, a look of mild surprise on his face. Whatever he'd expected, it wasn't this.

He held up a hand. 'You need to stay right where you are, Miss Scott.'

Aidan had emerged from the kitchen and was now in front of her. Eleanor was trapped behind them.

'Why can't you just leave me alone?' Aidan groaned.

'Because it's not safe to do that,' hissed the man.

He began directing both of them towards the kitchen. Aidan moved first but Eleanor paused. The man moved down the hall at a pace, grabbing her arm and wrenching it as he pulled her back towards the kitchen. He flung her into the room, her thigh slamming hard into the table. For a moment, she found the man's eyes staring at her, pupils blazing with anger.

But a second later, the man lashed out to the right. Out of Eleanor's vision, Aidan had clearly made a movement towards him, and the tall man had reacted with force. She watched in horror as the two men grappled in front of her, blocking her route out of the kitchen to the lift.

The man elbowed Aidan in the stomach. He let out a winded cry of pain and bent over, clutching his belly. He then dropped to his knees in the hallway outside the kitchen.

In a swift movement, the man was behind Aidan. He pushed him stomach-first on to the carpet and sat astride him. He then yanked both of Aidan's hands behind his back, holding them with one of his own. With the other, he pulled his tie from a jacket pocket.

Eleanor stood, frozen on the spot with terror. She wanted to run as fast as she could from the apartment. But she was trapped by the men blocking her path. At the same time she knew that, with Aidan almost restrained, the tall man would turn on her. She looked round frantically, then saw the red button. She darted towards it, pressing down firmly with the palm of her hand.

The sound of an alarm instantly broke out. It was like a repetitive klaxon, far louder than a fire alarm.

'You stupid bitch!' shouted the man over the deafening din. Beneath him, Aidan had started to thrash about. A leg shot out and kicked the tall man in his crotch. He momentarily lost his grip, groaning in agony. Aidan seized his chance, crawling forwards away from the kitchen and down the corridor towards his bedroom. But as quickly the tall man was on his feet and moving towards Aidan to leap on to his back.

There was now a clear path out of the flat. Eleanor grabbed her bag and Aidan's glass, dashing from the kitchen.

A moment later she was out of the apartment's front door and in front of the lift. The light above the doors indicated 'G'. She didn't dare wait, turning left through a door marked 'emergency exit'. She found herself on a staircase. It had to be the same service access that connected the kitchen with the ground floor. If she went down, she was confident she'd soon find herself back in the reception rooms – and close to the front door. In between the rhythmic screeches of the alarm she could hear other sounds, raised voices from downstairs, people running.

Chapter 70

Downing Street

Even from his position on Horse Guards Road, Sam could hear the alarm. The two policemen on the gates reacted immediately, visibly tensing, heads dipping as they listened to the crackle on their shoulder-mounted radios.

Moments later, four more policemen joined them. Two took up positions facing out, the remaining four facing in. Their machine guns were no longer loosely held, but gripped tight, aimed forward.

Had Eleanor activated a fire alarm? Or, judging by the policemen's reaction, something more serious?

Through the gates in the distance, Sam could see people spilling on to the pavement in Downing Street, moving towards the gates at the eastern end. If Eleanor was among them, this would be the direction she'd come. He had to get round the other side. He looked to the north. Horse Guards Parade Ground stretched across several blocks. There was no way he'd be able to cross to Whitehall through there. He turned south, breaking into a jog, his leg wound protesting with sharp jolts of pain every time his left foot hit the pavement.

Chapter 71

Downing Street

On the next landing Eleanor joined others, staff that had been working on the third floor. They pushed through double doors on to the landing. Behind them, Eleanor saw a corridor, doors opening and more people emerging.

'We need to evacuate the building fast,' said a man who seemed to be acting as a kind of marshal. Suddenly their path down the stairs was blocked by a team of police pacing up the stairs. They were dressed in flak jackets and clutching handguns.

The staff paused, united in their shock at seeing armed men move through what should have been one of the safest houses in the world.

With the police now on the next flight up, Eleanor joined the others on their journey out of the house. They moved down the service stairs to the second and first floors, where more staff members joined the exodus. There was a sense that they'd all been trained for this moment. The pace was calm, a shared understanding that, if they panicked, people would be trampled. Yet the expressions Eleanor saw on faces suggested another story. The woman next to her – in her fifties, with greying hair – was fraught, her eyes darting about as if she were a trapped animal.

Finally they were on the ground floor and then moving through double doors into one of the reception rooms Aidan had shown her earlier. She remembered the vast Persian carpet, a wall painted in deep terracotta. A moment later she could see the open door ahead.

Two armed policemen, standing right outside the front door, were directing them left, telling them to keep tightly to the side of the building and move in single file towards the Whitehall entrance. Ahead, at the open gates, police cars were streaming through, blue lights flashing. The gates were then closed again. Eleanor began to panic. Would she be stuck here?

As she moved slowly along the side of the building, she looked out at Whitehall. People were beginning to be ushered away. But across the road, a crowd of spectators was gathering. She scanned their faces, willing Sam to be there.

A moment later, she joined a group of around fifty people at the gate. She pushed herself through the throng and looked out at Whitehall. It was then Sam came into view. Jogging, with visible difficulty, from the direction of Parliament Square. He was on her side of Whitehall but she knew he'd soon be directed across the road.

Sure enough, he came up against a wall of police who gestured for him to move to the other side of the road. She watched Sam cross in front of the now stationary traffic, halted by a police car parked at an angle across the road, blue lights pulsing.

As if the bomb-proof steel of the gates wasn't enough of a barrier, there was now a line of police officers directly outside the gates.

Eleanor's stomach lurched as she realised what would happen next. She'd be interviewed – grilled as to why she was here, and what had happened.

She closed her eyes momentarily, attempting to form a coherent and plausible story in her head. She and Aidan were old friends; he was her father's godchild.

A terrifying possibility interrupted her thought process. What if the tall man caught up with her?

There was a crush at the gate as the group she was with was herded into a corner. She found herself pressed against the railings. On the other side, the police line had momentarily shifted. They seemed to be gathering around an officer, listening to instructions about what was turning out to be a rapidly developing situation.

To her left, another crowd had developed, held in check by a single officer. Another officer rushed over to him, cupping a hand over his ear. A moment later, he shouted at the crowd, asking them to stay where they were, then rushed to the huddle receiving orders by the gates.

It was then that Eleanor saw Sam emerge from the crowd to her left. He was walking towards the railings, mouthing the words 'You OK?'

Eleanor nodded. Sam was now feet from her. She turned to her right. The officer giving orders at the gate seemed to be winding up, the men around him ready to resume positions. It was now or never.

Eleanor passed her bag through the railings. Sam snatched it and walked quickly back in the direction he'd come.

Sam was half-expecting one of the police officers to call out. But there was no shout. He merged into the crowds, pushing past people too interested in the drama in front of them to notice him. Then, with a final shove of his shoulder, he was free.

As he moved further away from Downing Street, the pavements were eerily quiet. Up ahead, Whitehall had been sealed off at Trafalgar Square. The few people remaining were being ushered to a cordon at that point.

Sam sneaked a look inside Eleanor's bag. There, nestling on the soft bed of her scarf, was a wine glass.

They had the evidence they needed. But, in the process, he'd lost Eleanor.

Chapter 72

Downing Street

The police unit at Downing Street, part of the Met's Diplomatic Protection Group, is based in a small building at the western end of the street. Here, in addition to providing a 24-hour operations base for the officers protecting the PM, a small cache of arms is kept and there are briefing rooms and two seldom-used cells. While there are plenty of incidents outside the sealed-off zone of Downing Street which are dealt with by the Met, it's extremely rare that anything occurs within.

Frears stared at the blank walls of his cell, trying to form an action plan in his head. His brain longed for the comparative simplicity of a combat situation. Manpower and weaponry available, terrain, conditions, enemy position, objective. Sure, the situation could change rapidly, but at least you were trained for that. For this, he had no training.

He heard the door being unlocked and a man in a grey suit walked in.

'Major Frears, I'm Commander Lynch. This won't take long. Would you like a cup of tea? Coffee?'

Frears shook his head.

'Fine,' said Lynch. 'Then let's get started. Can you tell me why you were in the Prime Minister's private apartment?'

Frears looked up. It was then he realised what the best approach was.

'Major Frears?'

Lynch sighed. 'How about why you were found restraining the Prime Minister's son with extreme force?'

Silence again.

'Of course it's your prerogative to remain silent, but in time you will have to explain your actions. And in the meantime we will be listening to whatever Eleanor Scott says with even greater interest.'

The door shut behind Lynch. Frears clenched and then unclenched his fists. This was Stirling's mess and his alone to resolve. But did the PM really have the ingenuity – or the balls – to do that, wondered Frears? Or would other measures be necessary?

Two doors further down, Eleanor sat in more comfortable surroundings, in a small lounge where members of the DPG took their breaks. She was trying to slow her heartbeat as she struggled to convince herself that those who'd drawn her out of the crowd and gently led her to this room did not mean her harm. It was all too official somehow, wholly lacking the dark threats of the man from the pub or the violence of the tall figure who'd attacked Aidan. And of course there were now dozens of witnesses who could attest to her presence in Downing Street. They couldn't just make her disappear, surely? She thought of her mother, and her heart began to race again. She had to call her.

There was a brief murmur of conversation outside and then a man stepped into the room.

'Hello Miss Scott,' he said, with a stern expression, 'my name's Lynch. You realise you single-handedly triggered the largest security alert in Downing Street's history since the IRA fired a mortar into the garden in 1991.'

Eleanor smiled weakly. 'I'm sorry,' she said. 'I was terrified.'

She felt her eyes welling with tears, though for reasons Lynch could not know.

'You scared the hell out of a lot of people today, Miss Scott,' said Lynch. He appeared to soften. 'But I dare say they'll recover. And practising the evacuation procedure never hurts.'

He smiled, suggesting that this issue was resolved. 'Can I ask about the other man now?'

Eleanor nodded, a brief shudder running through her as she remembered how close she'd come to the man who, she now knew, had been hounding them so relentlessly.

'You say you were having a drink with Aidan, chatting about your late father.'

Eleanor focused her dark eyes, now rimmed with tears, on Lynch.

'And the other man arrived, unannounced, and attacked Aidan.'

'That's right.'

'This attack,' said Lynch. 'Can you tell me what might have prompted it?'

Eleanor closed her eyes, replaying the horror, while mulling over an adequate response. She now realised that, in all likelihood, the tall man was restraining a killer. But as an answer, that would not do right now. She settled, in the end, for a partial truth.

'I'm not sure,' she said. 'It all happened so fast.'

'Take your time, Miss Scott.'

'All I know is that he came in and Aidan seemed really angry about him being there, saying something like "why can't you leave me alone?" Then the other man said that it wasn't safe to do that. He moved us both into the kitchen and that's when it happened. I'm not sure if Aidan attacked him or whether the other man just lost his temper, but within seconds the two of them were on the floor.'

Lynch nodded. 'And then you got scared, and pressed the alarm.'

Eleanor nodded.

'OK,' said Lynch. His eyes remained locked on Eleanor's. She kept the contact.

Finally Lynch broke it, smiling again. 'I don't think there's any reason to keep you any longer.'

Eleanor felt a rush of such huge relief, she began to cry.

'Traumatic experience, I'm sure,' said Lynch. 'Would you like me to arrange for someone to accompany you home?'

Eleanor shook her head.

'I'll call a cab then. If we need to ask you anything else, we'll be in touch.'

As soon as she was outside the west gate, Eleanor dialled her home number. It began to ring. And ring. Eleanor wanted to scream.

'Hello?'

It was Jill's voice. Cheery, optimistic, and most definitely alive. Eleanor collapsed to the ground.

Chapter 73

Downing Street

The sitting room in the apartment had finally calmed. Aidan
sat on the sofa, heavily tranquilised, while Charlotte, in the
floor-length gown she'd worn to the state dinner for the
French President – ears and neck dripping in Bowlby family
jewellery – signed a series of forms at the table. Seated next
to her, a softly spoken psychiatrist was explaining where they
were taking Aidan now. Hopefully to a bloody big hole,
thought Stirling.

It had taken that man and two other burly male nurses
half-an-hour before Aidan could be restrained and finally, a
tranquiliser could be administered. Aidan had been railing
about Frears when they'd finally reached the apartment,
shouting about him being 'a bloody psychopath' and 'a
violent cunt'. By all accounts, that was all he'd been saying,
thank God, as members of the DPG had been waiting with
him when Stirling and Charlotte had arrived.

Aidan now sat, slack-jawed, like some stunned animal. It
was clear, immediately, that he hadn't been taking his
medication. But for how long? Stirling, himself still dressed

in white tie and tails, glared at his wife. He wanted to murder her right now. She was fucking hopeless.

Finally, the forms signed, the psychiatrist stood and nodded to the two nurses. Aidan was pulled up from the sofa, all floppy and compliant. He was gently led to the lift. They were to take him down to the service exit at the rear of the building, to a small minibus and, thankfully, not a big white ambulance with the words 'Nut House Transport' on the side.

At the door of the lift, Charlotte kissed her son on the cheek, hugging him briefly. Stirling wanted to vomit. The doors then closed and Aidan was gone.

'I'm finished,' Stirling muttered, closing the door of the sitting room behind them.

Charlotte collapsed on the sofa. It was clear she wasn't prepared to take her share of the blame just yet. She was rooting frantically around in the cushions. 'What the hell has Aidan done with the remote? We must find out what the media has made of this.'

She froze momentarily, shooting Philip an alarmed look.

'What is it?'

'Look at these,' she said. Her hand had emerged from beneath the cushion and was now held, palm out, in his direction.

Stirling moved closer and leaned down to get a better look. 'Fucking hell, Charlotte,' he hissed.

The palm of Charlotte's hand contained dozens of little white pills.

'The little bastard hasn't been taking his medication at all,' said Stirling. 'For Christ's sake, Charlotte, that was meant to be your department. After everything that has happened, how could you have been so stupid?'

For once, Charlotte was too stunned to come back at him.

Stirling's BlackBerry rang. 'Yes,' he snapped. 'OK,' he then said more calmly. There was a pause as he listened to the voice at the other end. Then Stirling spoke: 'I'll be down right away.'

He turned to Charlotte. 'The police want to talk to me. "A chat", they called it.'

'What are you going to say to them?'

'I don't know right now. Apparently Eleanor Scott has told the police that Frears attacked Aidan,' said Stirling. 'But who knows what else she saw and heard?'

He ran a hand through the dense thicket of his hair. Eleanor Scott alive and talking to Aidan. He wanted to crawl into a dark hole and disappear forever.

As Stirling left the front door of 10 Downing Street, receiving a nod from the officer on duty – how long will that deference last, he wondered? – he began mulling over his options. Apparently Frears had chosen to remain silent. Was that a sign of loyalty to the operation? Or was he simply weighing up his options?

There was a chill in the air as he moved down the deserted street. There were still plenty of cars parked outside the terrace. Vehicles left overnight by staff who'd fled the building and weren't allowed to return. The heels of his shoes clicked against the tarmac, the noise echoing around the surrounding buildings, their tall, grand frontages seeming to mock him. What's a Northern lad like you doing in a place like this?

Think, Stirling said to himself. Think. First and foremost, he needed to handle the soldier carefully. He couldn't afford to piss him off, let alone bollock him for allowing this to happen. Yes, Aidan had slipped out yet again. But the person really at fault here was Charlotte, who'd neglected the little bastard's medication regime. Frears needed to know that he wasn't going to get in shit. Right now, in custody, the Guardsman was probably feeling cornered.

Stirling, thanks to recent pay rises he'd driven through for the police, had a good relationship with them, certainly when compared to some of his predecessors. He hoped this might go some way to containing the fall-out from this event. Perhaps a leak could be avoided, at least until he'd had a chance to think through his options.

He was greeted by a man called Lynch, and led into a small kitchen and sitting area.

'Have you any idea why Frears was in the apartment, Prime Minister?' asked Lynch. 'Or why he might have attacked your son – and tried to restrain him?'

'None whatsoever.'

'Did Major Frears and your son have any kind of relationship?'

The inference lingered in the air. 'Not that I know of,' said Stirling. 'I mean, they'd met each other. I had meetings with Major Frears in the apartment, and they'd certainly been introduced, but beyond that, no.'

Lynch nodded. His forehead creased.

'Eleanor Scott said that your son was really angry about him being there, and he'd said something along the lines of "why can't you leave me alone?". Major Frears had apparently said that it wasn't safe to do that.'

Stirling felt his heart leap in his chest. 'Well, I've no idea what that means.'

Lynch paused, pursing his lips. 'And how is your son?

'Pretty shaken up,' said Stirling. 'He's not well, to be honest. Sedated.'

'We'd like to talk to him when he's better.'

'I'll be in touch when that happens,' said Stirling, who wanted Aidan tranquilised for eternity. 'Now, I wonder if I could have a word with Frears?'

Lynch raised an eyebrow.

'See if I can get some sense out of him,' continued Stirling, unfazed. 'Obviously he's not top of my Christmas card list right now, but we were friends, close colleagues. That might mean something. He might talk to me.'

'I appreciate the offer of help, but –'

'Please, Commander Lynch.'

Stirling watched as the policeman struggled with balancing a request from the Prime Minister and the constraints of procedure.

'Perhaps a couple of minutes,' said Lynch. 'But I should probably accompany you. And you'll need additional protection too.'

Stirling smiled. 'Commander Lynch, Major Frears has been a loyal adviser to me – and to Her Majesty's Government. He's also served in the armed forces, with distinction. Whatever he's done today should not wholly define him.'

'You're a forgiving man, Prime Minister,' said Lynch. 'If someone had attacked my son, I'm not sure I'd feel the same way.'

'I'm not forgiving him. I'm just saying that if I treat him with a little respect, he might cough up the information he's so far chosen to withhold from you.'

Lynch continued to squirm.

'You know what a fan I am of the police,' said the PM. 'All I'm asking is a moment with a friend. It may well provide the break you need. If he attacks me, I'll scream and you can be in the room in seconds.'

'Two minutes,' said Lynch.

Frears' cell contained a narrow bed attached to the wall and a small toilet in one corner. The room was harshly lit from high above. The soldier sat on the bed, his back to the wall.

Stirling perched on the end of the bed. 'You're in a hole here, Frears. And I want to help you out.'

Frears looked up at the PM, a deadened expression on his face.

'Look,' said Stirling. 'We're both fucked if this isn't resolved.'

There was no response. Stirling racked his brains for a solution.

'I'll make sure Aidan doesn't press charges. And of course we won't either.' He was on a roll now, winging his way forward. 'Perhaps your presence can be explained as a misunderstanding, that you were up there to see me – crossed wires or something – and that Aidan got shirty because he was trying to get Eleanor into bed. And that you'd had a long week and an argument turned into –'

'That won't wash,' said Frears bluntly.

'How so?'

'It won't tally with what Eleanor Scott has said.'

'We don't know what Eleanor Scott has said,' lied Stirling.

Frears' eyes narrowed. 'Just ensure Aidan doesn't press charges. I'll take care of everything else. And get me out of here.'

As he walked back down the street to Number 10, Stirling knew that Frears had seen right through him when he lied. And of course he was right: Eleanor Scott's evidence would contradict any story they concocted. So what could he do? Getting the charges dropped would be easy enough, but that line about it not being safe to leave Aidan alone would be the sticker. They had to find a way to explain it.

To add to his problems, it was clear Frears no longer trusted him. Stirling shuddered. He thought of the Guardsman's favourite word, 'containment'. Now it was Frears himself – keeper of his darkest secrets – who needed containing.

Chapter 74

Downing Street

In the apartment, Charlotte Stirling was confident that, for now, the real nub of the story wasn't out. According to the media, an electrical fault at Number 10 had triggered an alarm, prompting an evacuation of the entire staff. The Prime Minister and his wife were not present.

The story would not end there. Sooner or later, someone would get hold of the fact that her crazy son had been involved in a violent altercation. And than what?

She walked through to the kitchen. There was a bottle of Sauvignon Blanc on the table. Aidan must have offered Eleanor Scott a drink. What Charlotte wouldn't have given for a glass of wine now. She sat down at the table and put the tip of the bottle to her nose, inhaling the fumes deeply. It smelt amazing. She could imagine losing herself in a matter of minutes, the Stirlings' tribulations melting away in a river of booze.

The smell took her back to a time when alcohol was her constant companion, a far more reliable presence than her absent husband. And it was alcohol and unremitting loneliness, she liked to believe, far more than any degenerative trait, which had caused her to act the way she had.

She remembered, as if through a fog – those days had been so deeply clouded by the dual intoxication of self-harm and wine – the moment it had started. That holiday in Tuscany near Montalcino, a hill town famed for Brunello, its red wine – the finest, so they were told, in all of Italy. Charlotte had preferred the cheap rosé.

How the days had dragged. The humid afternoons were the worst. Lunch barely touched, at least two bottles down, she'd take a cooling bath, a place to pursue her destructive passions.

At the memory of those moments, and all that followed, Charlotte winced, pushing the bottle away.

She imagined Aidan and Eleanor Scott sharing a glass of wine. She was amazed that her son was capable of such civilised behaviour.

Looking at the table, she had a sudden realisation, a thought that caused a sickening feeling that spread upwards from the pit of her stomach. Where was the other glass?

Chapter 75

Kensington, London

The embassy, a white stucco building in a street of similarly grand properties, was closed for the night. A flag hung from a balcony above him.

Sam pressed a buzzer by the door.

Seconds later, a voice grunted back: 'Yes?'

'It's Sam Keddie.'

There was a pause. Sam wondered whether Maalouf had abandoned the whole idea, not told the embassy staff. He looked over his shoulder, convinced that, at any minute, a last attempt would be made to silence him and retrieve his crucial evidence. But then Sam heard a bolt being pulled, a latch turning, and the door was opened. A short man ushered him in, indicating that he was to wait at the foot of a grand staircase.

Sam sat. Opposite was another portrait of the Moroccan King – this time a more serious image, of a swarthy, unsmiling bruiser in a suit, who looked down at Sam with displeasure. Ten minutes passed.

Sam heard a door open some distance away, and stood. A tired-looking man with pale skin and glasses was coming down the corridor, his footfall on the carpet virtually silent.

They shook hands.

'You have the evidence?' asked the man.

Sam nodded. He then gently lifted the glass out of Eleanor's bag. The man produced a pair of plastic gloves and a small plastic bag from his jacket pocket. He snapped on the gloves then delicately took the glass by its stem between two fingers, lowering it slowly into the bag.

'Just so we're clear,' said Sam, 'the prints on the glass are Aidan Stirling's.'

'And the other man's prints?' asked the embassy official dryly. 'When can we expect them?'

'We've not yet had the chance to collect a set,' said Sam, which was true, although he wondered whether Eleanor would ever willingly hand them over. 'Please check these now.'

A minute later, Sam was back outside in the cooling night, hoping to God that Maalouf was true to his word.

Chapter 76

King's Cross, London

It was nearly 10pm when Eleanor rang.

'Where are you?' asked Sam.

'In a cab,' she said, 'coming to you.'

Sam could hear her crying at the other end.

'It's OK,' he said. 'You're safe now.'

The fragile, emotional person on the other end of the phone was some distance from the nervous but single-minded woman Sam had last seen in the pub. But it wasn't until she returned to the room, and he'd wrapped her in a tight embrace and she'd let her tension go and sobbed for over ten minutes into his shirt, that he realised just what a state she was in.

Finally she pulled away, her face crumpled and damp with tears, and sat down on the bed. She beckoned for him to sit by her, and then told him what happened.

Sam listened, first with a sense of guilt at having let her go in the first place, then rage as her account unravelled.

Towards the end, having managed to speak without breaking down again, she became emotional as she recounted the tall man's arrival.

'I was so scared,' she said, running the back of her hand across her nose. 'If he hadn't been fighting with Aidan, God knows...' She began crying again, her torso rising and falling with great heaves of emotion.

Sam pulled Eleanor's head into his shoulder, stroking her hair. Her description of Aidan before the tall man entered the flat suggested a gauche, slightly conceited young man, nothing more. But the tall man's behaviour – his comment that it was not safe leaving Aidan alone; and the violent restraining – suggested that they'd found their man. And if the glass proved Aidan was culpable, the operation mounted against them had to have been sanctioned by the man with the most to lose if that fact became public knowledge – Stirling himself.

'I handed the wine glass into the embassy,' Sam said, keen for Eleanor to know that her experience had not been in vain.

Eleanor acknowledged Sam's comment with a grateful nod, then lay down on the bed, her eyes drooping.

Sam knew that, while sleep would come, Eleanor was going to need more than rest to get over this experience. A professional – not him, he was too close, too prejudiced – would be needed to help her through the next few weeks, to process and absorb the trauma so that it didn't bury itself deep and begin to infect her.

'I want to go home tomorrow,' Eleanor said. 'Help get ready for the funeral.'

Sam lay down next to her. The muffled sound of London traffic – accelerating engines, horns being sounded – leaked through the windows. Elsewhere in the b&b, a couple argued and a man coughed repeatedly. Sam locked on to the sounds, desperate to drown out the thoughts in his head. They'd done everything they could. But was it enough?

Chapter 77

Sussex

Police outriders ahead, the Daimler swept past a village hall and then a terrace of thatched cottages.

Dressed in a dark suit, Charlotte next to him in a black dress and knee-length overcoat, Stirling looked out through the tinted windows at the honey-coloured stonework. A little boy whose mother had momentarily stopped to stare at the convoy passing through her village waved at the car as it sped by. Stirling instinctively waved back. Everyone was a voter, even a child who couldn't see him through the glass.

It was a risk coming here today. If Eleanor Scott decided to get lippy, and started throwing about accusations, then he'd have to beat a swift retreat. But having discussed it with Charlotte the night before, they suspected that wouldn't happen. It was a funeral at which Eleanor was likely to behave. Besides, there would be press there. Despite Stirling's plea to the media to give the Scott family some privacy, he'd made damn sure his mournful presence would be recorded today. And even if she did decide to fling a bit of muck his way, he was now confident that it would be her who was damaged by it, not him. After all, certain developments over the past two days had given him a distinct advantage.

The first one was thanks to his son. His decision to have him hospitalised and monitored by his psychiatrist – the only way they could guarantee he was medicated and safely supervised – had, as he'd expected, become news. The *Mirror* was the first to break the story, an anonymous source at the clinic had told the paper that Aidan had been recently admitted as a patient. The details were still a little hazy but the gist was that the Prime Minister's son was possibly suffering from a personality disorder and receiving treatment.

Stirling had decided to acknowledge it yesterday at a press conference in Downing Street. To a packed and unusually reverential room full of hacks, he spoke of 'rumours floating around in the press that, unchecked, had the potential to do a great deal of damage'.

'My son is receiving treatment for a mental health problem,' he then announced. Stirling noted with a degree of pleasure the attention that was being paid. You could have heard a pin drop. 'He has been suffering for a while now but his illness has become more difficult recently. Obviously, as concerned parents, we have sought the best treatment possible and we hope dearly that our son will soon be home.'

He paused then, dipping his head as if collecting himself. His tie was particularly off-centre today, the hair noticeably untamed. He had in fact been about to head down to the conference looking better presented, but Charlotte had halted him at the door of the flat, loosening his tie and slightly ruffling his hair. 'That's better,' she'd said. 'You look more vulnerable now.'

He then spoke of how, like many families in Britain, he and Charlotte had been forced to face mental illness head on, and acknowledge the pain and suffering it could cause. 'Aidan's experience has opened our eyes,' he said, 'to how commonplace mental illness is, and how stigmatised those who suffer it can still be.'

The reception, judging by the coverage it received the following day, was favourable. According to the Guardian, Stirling had proved, yet again, that 'he was very human, a man who knows only too well what it's like to face some of life's toughest challenges.' The Daily Telegraph claimed that 'the Prime Minister had maintained exceptional dignity in the face of extraordinary personal difficulties.'

In the midst of such favourable press, it surely made sense, Charlotte had argued, to be seen mourning a dear old friend, to build on the image of a very human leader.

The second development, rather more surprisingly, had directly resulted from the episode in Downing Street. He could feel himself salivating at the prospect of his forthcoming announcement. Christ, he was an operator. Who else was capable of turning a near disaster into an unmitigated triumph?

The car slowed, dropping down a narrow lane, the steeple of a church visible over the top of a line of trees. Despite his confidence, Stirling started to worry about the risk they were taking. It reminded him of a loose end that was still of concern – Frears.

Since his release, the Guardsman had gone to ground. Was he disappearing for good, or biding his time?

Given recent developments – not least Aidan's hospitalisation and the mess in the apartment – it made sense to distance himself from Frears, to conclude the business arrangement. This was not something they had discussed. He had tried to contact the soldier, but his calls and messages had gone unanswered. The PM felt a slight knot in his stomach at the prospect of Frears and what he was up to. Silly to worry, he thought, given how his announcement would turn the tables in his favour.

The car had dipped into woodland, the lane overshadowed by the boughs of centuries-old oaks. Trees that had seen mere mortals like him come and go. Yet Stirling was confident that, when his departure came, he'd be remembered as a good, maybe even great, Prime Minister.

Chapter 78

Sussex

The day Thou gavest, Lord, is ended,
The darkness falls at Thy behest;
To Thee our morning hymns ascended,
Thy praise shall sanctify our rest.

The hymn echoed through the church as the large congregation joined in song. It was a rousing sound that seemed at odds with the subdued feel of the building, an interior of cold, grey stone weakly illuminated by a pale light coming through the stained-glass windows from the leaden skies outside. It was a mild autumnal day – the unseasonal warmth only adding to the discomfort Sam already felt in the suit Eleanor had lent him from her father's wardrobe.

The hymn's words seemed a mockery to Sam, seated with Eleanor and Wendy Scott in the front pew. They suggested closure, catharsis, relief; some of the things you might ordinarily associate with a funeral. But today, if what had happened so far was any predictor, there was only tension to come.

Eleanor was steaming mad, so angry she could barely take in the coffin before her at the head of the church.

The night before she had discovered that Susan, her mother's sister, had invited the PM and Charlotte Stirling. It wasn't her aunt's fault; she was merely attempting to translate Eleanor's mother's limited communiqués into a meaningful plan for the day. There had been hymns to choose, catering to organise and, of course, a guest list to finalise.

Sam had drawn Eleanor aside and cautioned her against letting rip on her aunt. 'You have to remember,' he'd said, 'Stirling's presence is about a lot more than an unwanted guest. You don't want to start bad-mouthing him. And it's not something your aunt needs to know.'

Eleanor, who at that moment was angry enough to tell anyone who would listen about Stirling, his son and the murderous henchmen that protected him, stormed out of the house.

Sam found her a little later sitting on a bench in the garden, a smouldering cigarette between her fingers.

'I didn't know you smoked,' he said.

'I don't,' she said. 'These fags are the gardener's.'

'We can't afford to speak out about this,' said Sam. 'Not until we have irrefutable proof. And we must leave that to the Moroccans.'

Eleanor took another drag on the cigarette. Tears of frustration had started to well in her eyes. Sam could tell she didn't want comforting. He took the cigarette from her lips and drew on it.

'I know this is agony for you,' he said, exhaling, 'But we just have to wait.'

Eleanor's anger, while contained, was still evident the next day. She deliberately got her mother to the church early so she wouldn't have the ordeal of dealing with Stirling's arrival. That said, both she and Sam sensed the PM's entry. There was a murmur of voices, a wave of energy passing through the church.

Sam turned. There, in the midst of an extraordinary congregation – which he knew from the guest list contained diplomats, high commissioners, charity workers, journalists and numerous politicians – were Philip and Charlotte Stirling, moving down the aisle.

Sam was glad Eleanor kept her eyes fixed ahead. She would not have been able to stomach the scene. Stirling was literally working the room, shaking hands and managing a smile – thankfully a muted one – for all his well-wishers.

After the service Sam watched from a distance as Eleanor, with Susan and a handful of Charles' relatives walking behind, pushed her mother to the graveside for the committal, a family-only affair. The last stretch of the short journey took them from a concrete path across the grass of the churchyard, bumpy terrain that made the wheelchair's progress slow and awkward. Sam wanted desperately to go and help Eleanor but he could see from her pained expression that it would not be a good idea. This was her private hell and she would endure it on her own.

A message had got to both of them that Stirling would not be attending the wake and he had sent his apologies. But any sense of relief on Sam's part was soon shattered when, after the committal, he joined the family as they made their way out of the churchyard to the lane and their waiting cars. There, standing by the gate that led into the road – which meant they had to speak to the PM – were the Stirlings. Beyond was a semicircle of five policemen in suits, recognisable by their stance – hands clasped in front of them – and their constant scanning of the area immediately around. A pack of journalists – mercifully fewer than Sam had anticipated – were standing behind. Sam could see a handful of cameras, now raised and snapping away, and one cameraman. A ministerial Daimler sat purring to the side of the gate, waiting to whisk Stirling and his wife back to London. Further up the lane, other guests were now departing for the wake at the Scott farmhouse, car doors slamming and engines accelerating the only sounds in the still air.

Wendy, now pushed by her sister, was the first to get the Stirling treatment. He knelt before her and took both her hands in his.

'I'm so sorry, Wendy,' he said. 'He was such a loyal friend to me.'

Eleanor bit her lip and turned away. He feared that, at any moment, she would scream or lash out.

Other relatives filtered past, getting a sympathetic nod from Stirling, until it was just Eleanor and Sam. At this point, Eleanor simply barged past the Prime Minister and Charlotte Stirling.

Sam was about to follow when Stirling offered him his hand.

'Philip Stirling,' he said, a solicitous smile on his face. 'You must be a relative of Charles'.'

Sam took the proffered hand and looked the PM in the eye. 'Sam Keddie.'

Stirling's grip tightened. 'We meet at last.'

Charlotte Stirling cupped her husband's elbow. Sam noticed her sleeve ride up a couple of inches to reveal a raised scar of criss-crossed lines on the pale skin of her arm.

'We should go, darling,' she said, her voice strained. A smile fixed on her face, she shot Sam a poisonous look, pupils black with hatred.

Just up the lane, Wendy Scott's wheelchair was rising on a platform by the open back door of a people carrier. Eleanor was by her side but looking in Stirling's direction, her eyes blazing.

'You do know why Charles Scott committed suicide, don't you?' said Sam.

Stirling's eyes locked on to Sam's. 'I'm sorry?'

'What happened in Morocco haunted him. He felt hugely responsible.'

Stirling leaned towards Sam. When he next spoke, Sam could feel the PM's breath hot against his ear. 'I don't know what you're talking about.'

Stirling then pulled away, the smile returning in a pastiche of warmth.

'Dear Charles,' he said. 'Like all of us, full of flaws.'

The PM and his wife moved off. The Daimler's doors were opened, Stirling and Charlotte climbed inside and, seconds later, the car glided away, its exhaust hanging in the motionless air.

Chapter 79

Sussex

The guests had departed. The caterers were busy clearing plates and empty glasses from the Scott family home. To Sam, the silence was deafening.

He watched Eleanor struggle with well-wishers all afternoon. Friends, family and Scott's colleagues – some of whom were household names – circled around her for the chance to pay their respects. He thought she coped admirably well. Looking at her, no one would have been able to tell that the expression on her face wasn't just the strain of a family funeral, but the added anger and frustration he knew was bubbling away inside her.

Sam had drifted from one conversation to another, telling anyone who asked that he was a friend of Eleanor's and that he hadn't known Charles Scott well. The one guest who knew better was Scott's old neighbour, Donald. He pressed Sam for an explanation of what had happened that night at the apartment block, and Sam promised to explain at a later date.

'But you're both safe now?' asked Donald.

'Yes,' replied Sam, though he was far from convinced.

Eleanor was now nursing a glass of luke-warm white wine in the sitting room, the caterers moving quietly around her. It was clear she needed to be on her own so Sam moved into the kitchen – where Wendy Scott was refusing the drink she was being offered by Jill – and out into the garden.

The light of the day was dimming. Sam wandered among flowerbeds, many of the plants cut back in preparation for the oncoming chill of winter. Beyond the beds was a stretch of lawn and then the dense dark wall of woodland that he had emerged from days before.

Sam was watching the woodland – thinking about his encounter with Stirling after the funeral, how he'd all but admitted his guilt with that mocking denial – when he heard a twig snap from within it. It meant nothing of course. There were animals that could easily have made the noise. And yet Sam had the distinct impression he was being watched.

He turned to head swiftly back towards the house, tired of feeling frightened.

Chapter 80

Esher, Surrey

The Abbey Clinic was based in a large Georgian property on the outskirts of Esher. It was separated from its nearest neighbours by expansive gardens that surrounded the building. Unlike the more famous clinics near London that specialised in drug and alcohol addictions, the Abbey treated mental health problems only. Accommodation ranged from tastefully decorated bedrooms that looked out over the gardens to more basically furnished secure units.

Once patients had been assessed and their drug and treatment regimen established, they were often encouraged, if weather permitted, to take a walk in the afternoon. The strength of their medication often meant patients slowed down, suffered muscle weakening and put on weight. In many cases, a walk was the only exercise they got.

Aidan was being led by a male nurse through the lower end of the garden. Beyond the fence, the land belonged to a golf course. Other than the sound of planes overhead, it was quiet.

The nurse had noticed that Aidan had a film of sweat on his upper lip and concluded that he needed to rest. He sat him down on a bench. Aidan sighed heavily. The nurse had read all about his patient in the papers and felt sorry for him. Another staff member had leaked his presence at the clinic to the press and now everyone knew who he was. He only hoped he'd be left alone enough to fully recover.

Hiding behind a hedge just yards away was one of Frears' team, the narrow-eyed man. He watched as Aidan's nurse prattled away to his patient. Aidan appeared to be utterly out of it. Which was good. If you were extracting an unwilling target, and they began resisting, it made the job twice as hard.

He'd made two preparatory visits already that week. He knew the routine, had assessed the nurse and what physical threat he presented. Of course he was hoping that it wouldn't come to that but right now, with time pressing, he was beginning to wonder whether some engagement would in fact be necessary.

But just then the nurse got up. He muttered something to Aidan, then nipped round the side of a large shrub. The narrow-eyed man chuckled to himself. The call of Nature. How often people failed to factor that into situations.

The man was by Aidan in seconds. The PM's son looked up but seemed incapable of forming the facial expression that spelt out surprise. The man grabbed him by the waist and slung him over his shoulders with a slight groan, before turning and moving back in the direction he'd come. When he reached the fence at the end of the garden, he opened a gate and walked out on to a slip road to the side of the 14th hole. There, a grey people-carrier awaited, its number plates thick with dirt.

By the time the nurse had discovered that the padlock was no longer on the gate at the rear of the garden but lying in the grass, its loop cut through with a hacksaw, the people-carrier was on the M25, heading east.

Chapter 81

Sussex

The house became a cocoon. Small windows set in thick walls let in subdued autumnal light, giving the building a womb-like feel they both craved.

They slept together repeatedly. At first the sex seemed like a wave of relief, a celebration of their emergence from the darkest of periods. But latterly a cloud seemed to hang over them in bed – a sense that, without a genuine resolution to the whole mess, they would never be a couple.

Soon they were almost constantly glued to the internet or television, hunting like news junkies for some developments.

On the third day after the funeral, Sam and Eleanor were slumped on the sofa watching the BBC news at 10pm – the Scotts' elderly Labrador, Baker, sleeping at their feet – when a story broke that made them sit bolt upright.

A major investment project in the south of Morocco had been announced by the British Prime Minister, Philip Stirling. Sam, who'd been dozing off, rubbed his face. He felt his body tense.

'Let's go now to Downing Street,' the news reader was saying.

Sam and Eleanor, now sitting on the edge of the sofa, watched the journalist, positioned outside the glossy front door Eleanor had escaped from just days before, as he explained the significance of the deal.

'This is a gamble,' said the reporter, 'in a region that's had more than its fair share of unrest in recent years. But Philip Stirling is clearly confident that the time is right to invest on this scale in Morocco.'

The screen then jumped to an image of Stirling talking to the press in Number 10. He looked, Sam had to admit, years younger, beaming with self-confidence, his face alive with expression as if he were adoring every minute.

'– so I am delighted,' the Prime Minister was saying, 'to announce that a major partnership between our own Office for International Development, the Moroccan Government and British renewables firm, Future Systems, is to deliver a ground-breaking project in the south of the country.' Stirling paused, the great communicator teasing his audience. 'The photo-voltaic solar vineyard planned, which will be one of the world's largest, is about a lot of things. The exporting of British engineering and technological expertise, thousands of jobs in a very poor region of Morocco, and the provision of dramatically subsidised electricity in this area.'

The news reader interjected.

'Stirling has been criticised by some organisations – Amnesty International among them – for getting into bed with a country whose human rights record is far from spotless.'

The reporter in Downing Street smiled wryly. 'For years we conducted business with the Egyptians under Mubarak. We continue to do business with the Saudi and Bahraini authorities. We now exchange intelligence with the Algerians. Morocco is by no means the only tough government in the region. Besides, you'll notice how Stirling is diverting our attention – stressing the fact that this project brings jobs and cheap electricity to one of the country's poorest regions. It's a very canny mix of overseas development and business deal.'

Sam remembered a moment in the security services building in Marrakesh. When Maalouf had abruptly silenced Badaoui as he'd talked about intense discussions taking place. This had been a big secret on both sides.

The mention of Future Systems brought another figure into Sam's mind. Jane Vyner. The woman who'd become so close to Charles Scott – and now Sam knew why. She'd been at the heart of these negotiations.

Eleanor, meanwhile, was only concerned with one person.

'What about Aidan Stirling?' she said, her voice strained with incredulity. 'What the hell has happened to the fingerprints?'

The news had moved on. A gunman breaking into a school in Vienna and killing thirteen pupils.

Sam began to realise what had happened. The announcement today was no coincidence. Something both Governments had been working on for months had been hurried through. These negotiations would have been stalled when the riots broke out. But now, suddenly, everything was calm again. What had the Berbers been fobbed off with – besides subsidised electricity?

Sam got up from the sofa and went to a desk in the corner of the room, firing up a MacBook. As he waited for the computer to warm up he looked at the photo hanging on the wall above him. Charles Scott with Eleanor on his shoulders. She must have been about five or six then.

The screen settled and Sam opened the internet, typing 'Berber girl murdered Marrakesh' into Google.

The top result was an Al Jazeera story. The teaser read 'Man held on suspicion...'

Eleanor had now joined Sam. She stood behind him, the weight of her expectation hanging in the air. Sam opened the story and read aloud.

'The Moroccan authorities have arrested a suspect in the hunt for the murderer of a Berber girl, killed in Marrakesh on 9 September. The man, a Tunisian national – '

'Oh Christ,' whispered Eleanor behind him, interrupting his reading. 'They've nailed that man, haven't they? The assassin who came after us.'

'Looks like it,' said Sam. He abandoned the rest of the article, resting his head on his arms on the desk.

He could see it now. The fingerprints confirming Aidan's guilt. Some hastily convened meetings between the Moroccan ambassador and Stirling. Perhaps the Moroccans had won some vital new concession from the British. All Sam could be sure of was that Stirling, faced with the prospect of his son being accused of murder, would have bent over backwards to please. So then all that was needed was a convenient scapegoat.

It was as if their quest for the truth had been for nothing. A girl had died and her murderer was walking free. Sam and Eleanor had been hounded, nearly killed. All so that the inconvenient truth they'd uncovered could be twisted to achieve a political end.

'I need a cigarette,' said Eleanor.

It was a full moon, the garden bathed in a ghostly light that cast long shadows across the lawn.

They retreated to the shed. The small building creaked a greeting as they entered. Sam sat on an old wooden chair while Eleanor reached up to a top shelf for the cigarettes.

Around them the walls were hung with rakes, shovels and forks, the work surfaces strewn with loose earth and pots of all sizes. Sam imagined the gardener in here, sheltering from storms, seeding his pots, sharpening tools.

There was a musty, fungal smell to the space. Sam noticed that the timber to his side had a creeping patch of dark mould. The shed was slowly being consumed by the very land the gardener spent so much time keeping under control. Death and decay winning, yet again.

Sam brushed the loose earth from the work surface, then accepted a cigarette from the proffered pack. Eleanor sat on a stool by him and lit up, passing the still flaming match to Sam.

They smoked in silence for a few minutes. Sam noticed that Eleanor's hand was shaking.

'You OK?'

Eleanor nodded rapidly, sucking hungrily on the cigarette. She was staring ahead through the open door of the shed at the soft, eerie shapes in the garden. Suddenly she froze.

Sam, who'd been watching Eleanor, now followed her gaze out into the garden. At first he thought it was a trick of the light. But then he realised it wasn't. A figure had emerged out of the grey haze, and was walking towards them.

Chapter 82

Sussex

It was instantly obvious to Sam who the man was. Eleanor's reaction was animal-like. She stood, pressing backwards against the flimsy rotten wall of the shed, as if cornered. This wasn't about an intruder on her land, but something much more frightening.

But, as he entered the shed, the man made his intent very clear.

'I'm not here to hurt you.'

'Then what the fuck are you doing here?' said Eleanor, her voice struggling to register.

Sam knew that the tall man before them, a figure dressed in combat jacket, jeans and trainers, was the same man who'd so terrified Eleanor in the apartment in Downing Street. One of their pursuers, a man who'd only recently been trying to hunt and kill them. And now, despite his words, he had them trapped. Sam's hand reached across the work surface for something to attack with, gripping a piece of broken clay pot.

'Put it down,' snapped the man. 'That won't be necessary.'

'How dare you come here,' hissed Eleanor, a small trace of her steeliness beneath the fear.

The man leaned against the open doorway, dismissing her anger with a wave of a hand.

'You can get all angry and righteous, or you can listen,' he said.

'I don't want to hear anything from you,' she snapped.

'You'll want to hear this,' the man replied. 'It's about something we both want.' His face was lit from the side by the moonlight, giving his features a hard, etched quality. 'Stirling's head on a plate.'

Chapter 83

M25, east of London

It was nearly midnight.

The car sped along the motorway, Sam sitting in silence in the passenger seat, the tall man at the wheel.

Sam cast his mind back to the events in the garden an hour or so before, the extraordinary revelations that had persuaded him to join their former enemy for one last assault on Philip Stirling.

'Sit down,' he'd said. 'You're making me tense.'

They sat. A slight breeze wafted into the shed, bringing with it a hint of the man's body odour.

'I won't tell you my name,' he said, his plummy enunciation suggesting he was an officer, despite the scruffy appearance. 'That won't be necessary. All you need to know is that I was a soldier, and I was approached by Stirling to do a rather unusual job.'

He winced at the mention of the PM's name. 'It's the kind of thing any sentient person would have run a mile from, but Stirling had a hold over me, and the pay was generous. So I accepted.' He sighed at the memory.

Sam nodded. I'm listening, the look said, even though the rest of his body wanted to run screaming from the shed.

'The Prime Minister asked me to set up a small protection team around Aidan Stirling.'

The man scratched his scalp. Sam imagined that, ordinarily, a former officer would have been immaculately turned out. Such a drop in personal standards was anathema to someone like him. His appearance was clearly a necessity.

'As you can imagine, this was to be a quiet set-up,' the man continued. 'There would have been far too many questions asked if the press found out Aidan was getting his own protection, even if it was paid for out of the Stirlings' own pocket.'

'Like why he even needed protection in the first place?' said Sam.

The man's face darkened. 'Quite. Anyway, I should have seen the warning signs at the beginning. We were not there to protect Aidan from others, but from himself, which made things bloody complicated.'

It was clear that the Stirlings had seen the time bomb ticking away in their son. Which begged the question: just how violent had he already been?

'At first it was just about pulling Aidan out of troublesome spots,' the man said. 'He had a habit of cornering girls in nightclubs, getting a little rough with them.'

'I don't understand,' said Sam. 'If he was like this, why had no one ever spoken to the police – or the press for that matter?'

The man shrugged. 'Aidan, through no particular skill on his part, seemed to choose the ideal victims. Thick tarts who'd barely recognise a member of the Cabinet, let alone the PM's son. If any had talked to the police, we never heard about it. And as I said, thanks to us, he failed to cause any real harm. Until Morocco, that is.'

Sam cast a glance at Eleanor, her face glowing in the moonlight. She looked his way, her eyes wide with an acknowledgement of what they'd just heard.

'So,' said Sam, clearing his throat to stop the tremble he could feel developing, 'what happened in Marrakesh?'

The man sucked his teeth. 'I was out there with the delegation, ostensibly to talk about the security implications of the project – making sure the plant had sufficient protection, that sort of thing. It was a front of course. I was really there to keep an eye on Stirling junior. Most of the time, that wasn't necessary, as he was with his mother, sightseeing and shopping. To be honest, I didn't foresee much trouble. This wasn't a night out in Newcastle. But then Charlotte had to join Stirling at a few functions and she let the little bugger off the leash. That was when the trouble started.'

'One afternoon, I watched him go into a shop and start talking to the girl serving him. Even from across the road, I could see she was interested. She was making eye contact, flirting, that sort of thing. The thing is, Aidan Stirling could be quite charming, perhaps even more so to someone whose first language wasn't English.' The man chuckled at his own quip. 'Anyhow, they must have made an arrangement to meet that evening.'

'When he stabbed her.'

The man nodded. 'It happened, as I'm sure you now know, near the restaurant where the British and Moroccan officials met that night. I was at the function and the area was crawling with local secret service and police, there to protect the Moroccan Prime Minister and Stirling. None of us expected him to slip out. But late in the evening, Stirling approached me, looking all flustered. Told me I had to find Aidan. And suddenly Charles Scott was there too, asking what the matter was.'

'Stirling tried to fob him off but Scott knew something was up. In the end Stirling concluded that two were better than one and Scott and I set off into the medina.'

'Now you've been out there,' the man said, 'it's a bloody warren. We moved methodically through the alleyways, hoping that he wouldn't have gone far. Of course it was like looking for a needle in a haystack. Every now and then we'd regroup and then move on to another section. In the end we were about to give up when Scott called me on my mobile and told me to get to this address north of the restaurant. It took me a few minutes to get my bearings, but then I found the place.'

The man looked shaken and Sam realised that, despite his involvement in a great deal of violent acts – attempts on their life, and the murder of Jane Vyner – this event still shocked him. Perhaps it was the significance of the act, and what it then unleashed.

'I found Scott with Aidan in an old warehouse. Aidan was pacing the room, talking to himself, clearly agitated. Scott was trying to calm him down but the boy seemed to be in a world of his own. On the floor against a wall was the girl I'd seen that afternoon, dead as a dodo. Aidan was holding the knife in his hand. The blade was covered in blood.

'Oh God,' Eleanor gasped, her face clasped in her hands. She was clearly as upset by the murder as by her father's painful involvement – and what it had done to him.

The man was still speaking, oblivious to Eleanor's grief. 'Scott had given Aidan the knife that very afternoon. It was an antique he'd picked up in Marrakesh. It was clear to me at that point that there was only one thing to do. There was way too much at stake. So there and then, we decided it had to be covered up. We told Aidan to drop the blade and the three of us walked away.'

Sam thought of Scott and his enormous burden of guilt. 'Something happened,' he had said during that session. 'Something I cannot talk about. And I did nothing to stop it.' He repeated the phrase in his head. Its obvious meaning was that Scott hadn't been able to stop Aidan killing. But of course that was a given. How could he have stopped him when he wasn't with him? What now struck Sam was that Scott was talking about something else – that he hadn't stopped what happened next, the cover-up. Why? A deep political allegiance and friendship with Stirling? Realpolitik?

He remembered Stirling's venomous little phrase about Scott at the funeral. 'Dear Charles. Like all of us, full of flaws.'

Sam saw Eleanor's eyes moving from side to side as if she too were dwelling on her father's motivations.

'So when one of your men saw Charles Scott at my house,' said Sam quickly, desperate to interrupt the thought process in Eleanor's head, 'you became concerned. That, perhaps, he'd told me.'

'That's right.'

'And then he killed himself.'

'He was in a right state. Of course Aidan had wielded the knife, but he felt hugely responsible for giving him the blade, and guilty about his part in the cover-up.'

Sam remembered the description of Scott at the hotel in the Lakes, a broken, ranting man.

Eleanor looked up, her cheeks tear-streaked.

'And then,' continued the man, 'you refused to play ball. Hardly surprising. But we had to find out what you knew.'

'The irony is, I knew nothing. But your actions made me bloody curious.'

'After that,' said the man, ignoring Sam's last comment, 'it was about clearing up a mess. Translating Stirling's less than clear-cut instructions into meaningful action.'

The man looked embittered, as if he had a foul taste in his mouth.

'I'm sorry,' said Sam, 'but if you want Stirling's head on a plate, why don't you use this to nail him?'

The man laughed. 'You'll have noticed my timing tonight. I wanted you to see the news, to understand where that Moroccan announcement leaves us all. The evidence you gathered,' and here he glanced briefly at Eleanor with what Sam felt was a grudging look of respect, 'is now useless. Destroyed by the Moroccans. Who's going to believe me?'

'But surely –'

'It's like I said, even before this got complicated, Stirling had a certain hold over me. Events in my past that are best kept under wraps. But after Morocco, he and I both knew we were even. But then I went into the apartment and the tables turned. No one's pressing charges, but Stirling's still fucked me over. Dropped me like a hot potato. Stopped paying me – and my men. And he knows I won't complain, or use what I know. After all, there's now no proof. Whereas a number of police officers will swear they saw me in the apartment.'

The man's face tightened. 'I was only doing what he'd asked me to do.'

'So what do you want from us?' asked Sam.

The man raised a hand, the finger pointing at Sam. 'Your professional skills.'

The car had crossed the Dartford Bridge and taken a turning for Rainham. To the left, a power station, from which a trail of huge pylons snaked its way towards London, glowed in the night, lit up by hundreds of small lights. Two cooling towers sent steam into the night sky, the vapour soon evaporating.

Sam twisted in his seat, all too aware of what to expect when they reached the address. He missed Eleanor by his side. The strength she gave him. But the man had told her flatly that she was not needed. Sam watched her face rail against the order, then subside in compliance, some inner sense that resistance against the cold soldier was pointless. As they were about to leave, she clung to Sam hard.

Their destination was in a cul-de-sac, the first finished group of houses on an estate that was still being built. Elsewhere, the wooden skeletons of new homes rose out of muddy fields. About eight red-brick houses were clustered around a loop of tarmac. Apart from one property, there were no lights on, no cars parked in driveways.

The car stopped outside a house where a faint glow could be seen behind a drawn curtain. Another vehicle, a battered old transit van, was parked in the street in front of the property.

The tall man unlocked the front door and walked in, followed by Sam. The house smelt of fresh paint and new carpets and, lingering below, the salt and spice whiff of Chinese food. He followed the man to the rear of the property, the light and food smell getting stronger.

In the kitchen, a small camping lamp – the hiss of gas audible – was lit on the kitchen table. Its surface was strewn with tin-foil cartons. Seated at the table were two men, both of whom Sam recognised with a sickening jolt – the short bald man who'd visited him in Stoke Newington, and the narrow-eyed man who'd chased him through the cemetery and killed Jane Vyner.

The two men glanced briefly in Sam's direction, then looked away with the dispassion of cold professionals.

'Everything OK?' asked the tall man.

The two men nodded.

The tall man then turned and moved past Sam, gesturing for him to follow. They climbed the stairs. When they reached the first floor, he opened a door and stood waiting for Sam.

Sam knew what to expect, but couldn't help but feel a jolt of surprise, like he'd placed his hand on an electric fence and a pulse had shot through his system.

Lying fast asleep on a mattress on the floor, the dark room around him decorated and carpeted but otherwise as blank as a monastic cell, was Aidan Stirling.

Chapter 84

It was a denial of everything his profession stood for. He wasn't providing therapy to a willing client, nor was he offering unconditional positive regard. The young man seated on the mattress before him was a prisoner and Sam had very strong, prejudiced feelings about him.

But Aidan Stirling wasn't his client. And Sam wasn't here as a therapist. Some of that knowledge would come in useful, but he was also tapping other skills – the very existence of which made him nauseous to the core.

It was over eight hours since Aidan Stirling had been abducted from a psychiatric hospital in Surrey. Sam overheard the narrow-eyed man describe the job as 'a piece of cake'. Sam had the impression that these men had conducted a number of extractions before, ones fraught with far more danger than the hospital could ever have presented.

The day had dawned grey and overcast. Thick clouds hung low over the building site, its JCBs idle, not a worker in sight.

Sam woke just after six. He'd barely slept, his bed the hard floor of another upstairs room, the blanket he'd been given barely covering his body. He'd also been haunted by the thought, which came to him in the dead of night, that he was sharing a house with four killers.

'Who are you?' Aidan asked as Sam sat on the carpet across the room from him. The PM's son was sitting up, his back resting on a pillow against the wall, a mess of curly hair hanging over his forehead. He wore a t-shirt and jogging pants. He seemed detached, calm and lacking fear. Sam, correspondingly, felt no fear, just the weight and significance of the job in hand. The tall man, who'd observed Aidan under the influence of his drugs on many occasions, said they had a brief window of opportunity – no more than a day – before Aidan became more conscious. He'd then be more fearful, less compliant and potentially dangerous.

'A friend of Eleanor Scott,' Sam replied.

'Then what are you doing with this lot?' asked Aidan. 'She's nice. They're Nazis. My Dad's goons.'

'Would you believe me if I said I was helping you?' The words caught in Sam's throat. Aidan might eventually get help as a result of this, but that wasn't Sam's goal right now.

'I don't trust anyone who says they're trying to help me.'

'Lots of bad experiences?'

'Plenty,' he said, his lip curling slightly. 'Shrinks of various shades. Is that what you are?'

Sam sensed that Aidan would smell dishonesty a mile off. 'Yes.'

'Go on then,' said Aidan. 'Cure me.'

'What do you need curing of?'

Aidan's drowsy face flinched slightly.

'Depends who you talk to.'

No sense of personal responsibility, thought Sam.

'What would your father say?'

Aidan grimaced as much as his medication would let him. 'When I was a child, my father used to say I was an awkward little shit. These days he prefers to call me a "fucked-up train crash of an adult".'

'And what about your mother?'

'My mother says lots of things. And then she pretends she never said them.'

'Can you give me an example?'

Aidan's eyes seemed glassy all of a sudden. 'I don't want to talk about my mother.'

'Would you like a rest?'

Aidan shook his head. 'Have you got any food?'

Sam disappeared downstairs. The tall man was in the kitchen with the other two.

'How's it going?' he asked.

'Fine,' said Sam. 'But he's hungry.'

'He's a bloody pig when he's on the drugs,' said the tall man.

'Give him these,' said the narrow-eyed man, handing Sam a bag of cookies.

Aidan devoured the first quickly, taking the second biscuit at a more leisurely pace.

'Do you like architecture?' he asked, his mouth still full of cookie.

'I do,' said Sam.

'What sort?'

'Art Deco buildings,' said Sam.

Aidan nodded, but not with any enthusiasm. 'I think they're a bit decorative. I like more unadorned Modernist stuff,' he said. 'Frank Lloyd Wright, Denys Lasdun. Do you know the National Theatre?'

Sam nodded, happy for Aidan to pursue this train of thought. He clearly found it safe territory, a place to retreat to after the brief painful mention of his mother.

'It's called Brutalism, you know. I like all that concrete. It's kind of what it is. No fancy embellishments.'

'More honest.'

'Exactly.'

'That important to you?'

Aidan nodded sleepily. 'I hate bullshit.'

Sam saw an opportunity. An approach his Jungian would never have used, but that he'd employed once in the past with a client – a very buttoned-up public schoolboy who'd struggled with trust.

'If I tell you a truth about me,' said Sam, 'how about you do the same?'

'A game,' said Aidan, with a hint of relish. 'You're more fun than the other therapists, that's for sure.'

'Shall we give it a go?'

Aidan shrugged his consent.

'I'm an only child,' said Sam.

'Big deal,' said Aidan. 'Me too.'

'I'm claustrophobic when I get stressed.'

Aidan snorted.

Sam sensed the game had to be upped.

'My mother never loved me. She used to lock me in a cupboard as punishment.'

Aidan paused for a moment, drinking in this information. He seemed to be weighing up his response. Sam noticed his eyes were welling. Then came the response: 'My mother used to sleep with me.'

Sam felt his skin prickle. The small room fell utterly silent. Then shrunk around them.

Sam's brain raced with the implications of what he'd just heard. Was it true? He had to assume it was. What possible motive could Aidan have for lying about such a matter?

'You look surprised,' said Aidan, his voice betraying a distinct tremble, as if he were trying to remain calm and detached, but inside was beginning to unravel. 'I thought you shrinks had heard it all before.'

'I guess I am surprised,' replied Sam. 'You said it in rather a matter-of-fact way.'

Aidan shrugged, unconvincingly. 'That was how it was.'

'Go on.'

'We were in Italy when it started. A villa in the middle of nowhere. Another holiday hanging round waiting for my father to arrive. Mother did what she always did in those situations, and got pissed. She was also self-harming.'

Aidan's eyes were fixed on the wall beyond Sam. He was now back in Italy, one hundred per cent. Sam stayed silent.

'She was at her worst after lunch. In a cool bath, a danger to herself. I used to help her out, get her dried off, bandage her arms.' He paused, swallowing hard. 'And then I'd get her into bed. She called me her little man.'

He smiled briefly, then his face darkened.

'One afternoon she asked me to climb in next to her.'

The voice had risen a notch, as if Aidan were reaching a crescendo. Sam sensed a simmering rage under the medication, one just contained beneath the damp blanket of drugs.

'You're angry.'

Aidan shrugged again.

'Angry because it happened? Or because you've told me?'

Aidan shook his head. He then slumped downwards, pulling his blanket up around him. The session was over.

Chapter 85

Rainham, east of London

An hour later, a request for food came from upstairs. The tall man insisted on giving him more sweet junk. 'Apart from little rushes of energy,' he said, 'it helps keep him sluggish. The way we want him.'

'You're a nosey bastard, aren't you?' said Aidan to Sam, after devouring another cookie. There was a hint of combativeness about him. As if he were more present, and trying to gain the upper hand.

'Aren't all shrinks?' replied Sam.

'I guess. You don't seem as wimpy as the others. They were always tiptoeing around me. Like I was some delicate flower that might snap at the wrong intervention. I knew what they wanted to ask. They just didn't have the guts.'

'They're not really meant to ask questions. It's too leading.'

'What's that about?'

'In person-centred therapy, the therapist works in response to the content presented, without trying to manipulate the progress of the session, however strong his instinct may be.'

'Do you have an instinct about me?'

'Seeing as you're the client, then I feel obliged to answer,' said Sam. 'Yes, I do.'

'Enlighten me.'

Sam inhaled deeply through his nose. 'I think you're angry with your mother because she stopped sleeping with you.'

The effect was electrifying. Aidan froze, his eyes locked on to Sam.

'How,' he snarled, 'how, did you know that?'

Sam felt a charge in the room, some definitive threat of violence from the man opposite. He wanted to get out, but knew he had to press on. 'You implied it.'

The eyes narrowed. 'Fuck you, shrink.'

And with that, the violence subsided. Aidan slumped down again, retreating under the blanket.

Chapter 86

Rainham, east of London

Time was running out. Sam knew it. During the last session, Aidan seemed more animated, his reactions a degree more physical. He was now more aware of his captivity, and of the interrogation session masquerading as therapy. Which meant the danger had increased. It was time to take a leaf out of Eleanor's book.

'Go away,' said Aidan, when Sam entered the room, closing the door behind him and sitting down on the floor.

'No.'

There was silence. Sam had read of a therapist who'd been counselling a traumatised war veteran. The man was so disturbed – and so mistrustful – the therapist had endured weeks of silence before his client finally opened up. Sam did not have that luxury.

It had started raining gently, the window flecked with tiny droplets of water.

'You don't like me because I saw through you.'

'I don't like any shrinks,' hissed Aidan. 'I thought you were different but you're just the same. And why am I here?'

'So I can speak to you. The alternative is that hospital – and lots more of your medication.'

Aidan's eyes welled again.

'Your father has you locked away. Why is that?'

'My father hates me,' said Aidan, the tears now dropping from his eyes.

'You're the "awkward little shit".'

Aidan nodded.

Sam took another deep breath, trying to slow his heart, which had begun to hammer against his ribs.

'Did you kill that girl in Marrakesh?'

It was as if Aidan's mattress was crawling with insects. He suddenly shot up, and began pacing up and down.

Sam pressed back against the wall. He looked Aidan up and down. Although he was in poor shape physically, the man before him was agitated – scratching his head furiously, as if his scalp were riddled with lice – and that agitation would count for a lot if he got violent.

'The warehouse had mosaics on the walls and pillars,' said Aidan, the words spilling out. 'Geometric designs repeated everywhere.'

He let out a short cry. 'She lied to me,' he said, his voice now full of anguish. 'Just like Mum lied to me. She said we'd be together forever. But then she changed her mind. Told me what had happened was dirty, wrong. That girl was just the same. She promised everything with her eyes, then denied me.'

He stopped, his head falling forwards. He then looked up at Sam. His eyes blazed and he suddenly lunged, sinking to the floor on his knees as he grabbed Sam's throat with both hands.

Sam could feel the air supply abruptly cut off as his windpipe constricted. He grabbed Aidan's wrists, but his assailant's elevated position – and the strength of a man possessed – made removing them an impossibility.

Sam's eyes bulged. His chest tightened with an intense pain. Surely the men downstairs would come running?

'I was so mad with her,' Aidan was muttering.

Sam looked into Aidan's eyes, which were wet with tears. The last words Sam heard were clouded by the sensation of a dark wave about to engulf him, but they still resonated in his head.

'And so I killed her.'

Chapter 87

Rainham, east of London

The rain had stopped. Sam and the tall man stood in the back garden of the house, below the window where Aidan was now sleeping.

He'd been given another tranquiliser. Sam gently rubbed his neck. His fingers were trembling. He'd passed out just after Aidan had admitted killing the girl. According to the tall man, he'd come to shortly afterwards.

'Nasty piece of work, that boy,' said the tall man.

Sam closed his eyes then rapidly re-opened them as an image of Aidan descending on him invaded his head.

'You'll need to get checked out. You're probably fine, but just in case.'

Sam shook his head in slight disbelief. The man who'd been trying to kill him for days was now offering him health advice.

'And sorry we cut it so fine,' continued the tall man. 'But we needed a definitive confession.'

Sam asked if he could have a cigarette and the tall man went inside. He returned with one lit.

Sam drew hard then inhaled deeply. He felt sick, light-headed. This was probably the worst thing for a man who'd just been strangled.

Despite the rage and hatred Sam now felt for Aidan, he couldn't help but think of the damaged individual upstairs, and how those loathsome elements in him were a direct result of an existing condition made a hundred times worse by his ghastly parents.

Minutes after the tranquiliser had been administered, Aidan was curled up asleep on his mattress, his knees drawn into the foetal position, some natural echo of his earliest days in the womb. Sam thought of the woman who'd carried Aidan there, who'd brought him into the world – only to destroy his life.

Charlotte Stirling had drawn him close to her – no doubt seducing Aidan with a muddled, poisonous blend of mother's love and her own confused, damaged needs – only to push him away when she finally came face to face with the magnitude of her crime.

'You need to get Aidan back to that clinic as soon as possible,' said Sam, casting the cigarette to the ground. The smoke had done nothing to improve the bitter, acidic taste in his mouth and he felt too light-headed to inhale any more.

Sam sensed it was the first time Aidan had ever admitted to anyone, perhaps even to himself, what had happened in Marrakesh. It would ripple through him, like tremors after an earthquake. Part of Sam relished the thought of Aidan suffering with the knowledge. Another part worried.

'We've replayed the recording,' said the tall man. 'It's everything we need to force Stirling's resignation.'

The tall man would have his revenge – and the money owed him and his men.

For Sam, Stirling's resignation was not enough. Aidan would never be tried in Morocco. That case was now closed as far as the Moroccans were concerned. But Sam felt strongly that what he'd done couldn't be left untried. He wanted Philip and Charlotte Stirling to be exposed as the unspeakable parents they were, and for Lalla's family to have their day in court.

Sam briefly considered asking if a copy of the recording could be sent to the police, but quickly dismissed it. The tall man would never agree to that. Bound up in Aidan's crime was the cover-up, in which his unlikely ally had played a major role. No, there had to be another way.

Chapter 88

Sussex

They were walking Baker along the edge of a wood. To their left a view of the Downs stretched out in the distance, soft hills like gently undulating waves. A sharp wind whipped across the landscape, and Sam pulled the collar of his coat up around his neck. It was still bruised and tender, but Sam had ignored the tall man's advice. He felt fine and dreaded a doctor's inevitable questioning of why he had fingerprints on his throat.

Lynch, the policeman who'd interviewed Eleanor in Downing Street, had just left, having sat round the kitchen table, his eyes slowly widening as Sam and Eleanor told their story, revealing the real reason for the struggle in the apartment. The police officer promised to pursue every potential lead including, in the first instance, interviewing Aidan and his parents.

'It may not be enough,' said Eleanor.

'I know,' said Sam. 'You can be sure Stirling will have the best barrister in London. But at least we tried.'

Baker was sniffing the base of a tree. He then began waddling off again, a plump torso over narrow legs.

'If it does go to court, what will happen to Aidan?' asked Eleanor.

'I'm no legal expert, but I'm pretty certain he'll end up in a psychiatric unit.'

Sam thought back to the small room in that house – to the cold core within him that had pressed Aidan so relentlessly, and the violence that had erupted.

'Sam?'

Eleanor's voice brought him back into the moment. He shook the room's image from his head.

'You don't have to talk about him now.'

Sam smiled. 'You sound like a shrink.' He paused. 'No, I think I want to. The thing is, Aidan's screwed unless he gets the right treatment. A psychiatrist would probably label him with an antisocial personality disorder – he'd certainly tick most of the boxes on the checklist – and pump him full of more drugs.'

'But you disagree.'

Sam's eyes were looking over the hedgerow to the left, on to a vast ploughed field. Some distance below them a small group of deer were standing so still, they looked like statues. Baker's nose twitched but it was clear his body wouldn't tolerate a chase.

'There are certain traits in him that entirely conform to that type. He's arrogant and, at least in part, struggles to take responsibility for his actions. He doesn't appear to have formed any significant friendships, and relationships with the opposite sex are, understandably, out of the question. But psychiatrists also argue that antisocial personality disorder types tend to be heartless and lacking remorse.'

'That's not how I would describe him,' said Eleanor. 'I mean, when he went for the soldier in the apartment, he was actually defending me.'

'And although he attacked me, there was, underneath the rage, a huge sadness,' added Sam.

'Of course they'll probably make as little of that in court as possible – go for diminished responsibility.'

They walked on in silence for a few minutes until Baker made it clear he didn't want to go any further and they turned back.

Sam thought of Aidan's parents, the effect they'd had on their child. Stirling, largely absent, then hyper-critical and dismissive of his son when he was around. And then there was the mother. Sam remembered that brief glimpse of Charlotte's arm at the funeral, the tell-tale scars of a self-harmer, something Aidan had later confirmed. A deeply unhappy woman, drunk and without boundaries, getting the attention she craved from her husband from her vulnerable child instead.

Sam remembered something else, a fleeting glimpse of an image. 'Do you remember that photo of Stirling with the Moroccan Prime Minister – the one we saw in the restaurant in Marrakesh that evening? The figure Stirling had an arm around who seemed slightly distant?'

'We weren't sure if it was my father or someone else,' said Eleanor. 'It was Aidan, wasn't it, dragged into a chummy, artificial shot of the two families.'

They walked on in silence for a moment, Sam dwelling on the photo, that gap between the two men that was, in reality, a chasm.

Eleanor drifted to his side, slipping her arm into his, drawing herself into him.

'So,' she said, her voice brighter, 'when do you think we'll see Stirling exit the building?'

'A matter of days,' said Sam. 'Maybe even earlier.'

'Do I sound incredibly bitter and twisted when I say I can't wait?'

'Absolutely,' smiled Sam.

Eleanor stopped and turned Sam gently so that they faced each other.

'There's something else I need to talk about,' she said, her eyes flickering as she studied his face. 'Something I've been thinking about a lot recently. It's just that, what with everything that's been happening, there hasn't really been the right moment.'

Sam was suddenly aware that his heart was pounding in his chest.

'The thing is, Sam,' said Eleanor, 'I want us to be together.'

'Right,' he said, his throat dry.

'But there's one condition.'

'OK…'

A fresh gust of wind whipped across the path, but they both stood still, staring at each other. 'I want us to do normal stuff as a couple,' said Eleanor. 'Watch tv, go shopping, hang out.'

Sam smiled. 'You mean no car crashes? No chases through alleyways?'

Eleanor returned the smile.

'Deal,' he said.

Later that afternoon, Eleanor put on a CD in the sitting room and curled up next to Sam on the sofa. The fire was on, casting a warm glow into the darkening room.

Wendy Scott was sitting close to them in her leather seat with its large padded arms and headrest. She seemed still, her body taking a rare rest from its involuntary spasms. Sam could see that her condition was not only debilitating, but utterly exhausting. He couldn't even begin to guess how she absorbed her loss in the midst of battling her illness – she could no longer speak – but he sensed an incredibly tough woman within the now contorted shell of her body.

The song began with a noise like a scratched record, a breathy fuzz in the background, which was then interrupted by the sound of someone playing the piano, almost hesitantly. A man's voice, both soulful and sorrowful, then broke in.

'It's by Chet Baker,' said Eleanor. 'Dad loved him. So much in fact, that he named the dog after him. Isn't that right, Mum?'

Sam watched Wendy Scott. Her head was cocked at a sharp angle but he saw a smile play across her lips. A moment later, she began to cry. Eleanor leapt off the sofa and went to her mother, kneeling by her and holding her hand as the two of them cried and the song continued to its soft, melancholic conclusion.

Sam looked at them mourning together, acutely aware of the man they both ached for. Their grief would continue for some time to come. He wondered whether Eleanor would ever reach any sense of closure, whether she'd ever truly accept what had happened. Not that her father was dead, but that he wasn't the man she'd always believed him to be.

She hadn't mentioned it since that night in the shed when the man had come out of the shadows and told them what happened in Marrakesh. But for Sam, it had turned into a niggle – one that he constantly felt worming its way around his head.

Something had persuaded Charles Scott to cover up a murder. Would Eleanor – like Sam – continue to wonder what had motivated him to do this? Or was she the type who could accept a certain level of uncertainty, and let go? Only time would tell.

Chapter 89

Downing Street

Stirling watched from a window on the first floor as Ministers' cars left Downing Street one by one. He'd just endured the last of his Cabinet meetings, the talk dominated by a discussion on how to quell public anger over proposed pension reform.

The PM, who was confident that he'd be out before being tarred with that particular brush, soon detached himself from the heated proceedings. For the rest of the meeting he felt as if he were floating somewhere above the table, occasionally making intelligent remarks but essentially observing.

He had yet to breathe a word about his impending departure to anyone, apart from Charlotte, of course.

He'd told her over the phone of their predicament and heard afterwards how she'd collapsed. It was not a good sign. Being the PM's wife had given her strength. Losing that role so suddenly was going to be a huge challenge for her. She'd been reliant on all the therapy 'wisdom' she'd acquired over the years. Would that be enough, or would she slip back to the warm comforts of the bottle? He hoped to God not. Charlotte drunk was not just ugly, but potentially extremely damaging to a former Prime Minister looking to secure a lucrative lecturing career.

There was a rap on the door. It opened before he'd had a chance to answer.

'Need a quick word, Prime Minister,' said Gillian Mayer. She seemed irritated.

'Sit down, Gillian,' said Stirling, a carefree lilt to his voice. The business of Government seemed suddenly so petty, trivial, when once he'd gorged on its every detail.

'It's about this Moroccan deal,' she said, perching on the edge of a chair.

Stirling smiled as he returned to his seat. Amazing how that 'M' word had so recently caused him fear, when now it had no effect whatsoever.

'Go on.'

'I'm sure you'll have noticed that the maths has changed.'

'Right.'

'Right?' she repeated, with a hint of indignation. 'We're giving away another eight million quid. When did this happen?'

'Oh, a few days ago,' he said dreamily.

Mayer examined him like he was bacteria under a microscope. 'Didn't you think to discuss it with me, or the new Secretary of State for that matter, before you dipped your hands into his budget? And can I ask what prompted this sudden bout of generosity?'

Stirling had no answer and for once, he didn't care. He was about to shrug when there was another knock on the door. A press secretary poked her head in.

'Sorry Prime Minister, another visitor. Commander Lynch. He says he needs to see you right away.'

Stirling smiled sweetly at the Foreign Secretary. 'Sorry Gillian. Another time?'

Gillian Mayer fixed him with a steely look. 'This needs resolving.'

'All in good time, Gillian. Now, if you would.'

The Foreign Secretary stormed out and moments later Lynch entered, closing the door behind him.

'Commander Lynch, how can I help?'

The police officer stood just inside the room, as if reluctant to come any closer.

'I've had some new information,' he said.

Stirling felt a slight flutter in his chest, an awakening of the fear and tension that had been his bedfellows for weeks.

'Can you be a bit more specific?'

'It's about your son.'

'For Christ's sake, Lynch, get to the point.'

'We need to interview him. About a murder in Marrakesh.'

Stirling watched as the Foreign Secretary got into her car and the door was closed by her driver. There would be more questions about the Moroccan deal. But that matter would soon be eclipsed.

When he might have exited with some grace, he now faced the prospect of a gruesome court case, one in which Aidan's every last foible and twitch would be examined in detail. Inevitably his role as a parent would be questioned. And would Aidan finger him for covering up the murder? He certainly had motive. After all, he hated his father's guts.

He thought of Charles and how he'd chosen to keep things under wraps. It was not friendship that had prompted this unwavering loyalty. Although Scott had never said anything, Stirling was sure that it was a deal. A crowning, when his time was up.

The Foreign Secretary's car was accelerating down Downing Street. Stirling noticed a shape darting in front of the vehicle. He winced.

The Downing Street cat, Balfour, had been caught by the car's right front wheel. It appeared to have crushed the cat's spine. The driver had felt the jolt and stopped the vehicle to get out and inspect the damage. The cat was twitching slightly, what looked like dying movements rather than an indication that there was any hope. Mayer was out of the car now, a hand over her mouth as she took in the messy feline corpse beneath her Ministerial car.

So, thought Stirling, Balfour had lived his nine lives. He was reminded of a story he'd been told about Humphrey, the Downing Street cat during Thatcher and Major's tenures, and how it nearly copped it under the wheels of Clinton's two-ton armoured Presidential Cadillac.

Like Balfour, Stirling had also lived his nine lives. It was time to leave.

He was numb, unable to quantify what this meant to him. When you wished for something for so long, and then attained it, only to lose it, what effect did that have? Only time would reveal the true impact of this day upon his psyche.

One thing was for sure. That woman out there wouldn't be succeeding him.

A sly thought came to him. In a day or so, he'd leak the story of Balfour's death under the wheel of Mayer's car. That would ensure the instant hatred of a few million cat lovers.

He smiled to himself. Still playing the game, even as the casino closed.

Chapter 90

Sussex

The resignation dominated the news for days. Sam and Eleanor devoured every last column inch and news bulletin. It felt at times like they were indulging in some form of binge eating, a sickening feeling that frequent, head-clearing walks helped alleviate.

Stirling made the statement outside Downing Street. For once, the man was immaculately turned out, a precise orderly appearance quite at odds with the delivery. He faltered frequently to take steadying breaths or fight back tears, talking of his 'beloved child, a boy with complex health problems'.

'Aidan needs our support, more than I realised,' he said. 'And I have come to the conclusion that his ongoing care makes it impossible for me to serve the country I am so proud of. I hope you will therefore understand why I have asked Her Majesty to accept my resignation.'

He couldn't finish after that, breaking down in tears and, with a sad little wave, turning back, for the last time, to enter 10 Downing Street.

The tears, Sam and Eleanor agreed, were for his career, not for his son. Sam watched him with intense loathing. Stirling should have slipped away gracefully long ago to concentrate on getting his only child the treatment he so desperately needed, but Philip Stirling had clung on and in doing so, had undoubtedly made matters worse.

Despite his premature departure, praise was heaped on his short tenure as Prime Minister – his sound economic stewardship, crowd-pleasing measures and announcements, as well as his recent noble efforts at overseas development in Morocco. How long, wondered Sam, would the warmth be extended Stirling's way?

A clip began circulating on the internet of Charlotte Stirling collapsing in public. One afternoon, alone in the sitting room, Sam found it.

Wearing an embroidered long-sleeved top, the PM's wife had been at a south London primary school pursuing her work as the patron of a charity for children with autism. She was seen perched on a child's chair, chatting to a little girl who was tapping away on a computer keyboard. A woman approached her and whispered in her ear, and Charlotte Stirling became visibly rattled. Sam guessed that she had told her aides not to disturb her. Charlotte Stirling had never come across as particularly soft and it would hardly have helped if she were seen exiting a room full of small children to answer a call. You could see her asking what the matter was and the assistant, now squirming, urging Charlotte Stirling to leave the room. Eventually the PM's wife hissed at the assistant, who then whispered again in her ear. Charlotte Stirling then stood, her face draining of expression, and moments later, she collapsed to the floor.

Sam felt sickened by his reaction to the footage. There was nothing to relish in the imagery – of Charlotte's vulnerability exposed for all to see. He was all too aware of transference – of seeing the traits and personality of significant others in people you hardly knew – but he couldn't escape the fact that Charlotte Stirling reminded him very strongly of his own mother. So to see her in pain gave him pleasure.

Quite why his mother had locked him in that cupboard for the mildest of misdemeanours, leaving him there for hours on end, remained a mystery, despite his therapy. Perhaps, Sam mused, she'd done it to toughen him up. Perhaps it was simply about deliberately denying him the affection she'd obviously never experienced herself. Or maybe it wasn't that malevolent, just a re-enactment of her childhood experience. In other words, what felt 'normal' to her.

'What are you looking at?'

Eleanor was standing behind him. She draped an arm over his shoulder, clicking the mouse to exit the website.

'I think we should designate today a Stirling-free day,' she said.

Sam looked down at her hand, the fingernails no longer bitten.

'Agreed,' he said.

In the kitchen, Baker had begun beating his tail against the tiled floor, the sight of the two of them suggesting a walk.

Despite a gentle rain falling, the fresh air did its trick, clearing Sam's mind of the poisonous Stirlings. He and Eleanor talked of returning to London, of her going back to work and the possibility, which made his heart skip a beat, of her moving in.

On their return, Sam began building a fire in the sitting room. As he tore strips of newspaper up, he saw another image of Charlotte Stirling. She was walking a dog in a square in Mayfair, their new home. She looked ashen. He quickly layered kindling around the paper and struck a match.

But even as Charlotte Stirling went up in flames, he sensed another mother – and her poisonous legacy – waiting in the wings.

Epilogue

Days later

Chapter 91

North London

It was the middle of the night. Sam sat bolt upright, eyes wide open in terror. Eleanor was watching him.

'I think you need to talk about this.' she said.

Sam disappeared to fetch a glass of water then sat on the edge of the bed. The dream was never different, he explained to Eleanor. His mother, the scientist, in her cold, clinical laboratory, the tubes and beakers bubbling away, thickening the air with noxious clouds and vapours. Her plaintive call to him. And then the huge black horse, its coat covered in sweat, nostrils flaring, white foam around its mouth, and eyes bulging with fear. His mother would beckon to him again, this time with open arms, and then the horse would rear up, hooves flailing at Sam, a primal wall stopping him reaching his mother.

'You know exactly what it means, don't you?' said Eleanor, reaching across the bed for Sam's hand.

'Oh yes,' he said. 'It's not my mother beckoning to me; it's a part of her that's in me. An Arctic, cut-off place. And the horse is my unconscious, telling me, in no uncertain terms, to run a mile.'

'Tell me more about her,' said Eleanor. The bedside light cast a warm glow across her face. She looked beautiful.

He spoke for an hour, compressing the stories that he'd told his therapist into one long discourse, explaining how, while so much insight had been gained, there still remained the sickening thought that, inside, he was no different to his mother. It was something that had become more evident in the past weeks, during those moments when he'd drawn on a cold, calculating inner resource – while talking to Aidan, or keeping the case notes from Eleanor. He knew there were good reasons for this behaviour, but he couldn't help feeling that it hinted at something darker.

'Sorry to be blunt,' said Eleanor, once he'd finished, 'but you therapists don't half complicate things.'

Sam managed a smile. 'How so?'

'Do I need to spell it out?'

''Fraid so.'

'You're not your mother. I mean, you carry traces of her, but that doesn't make you her. You're way too aware of yourself to ever turn into a person like the one you describe. I'm not saying your fear isn't real, but it's not grounded. It's like you've got yourself into a rut with this dream. It's become habitual.'

Sam thought of how he had avoided discussing his fear in therapy, convinced that airing it somehow gave it validity, the chance to take root and grow. In doing so, he'd merely helped it develop in the dark.

And now Eleanor had gone straight in, told it like it is. Was she right? His mother was a cold bitch, but the evidence suggesting Sam was going in the same direction was flimsy. His thinking – both conscious and unconscious – had become ingrained.

'I'm right,' she said. 'You know I am.'

Sam felt light, unencumbered, as he queued for a ticket at a cinema on the South Bank the following day. Two clients had cancelled and Sam had suddenly found himself with a free afternoon. He walked to the river where he discovered that a Hitchcock retrospective was on. The day was cooling, so he decided to take in a movie.

Sam opted for Psycho, which might, until today, have seemed a poor choice for someone trying to escape the poisonous shadow of their mother. But the fact was, Eleanor's comments had definitely had an effect. There was a shift. An understanding that had slotted, finally, into place. He looked forward to meeting her later. They were having dinner at a restaurant near her workplace.

But at the front of the queue, Sam discovered that the film was sold out. He smiled to himself at the thought of so many people escaping a sunny, late autumn day to sit inside and watch an utterly terrifying examination of the Oedipal myth.

He opted instead for The Man Who Knew Too Much, which he'd never seen.

In less than ten minutes, Sam was back outside, clinging to the wall of the Embankment, his head spinning. He watched the Thames move with speed downstream, its grey, moody surface churning with dozens of different currents, any one of them strong enough to drag a man underneath.

The movie was a thriller, the opening scenes set in Marrakesh. Watching them, Sam felt increasingly nauseous, as if a curtain were slowly being opened to reveal a gruesome autopsy.

The film starred James Stewart and Doris Day as an American couple holidaying with their son in Marrakesh. Shortly after arriving in the city, they witness a murder. James Stewart then overhears the dying words of the victim. And before long, their son is kidnapped.

Sam looked up at the opposite bank of the river. A few miles north was his house, which Eleanor had just moved into. Their relationship felt quite different to any he'd previously had. It was built on a shared experience that had bonded them deeply. And on trust.

He gazed down at the opaque water again. At first the film had reminded him of his own experience in Marrakesh, which was unpleasant enough. But then a darker memory had emerged – Scott's dream. Sam remembered the Minister recalling it. The description of him frantically searching a maze with high walls. Looking for someone called Hank.

What was it Eleanor had said that first day they met at the farmhouse? That her father was a massive fan of Hitchcock. Scott must have watched the movie. And somehow it had become embedded in his subconscious.

James Stewart often played principled, decent men. It was entirely logical that Scott, who enjoyed a similar reputation, would identify with him, if only unconsciously. And a high-walled maze was a description you could easily apply to Marrakesh's souk.

But most telling of all was the name of the kidnapped boy in the film – Hank.

Equally revealing was how Scott reacted straight after mentioning the dream. The sudden alertness and detachment. It was, Sam now realised, as if Scott had exposed more than he'd anticipated and was girding against further incriminating revelation.

And of course that was what had happened. As Scott described his dream – possibly for the first time – he understood what it meant. Like James Stewart, he was looking for his son. And in Scott's case, that was Aidan Stirling.

What had happened? Had Charlotte Stirling seduced Scott, using every ounce of her neediness to lure him to her? Had it been a single event, or a longer affair? It mattered little. Because now Sam knew why Charles Scott had been prepared to cover up a murder. He was protecting his own flesh and blood.

What did one do with this kind of poison, Sam thought? Could he tell Eleanor that her beloved father slept with Charlotte Stirling, that she was the half-sister of a murderer?

The surface of the Thames betrayed no hint of what was below. Perhaps it was better to leave this knowledge where it was. Could he do that – keep the toxic secret to himself – or would it slowly worm its way to the surface?

He'd only just emptied his head of its darkest contents. And now something equally destructive was taking its place.

Acknowledgements

Disorder was inspired by a trip I made with my dad to Syria in 2007. With its winding alleyways and ancient buildings, the Old City of Damascus seemed tailor-made for a thriller about hidden secrets. In those early days, I made contact with Professor Joshua Landis at the University of Oklahoma and Dr Eugene L. Rogan at the University of Oxford, both of whom were invaluable sources of information on Syria and the Middle East. But as the events of the Arab Spring took hold in increasingly destructive ways, it became obvious that it was completely inappropriate to base the story in Syria and so the action switched to Morocco. All I can add is that my memories of travelling in Syria were of a warm, friendly, courteous and hospitable people. It's heartbreaking to witness their plight now.

When the manuscript was still in its infancy, Nigel Magrane (my dad), Jan Coman, Stef Evans and Julie Lockwood read it and offered encouragement and criticism – both of which I needed badly. As the book matured, the editorial guidance of Jo Unwin and Robert Dinsdale was invaluable, as were the suggestions of Broo Doherty.

I owe a huge debt of gratitude to The Writers' Workshop and, in particular, Eve Seymour. A seasoned thriller writer herself (writing as E.V. Seymour), Eve wrote an incredibly insightful critique of the book, helping me move the manuscript forward in so many ways.

Thanks also to copy-editor Steve Haines. He has an eagle eye for typos and grammatical howlers, and spotted a scandalous continuity issue at the ninth hour.

Finally, I'm grateful to Dr Rob Daniels and paramedic Tony Thompson, who gave of their time and knowledge generously to help me out with matters medical and pharmaceutical. Any mistakes in those departments are entirely my own.

Disorder's route to publication wasn't the smoothest. I thought I'd made it when Zoe King of The Blair Partnership decided to represent the book and pitch it out to publishers. But that route wasn't to be and in 2014, I self-published.

In 2015, the book was taken on by the mighty Fahrenheit Press. I am indebted to Chris McVeigh for his faith, enthusiasm and cojones, surely the biggest in publishing.

I really hope you enjoyed reading Disorder. If you want to hear more about Sam Keddie and his next adventures – or me, for that matter – get in touch at www.paddymagrane.com/books. I'd be delighted to hear from you.

Paddy Magrane
November 2015

Denial the 2nd Sam Keddie book is now available from Fahrenheit Press

20103358R00208

Printed in Great Britain
by Amazon